adviser. She bred sheep and alpacas, reared calves, broke ploughs, represented the UK in international negotiations, specialised in emergency response from Chernobyl to bird flu, managed controls over pesticides and GM crops, saw legislation through parliament and got paid to eat KitKats while on secondment to Rowntree.

In the second half she chaired an NHS Trust, worked on animal welfare, sailed a boat on the Norfolk Broads, volunteered in Citizens Advice and the Witness Service and vaccinated humans against Covid. Two golden threads have run through everything, her fascination with words and her Gran's wise advice: 'You can do anything if you try hard enough.'

She writes about the countryside and the animals she loves, the industry (farming) she holds in deepest respect, and issues she is passionate about.

Peck's main protagonist has grown with each story and his life has changed in ways she couldn't have predicted at the start. She'd like to meet him.

www.heatherpeckauthor.com.

Other books by Heather Peck

DCI GREG GELDARD SERIES

Secret Places
*Glass Arrows**
Fires of Hate
Death on the Rhine (novella)

****shortlisted for the East Anglian Book Awards prize for fiction 2021***

Coming soon:

Dig Two Graves (Greg Geldard No 5)

THE TEMENOS REMAINS

DCI GREG GELDARD BOOK 4

Heather Peck

Published in 2023 by Ormesby Publishing

Ormesby Publishing
Ormesby St Margaret
Norfolk
www.ormesbypublishing.co.uk

ISBN 978-1-915769-00-8 (paperback)
ISBN 978-1-915769-01-5 (ebook)

British Library Cataloguing in Publication Data
A CIP catalogue record for this book is available from the British Library

Page design and typesetting by SilverWood Books
www.silverwoodbooks.co.uk

To Gary

still loving and still laughing

Acknowledgements

My thanks to British Sugar for being willing for me to use one of their processing facilities as a location, and especially to Andy Cowan for showing me round the factory at Cantley and answering all my questions. Any errors relating to beet processing are entirely mine and my use of the location is entirely fictional!

Huge thanks to my beta readers, Geoff Dodgson and Alison Tayler, for all their detailed comments and suggestions.

Thank you also to Alexandra Atherton, fellow alto in the Bure to Yare choir and archaeologist, to whom I am deeply indebted both for a tour of the dig near Caister St Edmund and the idea that gave me the title of this book.

List of Characters

Police
The big boss: Chief Superintendent Margaret Tayler

Main investigative team:
DCI Greg Geldard

DI Jim Henning

DI Sarah Laurence

DS Chris Mathews

Constables Bill Street, Jill Hayes, Steve Hall & Phil Knight

DC Jeff Fellows, recent transfer from the Metropolitan Police

Ned George, senior crime scene investigator

PC Bates from North Walsham

PCs Morris and Ford from Cambridgeshire

DI Newton – of the 'funny buggers' otherwise known as MI6

Roger Makepiece duty defence solicitor

Medical experts
Dr Paisley, pathologist
Dr Fish senior registrar, Westgate Hospital

Characters from other books making a reappearance

Bobby, Greg's cat

Isabelle Fontavelle, Greg's ex-wife

Paul Fontavelle, her new husband

Colm Fontavelle, their son

Crook from *Glass Arrows* and *Fires of Hate*

Dragan Bakalov

Archaeologists

Jason Oakes, project lead

Miles Sandiford, volunteer

Other participants

Henry Tipton
Mrs Caroline Tipton, proprietors, St Edmunds Farm

Joseph Woods, Cantley Sugar Beet factory HR

Julie Bolton, community nurse

Angela Freeman, a relative of Julie's

Madame Trieste, proprietor, Nails Galore

Marilena Dalca, employee, Nails Galore

Krystina Kaminska, care worker

Krystal, Joey Asher and Kay Norton, sex workers

Colin Brown and Ray Bennet, lorry drivers

Tom Howe, cab driver

Prelude

October 2018

The early hours of a chilly morning, and Greg was woken by an unmusical cacophony from his iPad. Barely awake he lifted the cover and clicked yes to a FaceTime call. Behind him Chris rolled over in bed with a sleepy complaint. He realised with shock that the figure on the screen was Isabelle, a small child clutched to her shoulder.

'Greg, we need your help.' Tears streaked her face and sobs distorted her voice. 'I've had a phone call. We've been threatened. They said they'd do terrible things. To me and my baby.

'Please help. He's all I have now. He should have been yours. You have to help me, Greg.'

1

Night Call, October 2018

Chris rolled out of bed so fast she almost fell off the edge as she clutched for a dressing gown and her mobile phone. By the time Greg turned from his iPad she was through to Control.

'Here you are,' she said, handing him the phone. 'I'll leave you to give them details of address and threats made. They'll get a response car there soonest.'

'But I need to go,' he said staring at the phone.

'I'm sure you do, but make the call first. This needs to be done by the book, for all our sakes,' she said.

Suppressing his instincts to fly to the rescue like a reconstituted Clark Kent, Greg took the phone and issued crisp instructions, then turned to find some clothes. Chris had already laid out trousers, shirt and pants on the bed and was flourishing a mug of coffee.

'Get yourself around this then get yourself off,' she instructed. 'I'll go in to Wymondham and see what's happening at that end. See you there?'

'As soon as I can,' he promised. 'I have to go to her, Chris; I hope you see that.'

'I do,' she replied briskly, 'but don't run away with the idea that I like you running to the rescue of your ex-wife. Find out what you need to, hand over to uniform and meet me in Wymondham so we can plan.' She took hold of his shirt front. 'I'm not immune to the green-eyed monster,' she said. 'Just remember that while you're playing Robin Hood to Isabelle's Maid Marian. There're ways of dealing with this sort of thing, and knight errantry will not go down well with Margaret, think on!'

Through the worry, a smile forced its way onto his face and he kissed the lips offered. 'I won't forget and I'll be in Wymondham as soon as. Thanks for keeping my feet on the ground, Chris. Who's attending from uniform?' he asked on his way out the door.

'Phil Coleman is for one,' she shouted after him. He waved as he got into the car and shot off down the gravelled drive with a spray of stone.

By the time DCI Geldard reached the Norwich address Isabelle had given him, a patrol car was already outside. He paused by the driver's window.

'Thank you for being so prompt,' he said. The constable looked up with a smile.

'When Chris Mathews says jump, you don't stop to ask how high,' he remarked. 'Phil is inside calming down your ex-wife.'

'Thanks.' Greg took the short flight of steps to the front door two at a time. A sharp rap and it was opened by Phil, sporting his new sandy beard with pride but otherwise looking reassuringly familiar.

'All well here,' he said. 'I've made the lady a cup of tea and sat her down. She's a lot calmer now and she's rung her mother to come and stay for a while. I think a lot of the panic was because she was on her own with the little 'un.'

'I'll go and see her now, thanks Phil. Has she said who did the threatening?'

'No name given apparently, but she's sure it was a man. He had a strong East European accent and made reference to you,' he flicked through his notebook, '"meddling where you weren't wanted."'

It felt very strange seeing Isabelle seated on a familiar brown leather chair, surrounded by other familiar furniture, but in an unfamiliar room. He noted white walls and white woodwork, ornamented solely by concert posters and huge blown-up black and white photos of a conductor (most of them) and Isabelle singing (a few.) On the table, shared by an immense bunch of lilies scenting the air, he saw a sole photo of a toddler, leaning on Isabelle's knee and apparently taken by an amateur snapper.

'Where's Paul?' he asked.

'In the US on a tour,' she replied. 'I've rung and left messages.'

'Is he on his way back?'

'Don't know.' She shrugged and hid her face in her coffee mug. 'I doubt it. Not until this tour ends anyway. That would disrupt too many plans. Anyway,' she said, 'it's your fault, isn't it? So I don't think it's unreasonable to expect you to put it right!'

Greg could feel his hackles rise, and had to swallow hard to suppress the first words that came to mind. He sat down in the chair opposite and took some time to take a notebook out before he could bring himself to speak.

'Let's just go back a step, shall we?' he said as calmly as he was capable of. 'When did you get the call?'

'Around midnight,' she said.

'And did you get the number?'

'No. Nothing showed on the handset and it didn't occur to me to try 1471 until I'd already had other calls.'

'Calls from where?'

'Well, I rang Paul obviously and left messages. The orchestra secretary rang me back. And so did my mother. Then I left more messages. Then I rang you.'

'So, you'd already rung several people before you rang me.' Greg's blood pressure was rising. 'I thought it was an emergency and you'd just had the call. That's why I came straight round. And why we got uniform out to you so fast.'

'Disappointed you weren't my first thought? Spoil your evening with your new squeeze?' asked Isabelle with understated, but clear, malice. 'So sorry! And it is an emergency. I told you; I had threats made to me and to Colm.'

'Colm?'

'My son. Our son.'

'The one that should have been mine?' Greg couldn't resist the dig. Isabelle had the grace to blush, just a fraction. Greg couldn't help but notice how pretty the extra colour made her look. The new longer blonde hair suited her too.

'I was upset,' she defended herself. 'I'd had a chance to think about it. About how isolated I am. And he *would* have been yours if you hadn't been so career-obsessed.'

Greg got up and walked over to stare out of the window. He had a clear recollection of raising the subject of parenthood and being knocked back by an Isabelle keen to pursue her singing career. It seemed this part of their collective history was also being rewritten.

'Look, Isabelle,' he said without turning round. 'I'll help all I can but this's only going to work if we keep it on a friendly footing. So can we quit the digs please? We should be past that. You have a new life and so do I.' He turned back in time to see Isabelle open her mouth for a retort, then she seemed to think the better of it and buried her face in her mug again. Phil looked in through the door, said 'sorry' and backed away, but Greg called out, 'Phil, come in please and take some notes would you? Now, I know you've told Phil here that it was a man's voice and he had an East European accent. Was it just the one voice?'

'Yes,' said Isabelle. 'But it wasn't the first time.'

'Did you hear any background noises? And can you narrow down the accent any more than that? Hang on a minute! What d'you mean? It wasn't the first time?'

'Which of those questions do you want me to answer first?' demanded Isabelle. 'No, no background voices. I heard nothing but the voice. And he just sounded vaguely Ukrainian or Romanian. We used to have a Ukrainian window cleaner. He sounded a bit like him, only not exactly like him. And I've had calls before from that voice, or a similar one.'

'Did he use any foreign words?'

'Not that I noticed.'

'What exactly did he say?'

'I'm not sure I can remember any more. But the sense of it was that, unless you stopped meddling where you weren't wanted, I would regret it. Then he said something about making sure my face was never pretty anymore, or making my son disappear. He said, if they were feeling kind, they might give me the choice.'

'What did the earlier callers say?'

'Nothing much. Just asked for you and I kept saying you didn't live here.'

'He definitely referred to a son, not just a child?' asked Greg.

'Yes, he definitely said son. But that wouldn't be difficult to find out, would it? His birth was on my Facebook page. And Twitter.'

'What about the other phrases you've quoted? Did he definitely say he'd make your son "disappear"?'

'I think so.' She was only slightly uncertain. 'And what he said about my face, I think that's right too. It's been ringing round and round in my head. I thought straightaway of acid. It terrified me. And to be offered a choice! That would be even worse!'

Greg turned to a knock on the door and Phil looked up from his notebook. The constable put his head round.

'I thought I told you to stay at the front door,' started Phil.

'Yes. Sorry,' said the constable. 'But I've had a call from HQ. They say to tell you,' he was addressing Greg, 'that you're to call in on the chief super once you get to Wymondham, and that DI Sarah Laurence will be here in a few minutes to take over this case.' He withdrew, leaving a pregnant silence behind him.

'Oh no,' said Isabelle, 'oh no, you don't get off as easily as that, Greg. This is down to you and you don't just walk away leaving me in the shit again.'

'Again,' said Greg in rising tones. 'What the devil do you mean by again?' Then getting a grip on his temper and interrupted by the sound of infant wails coming through the closed door he said, 'I'm sorry, Isabelle, but it's pretty unlikely I'd be allowed to handle a case where I'm so closely involved. But I will keep an eye on things. And DI Laurence is a good officer. One of the best.'

'I bet this is your sweet sergeant's doing,' almost snarled Isabelle as she headed for the door. 'Out of my way, Greg. I need to go to Colm. You woke him up with all your shouting.'

Aware that Chris probably had, indeed, had a hand in this development, and guiltily aware that what he mainly felt was a strong sense of relief, Greg swallowed his indignation as he followed Isabelle to the foot of the stairs.

'Isabelle,' he said, 'I *will* make sure you're protected and that we follow this up. We'll find out who made the call and get him put away, I promise. It's best someone else takes over here, but I won't leave this, I promise that too.' As an afterthought he added, 'And don't forget to mention the earlier calls too.'

On the A11 near the Thickthorn roundabout, had they but known it, Greg and Sarah passed each other travelling in opposite directions. Greg in his red BMW, en route to Norfolk Police HQ at Wymondham, was rehearsing what he would say both to the chief superintendent, Margaret Tayler, and to Chris. The first would be looking for an explanation of his departure from protocol, the latter – although she would never admit it – for reassurance. Greg, feeling equally inadequate to both tasks, found himself longing for the simplicity and certainty of major crime.

*

Sarah, heading north, also had mixed feelings about her new assignment. On the one hand, she was curious to explore the intricacies of the relationship between Greg and his ex-wife. In her heart, she still cherished a half hope that she could, one day, step into Isabelle's discarded shoes. On the other, she resented both Greg's superior career success and his rejection of her in favour of a mere sergeant with strange fashion sense and no particular beauty. The muddle of emotions found common cause only in the solution – a stunningly brilliant and career-enhancing resolution of the task she'd been given.

2

Remains, October 2018

Entering HQ after his dash from Isabelle's, Greg missed Chris in his headlong rush up the stairs to the chief super's office.

'Sorry, Margaret,' he said before he was barely through the door. 'I know I should've stood back on this one, but I did feel an obligation to at least show up. She was panicking and...' He paused, aware his audience was not with him. Margaret Tayler, soft brown fluffy hair as wild as usual, looked up from the phone pressed to her ear and waved him to the seat in front of her desk. The top layer of papers did not, as far as Greg could see from upside down scrutiny, appear to relate to East European threats against the former wife of a serving officer.

Concluding her conversation, she put the phone down and ran her hands through her hair, rendering it yet wilder.

'Sorry, Greg, missed what you said on the way in. These folk use such arcane terms I have to concentrate to make sense of them. Sorry to hear about your ex by the way. I've detailed

Sarah as OIC.'

'So I heard,' said Greg, but Margaret hadn't finished.

'I've got a little job for you too. Hopefully it'll keep you out of mischief.' She shuffled the papers on her desk and came up with a map, which she turned to Greg. 'Had a call from these folk,' she stabbed her finger at the name across the top, 'well, several calls actually. The first was to report they'd found a body. The remainder were all about how quickly could we get it out of their way so they could get on, the last one with a distinct overtone of, "if they'd known it was going to cause this much trouble, they'd have buried it again."'

Greg looked at the inscription along the top of the map. 'Norwich Archaeology,' he read.

'This,' said Margaret, 'is the map they emailed me of their current diggings near Caistor St Edmund. It's an area some distance from the main site that everyone knows.' Greg tried to look as though 'everyone' included him, but was fairly certain he wasn't very convincing.

'Mainly they've been doing some more work on a temple site they found a few years ago, and exploring what they described to me as the whole entrance area and approaches. What they call the "temenos", which they have been kind enough to translate for me as, and I quote, "an area dedicated to the gods".'

'And we're interested why?' enquired Greg.

'Oh, didn't I say? They've found a body.'

'So, do we need the forensic anthropologists again,' asked Greg, his heart sinking slightly, 'to tell us whether it's one we need to worry about or ancient remains?'

'It's definitely one for us. The archaeologists are used to finding bodies and used to identifying them as ancient or not.

In this case it seems it was pretty obvious. The skull includes teeth with modern dentistry. No older than ten years according to Jason, the man in charge. So get yourself over there, Greg, and see what needs doing.

'One other thing they found,' she added. 'A bit odd too. There was a coin in the skull's mouth. A silver thruppence.'

A quick visit to his office, and Greg was ready for the road again. All he was missing was his sergeant. He stuck his head into the general office.

'Anyone seen Chris?' he asked.

'At risk of sounding like panto,' replied a woman seated in front of three screens showing CCTV footage, 'she's behind you.'

'Thanks, Jill.' Greg whipped round in time to get a bad attack of photokeratitis from today's ensemble of bright pink tunic and yellow leggings. The weak autumn sun peering in through the window was fighting a losing battle with the leggings and the pink tunic made an interesting clash with the fuchsia tote slung over Chris's shoulder. Even in these circumstances, Greg found himself suppressing a grin.

'You're back,' she said, somewhat unnecessarily.

'And now off again,' he replied. 'I'll brief you on the way. OK to leave now?'

'OK,' she said, and followed him down the corridor and out to the car park.

They walked in silence to Greg's car, each waiting for the other to speak, then both spoke at once and fell silent again.

'You first,' said Chris.

'I was just asking if you were OK, and had you been briefed on this case at the Roman remains?'

'No, and yes,' replied Chris. 'And I was asking how your meeting with Isabelle went.'

Greg thought about that response as he unlocked the car, and decided to postpone answering until they were both seated and on their way.

'No, you're not OK?' he asked.

'Not 100 per cent, no,' she said. 'What did you expect really, when you go rushing off to your glamorous ex-wife without hesitation the moment she rings and crooks her finger?' Greg waited until he'd pulled out of the car park and joined the northbound traffic.

'That's a little unfair,' he said. 'She wasn't asking me to unblock a sink or replace a fused light bulb. She said she'd been threatened, and threatened because of my job. I *did* need to check she was OK. And I came back as soon as.'

Chris sighed. 'Yes, I know,' she said. 'And I've tried hard to be rational about this. I didn't try to stop you going, did I? But the fact is I can't compete with your beautiful, talented ex-wife and I'm very aware of that.' She turned as far as her seat belt permitted to look at Greg's profile. 'I never expected to feel like this, and I certainly never expected the green-eyed monster to be paying me a visit. I'm sorry, Greg, but I'm struggling.'

Without taking his eyes from the road, Greg briefly took one hand from the steering wheel and squeezed the hand lying in her lap.

'You're right, you can't compete,' he said. 'You're honest, loyal, and balanced. You support me even when it hurts you. You back me up even when you think I'm wrong, and you never hesitate to warn me when I *am* going wrong. You're smart, wise and the most emotionally intelligent person I've ever met, man or woman. On top of all that, you're beautiful and I fancy you something rotten. So no, you can't compete because you don't need to. There are no grounds for competition between you and an ex-wife who is so utterly different and untrustworthy that she's not even on the same playing field let alone a level one.'

There was a silence while Greg waited for a response and Chris looked hard out of the side window. He sneaked a glance across just as she wiped her eyes on her sleeve.

'Bastard,' she said, 'now look what you made me do,' and they both laughed.

'OK, now that's dealt with,' he said briskly, 'how much do you know about the Roman remains?'

'If you mean our body,' she said, 'mainly that they're definitely not Roman. SOCO got there about fifteen minutes ago and have confirmed they have modern dentistry, specifically a filling or two. They're taking all the details to do a round of local dentists to see if they can find a match. Otherwise, they're checking around the area and everything else the archaeologists dug up, including the coin in the mouth.'

'Which I gather was a silver thruppence.'

'So I'm told. Dated,' she consulted her notebook, '1911.'

Turning off the A47, Greg asked, 'Where now?'

'Follow the signs to Bungay, then the notes I've got say head for Framingham Earl, then the by-way to Caistor St Edmund.'

'That's not what my satnav said,' objected Greg.

'Yes, but you probably entered the details for Roman Norwich, didn't you?'

'Probably,' agreed Greg. 'I thought that was where we were going.'

'No. The find is on another dig nearby. We have to pass

a farm on our left, then I'm told we'll see a field with spoil heaps, a big white marquee and other tents. Yes, there it is,' she said, pointing. 'Just past that field with horses. I can see the SOCO van too.'

They bumped in through a field entrance and over the grass to park near the SOCO van, then got out.

'Better suit up,' remarked Greg, and they pulled on coveralls and over-shoes before venturing inside the blue and white tape surrounding one of several holes in the ground. A small group of similarly clad people stood around the hole, just outside the second layer of tape, this version red and white. Inside, Greg could see Ned, his senior crime scene investigator, and one of his colleagues measuring various bones of the skeleton partly revealed at their feet. One of the other white shapes turned round with a crackle of plastic overall straining over well-fed torso.

'Jason Oakes,' he said, holding his hand out. 'I'm the lead archaeologist here.'

'Was it you who found these remains?' asked Greg.

'Not the first,' replied Jason. 'That was Tom and Anne here.' He pointed to two more plastic-suited figures, who turned and nodded to Greg. 'They called me over, so I'm the only other person who's been in the excavation since the remains were discovered.'

'Why are you digging here?' asked Chris. 'Especially why this precise spot?'

'It's the north-east corner of a temple complex,' explained Jason. 'This complex was discovered and mapped some twelve years ago, then the remains covered over again for further exploration at a later date. This *is* the later date. We excavated this corner of the temple and then found the skeleton as you see.'

'Did you move it at all?' asked Greg.

'A little maybe, as we were uncovering it, but as soon as we spotted the fillings,' he pointed down into the trench, 'we stopped and rang you.'

The skeleton was laid out in the centre of the neat trench cut down about four feet into the earth. Two sides were bordered by a low brick and flint wall, which met at a neat right angle in the north-east corner. The skull and part of the neck were fully exposed. Lower down the torso Greg could see the rib cage with arms crossed neatly over the sternum. The second half the spine disappeared into a thin layer of soil. One of Ned's chaps was brushing gently at the soil with a brush, and as Greg watched, the lower edge of the pelvis appeared into view.

'He's good,' said Jason approvingly. 'Would he like to moonlight for us? We could use some more volunteers.'

Ned looked up as Greg's shadow fell across the excavation. The sun was now low in the west and a skein of geese flew over as he spoke, heading for the east coast and the North Sea.

'Hope the tent and floods are on their way,' he remarked, speaking over the geese calls from the sky above. 'Or we'll have to stop soon for lack of light.' Chris looked round at a small truck bouncing into the farm track.

'Looks like they're arriving now,' she replied as Greg asked, 'What do you have for us so far, Ned?'

'Doctor's been and gone,' he replied. 'She reckons it's a young woman, no obvious cause of death. She also agrees she's probably been in the ground around ten years or so. Says she'll take a closer look once the bones are recovered to the mortuary. Nothing much else here so far except a few hairs and the coin the archaeologists found. 1911 silver thruppence.'

'Which was exactly where?'

'Resting against the occipital bone and the atlas vertebra,' said Ned pointing, and Jason chimed in, 'Which is why we thought it had been in the body's mouth. I've seen similar placements when looking at early undisturbed burials from Ancient Greek or Roman times.'

'But this definitely wasn't ancient, not with a relatively modern coin,' said Greg.

'Precisely,' replied Jason.

Greg took a step back as the crew with the tent and flood lights approached the trench.

'Nothing much we can do here at the moment,' he said. 'Ned, can you keep me posted if you find anything else? We'll go and start on dentists and missing persons, the usual.'

'We'll be a good while here,' answered Ned. 'We have all that to sift through too.' He nodded at the spoil heap that constituted the material taken out of the trench.

'Christ,' said Greg, then turning to Jason asked, 'In your historic burials, what was the significance of the coin?'

'No one knows for certain,' said Jason. 'There're various explanations, mostly centring around the dead paying Charon an obol to ferry them across the river Styx. It was sometimes thought the money in their mouth was the only money they could take with them in death. Other versions describe it as sustenance for the journey or a seal to protect the deceased's soul or to prevent it from returning. Take your pick.'

Entr'acte 1

In the shadows

Looking back, I've always felt I lived in the shadows. To be honest, I feel most comfortable there, unobserved but observant. Unseen but all-seeing. I have a recurring fantasy that I died without noticing the event; and the reason no one takes any notice of me, or speaks to me, is because I'm not really here. I'm a ghost, moving silently and invisibly through the world.

Being a ghost has its advantages. You don't have to engage with people you'd rather not. You don't have to get close to people. They naturally keep their distance because, while they don't know you're there, something about your echoes or vibrations alerts them and makes them uncomfortable. Also, as I've often read, the observer sees more of the game.

I certainly see things other people don't. I see other ghosts, for example. Other shapes that drift through the world amid the shadows. Only, unlike me, they're not always good ghosts. Some of them are dangerous. Luckily, my voice warns me off them. And if I can't avoid them, I've learned how to protect myself.

3

Threats and promises

'This case might be my step to promotion,' thought Sarah, 'but it's going to be a bloody big and difficult step!' And, as someone not normally prone to mental swearing, this said a lot about her reaction to Isabelle Fontavelle ex Geldard.

As first meetings go, it wasn't the best. Isabelle had been anything but welcoming when she opened the door. Trying to be fair, Sarah put this down at least partly to the fact she had not been looking her best. Baked-bean appliqué on a silk blouse is never a good look, and even worse when the blouse is salmon pink and currently a pretty good match for the wearer's complexion. Applying her powers of deductive reasoning at full strength, Sarah concluded the young Master Fontavelle had recently been throwing a full-on tantrum as well as his, surprisingly plebeian, lunch.

'And you are?' asked Isabelle unpleasantly.

'DI Sarah Laurence,' replied Sarah. 'I'm the officer in

charge of investigating the threats made against you.'

'Oh, another of Greg's geishas,' was the reply. 'Or is it gofers? I can't keep up these days. I suppose you'd better come in. So, what did you do to get landed with Greg's problems?' she asked, indicating a seat on a sofa, only partly cleared of changing mat, tissues, various salves and what looked unpleasantly like a used nappy. Sarah wrinkled her nose and sat down cautiously, keeping as far as possible from the other contents of the sofa.

'Sorry,' said Isabelle, sweeping most of the clutter cursorily onto the changing mat and away into the kitchen. A couple of tubes of ointment fell to the floor and rolled away. Sarah considered retrieving them, then decided that her welcome so far did not merit favours. She left them where they lay and got out her iPad.

'I've had a report from the officers who attended first thing this morning, and of course from DCI Geldard and DS Mathews.'

'Oh yes, DS Mathews,' said Isabelle meaningfully, then seemed to change her mind about what she intended to say next. 'So, how are you going to protect me?'

'We currently have an officer on duty in a car down the street,' replied Sarah, 'and when he leaves, a patrol car will make regular passes during the night. The other option, of course, is that you move to a discreet hotel while we find the people who made the threats. We can recommend somewhere suitable.'

'And Greg, is he going to comply with their request?'

'Well, as I understand it, it wasn't a very specific request,' responded Sarah. 'Just a generic "keep out of our hair or else"? And…'

'The threat was specific enough,' interrupted Isabelle. 'Acid in my face or my child kidnapped. Or both perhaps.'

‘Yes, I understand it must have been terrifying,’ replied Sarah. ‘We’ll do all we can to keep you safe and we will find the perpetrator. But I do need to be clear on this. Under no circumstances will we allow threats to influence an investigation!’

She had then run through the benefits of moving to a safer, more supervised location, but Isabelle had remained obdurate. She was going nowhere. Sarah had then explained the form the investigation would take, the checking of phone calls for both the recent threat and the earlier calls, numbers that had been rung from, locations pinpointed via radio masts, the review of recent visitors to the house or even street, then her voice had trailed off as it had become clear that Isabelle was not listening properly, if at all.

‘I’ll be off then,’ she said and left abruptly, heels clicking sharply on the wooden floor and narrowly avoiding a slam of the door.

Striding down the drive, she’d looked round enviously at the neighbouring houses. All were substantial properties, set back from the road in gardens that showed evidence of expert, or at least enthusiastic, care. Most were still benefitting from the elusive fragrance of late roses, sagging gently on end-of-season stems. A few had tarmac drives sweeping round to the house, but most, including the Fontavelles’, had gravel drives and parking areas occupying most of the space between house and road. Sarah tapped her pen reflectively on her teeth, then went for a chat with the constable parked two doors down with a good view of the target location. He rolled the window down as she approached.

‘Don’t suppose you’ve got a cuppa for me have you?’ asked Phil Coleman.

'Do I gather the lady of the house hasn't offered you anything?' asked Sarah with a grin.

'Her? Mean cow!' he replied. 'She's in too much of a temper for that. I reckon the boss is well out of it with that one.'

'She's scared, short of sleep, and coping with a baby on her own,' said Sarah, trying to be fair with a bit of a struggle. 'One of you could nip down to the garage for a coffee.'

'No problem,' he replied. 'Steve's gone to fetch us coffee and sticky buns. Look, he's coming back now.' He nodded down the road to where a uniformed figure holding two coffees and a paper bag was coming round the corner.

'Good, glad you're OK for the moment. I'll review the threat level when I'm back at HQ and we'll decide then what's happening this evening.'

'Any overtime?' asked Steve hopefully, as he arrived at the car.

'Doubtful, but I'll see. Anything I should know from the house to house?'

'Nothing. Zip. Nada,' he replied. 'These places are too far apart, and too surrounded by greenery for anyone to see much. But even the nearest neighbours say there's been no unusual visitors or workmen of any kind. One thing they did say. The Fontavelles are renting. That house isn't theirs, and according to their neighbours the rent is sky high. An arm and a leg were mentioned.'

'Have to see what the phone data can tell us,' said Sarah.

Back at Wymondham, the news from the civilian assistants interrogating BT and the mobile-phone companies sent her straight to the chief super.

'She's lying,' Sarah said bluntly. 'At least as far as this call is concerned. According to the records there was no incoming phone call other than one from the States in the early hours of the morning. That went to the landline. The mobile-phone records, by contrast, show lots of calls made from Isabelle Fontavelle's phone to a couple of numbers. One a mobile, the other a landline belonging to a hotel in the US. Fourteen in total. The mobile belongs to Mr Paul Fontavelle. The one to a hotel is to the room booked in his name. All the calls are outgoing. She seems to have left numerous messages and as far as we can see, he hasn't responded.'

'Apparently she told Greg that wasn't unusual when in rehearsal,' remarked Margaret, 'and you'd expect her to be trying to contact her husband when she was threatened.'

'That's just what I'm not sure of. We can't find any record of a call from within the UK in the time period she says she got the threat,' objected Sarah.

'I suppose that call could have been the one that frightened her?'

'But from the US? And from the exact same hotel her husband is staying in? Something's not right, ma'am.'

'So, what do you want to do about it?'

'I'd like to find out who made the call from the US. I'll speak to the hotel in the first instance, then take it from there. And I'd like to talk to DCI Geldard about his more recent contacts with the Lithuanian links from the last investigation. Just in case there is a link I've not found.'

'Could she have a second phone?' asked Margaret.

'Always possible,' agreed Sarah, 'but if so, why keep it secret?'

'And what about the earlier calls?'

'Still checking. But she's so vague about when they occurred it's probably an impossible task.'

Sarah's next stop was Greg's office. It was empty. The desk was clear except for the morning's post, the computer monitor blandly uncommunicative. Sarah hesitated by the door, then, prompted by a random impulse, she entered and closed it behind her. The room smelt faintly of coffee and an elusive male fragrance, which she traced to the jacket hanging on the back of the door. She moved closer.

And inhaled. The jacket undoubtedly smelt of Greg: part soap, part aftershave, and part something more personal but yet pleasant. 'Pheromones,' she thought and inhaled again before moving towards the desk, then jumped almost out of her skin as the door swung open abruptly. Greg came in briskly with Chris following closely on his heels, her phone to her ear. She was still talking.

'Let's have a word later,' she said into the phone as Greg said, surprised, 'Sarah? What can I do for you? I thought you were looking into the threats made against Isabelle.'

'I was. I am,' she said, mentally kicking herself for sounding stupid. 'Not much intelligence to be had on the ground, so I came back to check out the phone data. Now, that *is* interesting.'

She laid out for Greg's benefit what they'd found so far. He nodded, made affirmative noises, but said little.

'Was that what you came to tell me?' he asked.

'Not exactly. What I wanted to ask about were your further investigations into the Lithuanians behind last year's modern slavery case.' Greg exchanged a lightning glance with Chris, which did not go unnoticed by Sarah.

'What further investigations?' he asked, prevaricating.

Chris snorted and Sarah glanced across at her before sitting down, uninvited.

'It's an open secret in the office,' she said. 'We all know you've been looking at links between Dragan Bakalov in gaol, and the supply chain that provided Semtex to the defendant in your last case. We know you think the same Lithuanian gang was behind both crimes and that the ringleaders are still free and still operating in Norfolk. Clearly this has to be a possible reason for threats made against your ex-wife, if any.'

'What d'you mean, "if any"?' pounced Chris.

'I mean, that so far there just isn't the evidence there was a threat, at least, not today, not by phone and not to any phone we've had access to.'

4

Discussions, October 2018

As the door closed behind Sarah, Chris sat down in the chair opposite the desk.

'If everyone else knows, so will Margaret. Have you told her what you're up to?'

'Not yet.' Greg was brusque. 'Not much to say yet. Right, let's go and brief the team on our Roman case.' After gathering up his notes, he left the room. Chris waited a moment, sighed, and stood up to follow the figure disappearing rapidly down the corridor.

By the time she got to the main office, everyone else was ready to listen, except for Ned, presumably still busy on site at Caistor St Edmund, and Phil Coleman, minding Isabelle Fontavelle. It was the usual team. Constable Bill Street, struggling with his homework for the sergeant's exam, was there in uniform and leaning dangerously back in his chair as normal. Jill Hayes, CCTV whizz kid, was dragging her attention from her three screens; Steve Hall was wrapping himself round a doorstep sandwich, also as normal.

'No Jim?' she asked.

'Jim's still winding up his last case with CPS,' said Greg. 'He may join us later depending how big this gets.

'Now, I have an interim report from Ned, and this is the position so far. We have a skeletonised body in an archaeological dig just outside Norwich. The rough estimate on the basis of the state of the bones etc is that it's been there for around ten years. That coincides with the last time the trench was opened by the Norwich history team, so the working hypothesis is that it was dumped there after the excavation was back-filled at the end of the last dig, but before it set hard and the grass grew again on the top. Preliminary data from the pathologist suggests it's the body of a young woman, estimated age between twenty and thirty, but obviously with room for error at either end of that spectrum. No cause of death apparent from the bones, by which I mean no breaks or cut marks. The body was placed carefully with arms crossed on her breast and a coin in her mouth. An old silver thruppence.'

Bill Street looked up from his notes. 'Ritual killing?' he asked.

'No way to tell at present, but certainly it looks like there were elements of a ritual in the disposal of the body.'

Bill nodded, noting the distinction.

'Are any of those archaeologists involved ten years ago still at work today?' asked Jill.

'Good question, Jill. I don't know. We have a list of all those who've been working the site this month, but we're still waiting for someone to come up with the ten-year-old list of team members from the archives. The problem they have is that many were and are volunteers, and the records don't seem to be as good as those for employees.'

'Or, one of them has a good reason for hiding the fact they were around when the body was buried,' said Bill.

'Clearly we can't rule them out as suspects,' replied Greg, 'but the first thing to check is whether anyone was reluctant to reopen that trench. If one of them deposited the body there, they'd know it would be found as soon as the latest dig went down more than a few feet. OK, enough speculation. We have some work to do.

'First, check out missing persons ten years ago and see if we have any matches. Second, as soon as we have the dental details from Ned, start on the local dentists to see if we have a match. Third, background check on the archaeological team, both past and present. Fourth, a search on HOLMES for any similar cases, especially the coin in the mouth touch.

'Chris, can we have a word please?'

Back in his office, Greg sat at his desk and Chris resumed her seat opposite.

'I *was* listening,' he said. 'I'll have a word with Margaret as soon as she's free. First, let's just pool notes on what we know, or think we know.'

Chris smiled, relieved he was taking her advice at last, but too wise to say so. Greg smiled back, perfectly well aware of what she was thinking.

'Yes, OK, you can say "told you so" later. First, where did you get to following up Bakalov's contacts?'

She flipped through screens on her iPad, then paused

on one. 'First off,' she said, 'I checked whether any of the few contacts he'd had in prison matched with those we turned up during the modern slavery investigation. Two did. One a phone number from Lithuania. The other a visitor. A woman.'

'What do we know about her?'

'Not much more than a name and the address she gave the prison service when the visit was arranged.'

'Girlfriend?'

'No idea. Obviously Bakalov had to agree to the visit, or she wouldn't have been let in in the first place. Whether they had a prior relationship, who knows? He isn't going to tell us. But, get this, the visit was arranged a few days after Bakalov's phone call from Lithuania and I've done some digging. She runs a nail bar and beauty parlour in Norwich.'

'Was it one of the ones using slave labour the other year?' asked Greg.

'It was on our list, but it checked out then. I think it's worth another look and I've asked the Gangmaster and Labour Abuse people about it, but nothing so far. I was going to carry out some checks myself, but then the Roman case came up. What about you?'

'I followed the money, as we agreed. I got an old friend now on the Serious Fraud team to do some digging. The cash that came to the man running the gangmaster and smuggling scam.'

'Yes, Metcalfe,' said Chris.

'That cash came from the same bank account in Vilnius. I mean, the same one that Lily Lai paid money into when she bought the Semtex to blow up the Agricultural Science lab.'

'Wow.' There was a pause, then Chris said, 'Confirmation

of what we suspected. A definite link. We have to take this to Margaret.'

'Yes. My next job. But I only got the confirmation this morning. So, we have evidence there is a Lithuanian link, which runs from my first case here in Norfolk.'

'The modern slavery case and the murders,' interpolated Chris, nodding.

'To the explosion at the National Agricultural Science Agency,' went on Greg. 'And who knows what else? Question is, how does that tie up with the threats made against Isabelle?'

'If there were any,' remarked Chris, only half under her breath.

'So you're with Sarah. You think Isabelle was making it up.'

'I think it's a possibility, Greg. Look at the facts,' she went on, watching the expression on the face downturned to the papers on his desk. 'There was only one incoming call last night to any of Isabelle's phones. All the other calls are outgoing, and except for the call to you and one to her mother, they were all to her new husband in the States. Who did not return her calls. The threat made was general, not specific. The description of the voice is also very general.'

'She did say he sounded East European.'

'Yes, and she also said it sounded like someone she'd employed from the Ukraine. Maybe that's where she got the idea.'

'What're you saying, Chris? What d'you think happened?'

She paused before answering, then chose her words with care.

'This is hypothesis,' she said. 'I need to know who spoke to her from the States and ideally what was in the recorded messages she left. But to me it sounds like...' She hesitated.

'Just spit it out,' said Greg.

'It sounds to me like not everything's well between her and her husband, that she got a malicious call of some kind from the States, perhaps someone blowing the whistle on him, that she's been trying to talk to him since, and that the call to you was an attempt to get you back in her life.'

'That's a pretty big hypothesis based on not very much. And what about the reference to our "meddling" by looking into the Lithuanian links?'

'Well that's just it. If you look at the words used, there's no reference to Lithuania. None. Just a mention of an East European accent. And she'd know from the papers about your last couple of big cases and the Lithuanian link. They were reported pretty faithfully.'

'What about the earlier calls?'

'Well, they're even more vague. No threats, nothing specific except your name, and she can't remember the dates. Given we've pretty much proved the latest cry for help was a total lie, where does that leave us with the other calls?'

There was a silence then Greg asked, 'Is this what Sarah thinks?'

'She thinks it's a possibility. She's checking just in case it was a real threat, but…' Chris shut up. Greg was shuffling his papers together.

'Well, let's get on,' he said. 'We've both got stuff to do and I'll try and see Margaret.' He paused on his way out the door. 'Just one thing, Chris,' he said over his shoulder. 'Whatever the truth of Isabelle's allegations, there's no chance of her getting me back, as you put it. You're my life now. Don't forget that.'

*

On his way to see the chief super, Greg was waylaid in the corridor by Jill. What she had to say pushed all thoughts of money transactions, Vilnius and the imprisoned Romanian fixer, Bakalov, straight out of his head.

'I've got a match on HOLMES,' she said. 'Well, to be precise, I've got two. Seven years apart.' Greg stopped dead.

'Show me,' he said, and followed her, almost running, to her desk in the corner. He pulled up a chair beside her and she pointed to the screen.

'I'm printing all the detail off,' she said, 'but the essentials are here. First hit was for 27 Feb 2002. A body was found in a drainage ditch on a farm near Cambridge. According to the notes made at the time, it was the partly decomposed remains of a young woman. Dark hair, slim build, poor teeth, no clothes found at the scene but there was a silver thruppence in her mouth. The body was never identified. The post-mortem report states that the death was due to suffocation, but there was some doubt owing to the condition of the remains, which they reckoned had been in situ for around a year.

'The second hit was November 2008, and this time in Suffolk, near Lowestoft. It seems a street in Oulton Broad had been dug up to repair a water main a few weeks earlier. The repair seems to have been unsuccessful and the road was dug up again. This time they found a body. A slim young woman with dark hair, estimated to be in her mid-twenties, but again there was no firm ID. The file states that there was some suspicion she may have been in the country illegally. They tried really hard with reconstructions of her face, touting them round all the possible places where someone that age might have been working, care homes, processing plants, fruit farms etc. Nothing.'

'Did either Cambridgeshire or Suffolk check HOLMES?' asked Greg.

'It seems they did, but it also seems that Suffolk didn't turn up the 2002 case. I'd guess, looking at the dates, that perhaps the earlier data hadn't been entered on the system by Cambridge police until later.'

'Did they work out how the body got into the hole in the road without anyone noticing?' asked Chris, standing unnoticed behind Greg.

'Apparently after the first excavation and repair, the hole was back-filled then left overnight before being re-tarmacked in the morning. The roadworkers suggested the body had been placed in the hole during the night and the ground smoothed over again before the tarmac team arrived the next day. The road was a quiet one, overlooked only by the railway line and the back of a pharmacy. It'd been closed to traffic until the repair was complete, so there'd have been nothing going past.'

Greg went over to the whiteboard and started making notes. 'So, we have a body found in 2002 that dated from, according to the pathologist at the time, early 2001. And another found in late 2008, this one discovered relatively shortly after the death. Then,' he made another note, 'not forgetting our local body found this week in the temenos of Roman Norwich but killed probably also around 2008. The first two were dark, slim females. The last one is also female and of similar age. No idea about hair colour. All three were laid out ceremonially with a coin in their mouths.' He paused and looked round, his facial expression caught between horror and excitement. 'Team, I think we have a serial killer on our patch.'

5

Priorities

Margaret Tayler was more restrained in her reaction to his news than Greg had expected. She sighed heavily, pushed her hands through her hair, sighed again, then leaned back in her chair, twiddling with a pen.

'Let's not get carried away yet, Greg, and whatever you do, don't start any hares running in the press about a serial killer in Norfolk. We've already got more major investigations running than I know how to resource. The county lines case isn't going away any time soon. We have knife crime in Norwich and Great Yarmouth, drugs being run into both our local prisons with apparent impunity, ongoing modern slavery cases, and that's before I mention your self-inflicted activities relating to a possible Lithuanian Mr Big and the sources of the Semtex that blew up our local science park not long ago. Do you really think we need Jack the Ripper on top of all that?'

Greg sat down looking stubborn. 'We don't need it, no,' he

agreed. 'But what we need and what we've got are two different things. I can't see any other way of interpreting the data we have. Three deaths that we know of within East Anglia within eight years, all apparently with similar victims and all with identical approaches to disposal of the body. I don't see how it could be a copy-cat, because nothing was known about the deaths or the burials. The last two deaths took place within around a year. What would you have me do? Ignore it?'

Margaret sighed again. 'No, I'm not asking you to ignore it. Someone killed those poor women and got away with it for more than sixteen years and counting. But that's my point. That makes this a priority cold case. It doesn't make it a live investigation of a currently active serial killer on our patch. You must see the difference.'

Greg's expression hadn't changed. 'No evidence of crime is not the same as evidence of no crime,' he argued. 'No one seems to have missed these three women that we know about. And each was discovered by accident. We've no idea how many more might be out there. And for all we know, he may still be active. We won't know until we look.'

'So what do you suggest? Excavating all roadworks undertaken in the last seventeen years?' scoffed Margaret. 'Checking all the other archaeological sites we have in a county rich with history?'

'Give me some credit for common sense,' replied Greg, with the closest he had come so far to blatant disrespect. 'No, what I have in mind is a twin-track approach. Here in Norfolk, we need to follow up on the temenos remains. The usual search for identity, and then see where that takes us. We'll check out everyone who knew about the earlier dig too, all the normal research that we do in every major crime. In parallel, I'm proposing a thorough check on missing persons over that period with the characteristics we've identified. We might get lucky with some leads. I'll need to involve our colleagues in Cambridgeshire and Suffolk on that, so I'll need the go-ahead from you.' He paused. 'I don't think we can ignore this and hope it goes away,' he added. 'If this chap's still active, whether here or elsewhere, he's a potential major threat. And he will slip up some time. When he *is* caught, we'd be very exposed if we'd done nothing.'

There was a silence, broken only by Margaret tapping her pen on her desk, and the wind howling through the ill-fitting window.

'You seem to've decided it's a man, and that he's still active,' she remarked. Greg laughed.

'I'm pretty safe on both assumptions,' he said. 'Over ninety per cent of serial killers are male. And they don't usually stop until stopped by us. Or until they're dead.'

Another pause, then Margaret said, 'The wind's getting stronger. OK, Greg, I'll support approaches to Cambridgeshire and Suffolk, and investigations along the lines you've outlined, but one whisper of serial killer outside these four walls and I'll have your guts for garters.'

'Understood.' He got up. 'I've got a lot to do, then.' And he left the room at a brisk walk.

Back in his office and a few phone calls later, Greg was surrounded by his top team and a small pile of wrapped sandwiches, packets of crisps, and cans of coke. He looked round the table at Jim, Sarah, Chris and Ned.

'Tuck in, folks. We've got a lot to plan and even more to do. Ned, I've asked you to join us because, ultimately, the forensic evidence is going to be key and I'd like you to be up to speed from the off. Neither of our immediate problems is recent in origin. OK. Let me lay out the challenge and my first thoughts, then you're all welcome to comment.

'We have two priority cases and we're going to struggle to resource them. First, the remains found near Caistor St Edmund. In case you haven't heard already, HOLMES has come up with two similar cases dating from 2002 and 2008 respectively. Our assumption has to be that they were committed by the same person, and that there may be more, so far undiscovered. Margaret wants us to treat this as a priority cold case, and will herself slaughter anyone who mentions the "s" word, so think on! We have some hard work coming up, both to identify the body we have, and to check missing persons data to see if we can identify any more possible cases.

'Second, we now have information that the Semtex sourced for and used in the bomb attack on the science lab came via a Lithuanian gang operating out of Vilnius. At least that's where the money went. We need to engage with the national team to trace the money movements further, and to follow up on what we know about Bakalov's contacts beyond HMP Norwich.

'My suggestion is that Sarah leads on the Lithuanian case, and Jim on the silver threepenny murders, both reporting to me. Working to Jim, Chris will lead a team of Jill and Steve. Sarah will have Bill and Phil. I appreciate that leaves you without a sergeant in support, Sarah, but Bill is taking his exam shortly and the experience of working for you would be good for him. He's keen to step up. OK, reactions, everybody.'

There was a pause and then Sarah asked, 'What about the threats made to your ex-wife?'

'Oh God.' Greg clutched his head. 'This latest stuff on the killings in Cambridgeshire and Suffolk had completely pushed that out of my head. Where are we on that?'

Sarah turned to her iPad and flicked through a few screens.

'Are you OK with me reporting back now?' she asked, carefully not looking at Chris.

'Yes, please go ahead. Everyone here knows the position.'

'Well, to be brutally honest, in my opinion this is a hoax. A cry for attention. There were no calls made to any of Mrs Fontavelle's telephones that evening other than the one from the International Hotel, Washington location. That call was made from the room occupied by a cellist in the orchestra being conducted by Mr Fontavelle. A female cellist. All the outgoing calls made by Mrs Fontavelle, apart from the one to yourself, Greg, and two to her mother, were made either to the room occupied by her husband at the same hotel or to his mobile. None of them were answered or returned. My assessment is that the call from the female cellist was a malicious call from her husband's mistress, and no more than that. The rest of the events of that evening were an attempt to get an answer from her husband, followed by an attempt to get your attention. As for the earlier calls with an East European accent asking about you, we've so little detail it's impossible to take that further. I think those allegations are a smokescreen, designed to make the most recent accusation more believable. The response from Norfolk Police did, I think, take her by surprise and the whole thing took on proportions she wasn't expecting.' Sarah paused. A red-faced Greg was shuffling papers and the rest of the room was silent.

'Then there's no reason to take that farther,' he said. 'I'll have a word about wasting police time, and there's an end to it. We have more important issues to consider. Any other feedback?' Heads were shaken, and Greg responded, 'Then let's get to it. You all know what to do.'

The wind was rising further as Greg left, reluctantly, to pay a visit to Isabelle. The sky was filled with ragged grey clouds, scudding fast to the west and the reddening sky. 'On-shore wind,' he noted vaguely, as he drove to his uncomfortable assignation.

Isabelle was waiting in the sitting room. Her mother was flitting nervously from kitchen to sitting room and back again. 'Greg,' she exclaimed, 'lovely to see you. I think it's very kind of you to help Isabelle out.'

Isabelle didn't seem quite so grateful. She was folding children's clothes and dropping them into the wicker basket by her side. She didn't meet his eyes, as she demanded, 'So what progress? Have you found the man who threatened me?'

Greg sat down, taking his time to consider how he was going to answer. 'Thank you, Fliss,' he said to his ex-mother-in-law's question about coffee.

'I know how you like it,' she said, and returned to the kitchen briskly, relief evident in every line.

Greg leaned back. 'We've investigated your allegations thoroughly, Isabelle,' he said, as dispassionately as he was capable. 'How long did you think it would take us to find there were no calls in to you at the time you claimed?' There was a pause as she flushed bright red, more with anger than embarrassment, he noted, then she replied. 'Perhaps I got the time wrong. There was definitely a call.'

'One call,' said Greg, consulting his notes, 'from a room at the hotel where your husband is staying. The room is occupied by a female cellist named Flo Pedersen. All the other calls are outward from your mobile and the landline. Multiple calls to your husband's numbers, mobile and hotel room, one call to me, and a couple to your mother.'

His ex-mother-in-law was standing transfixed at the doorway, a tray of coffee mugs and a cafetière wobbling in her hands. Greg leapt up and grabbed the tray before it tilted too far, and put it safely on an occasional table.

'Oh, Isabelle,' exclaimed her mother as she sank into the nearest chair. It was a measure of her distress that she failed to notice that her elegant trousers had rucked up to reveal the tops of her pop socks.

Greg sat down again. 'I don't want to speculate about why you called me, Isabelle, but you do need to know you stepped over a line when you involved me professionally. Technically what you did is known as wasting police time. And it's an offence. The only reason no action is being taken is because I said I would have a word.'

'What about the earlier calls?' asked Isabelle.

'What earlier calls? Give us dates and times and we'll investigate. But you can't, can you?'

'Oh, Isabelle,' said her mother again, and Isabelle rounded on her.

'You're very quick to believe him, I note. The man who abandoned your daughter.'

'Oh come on, Isabelle,' her mother replied. 'Even I know

that isn't true. Whatever went wrong between you and Greg, and no matter where any fault lies, *he* didn't leave *you*.'

Isabelle burst into stormy tears and fled the room, leaving a difficult silence behind her.

'You might as well have your coffee,' said her mother, and she got up to pour. 'I don't know what's got into that girl, Greg, I really don't. And I apologise that she involved you like this. I can only think that she's belatedly realised what she threw away when she ran out on you.'

Greg sipped his coffee, then said with some hesitation, 'I guess the faults weren't all on one side. Policeman's wife is a tricky role at any time, and changing job and location.' He shrugged.

'But you've moved on haven't you, Greg?' There was a note of hope in her voice that perhaps the answer might be no, and her face fell a little when he replied.

'I have, very unexpectedly I must admit; but I could never trust Isabelle again, so I'm afraid that part of my life is over, Fliss.'

'I was afraid you'd say that. That man Paul is no good for her,' she added. 'He's a bully and a serial philanderer. Watching him round a woman, any woman, is like watching a dog round a lamppost.' Greg couldn't help but snort with laughter, a noise he suppressed hurriedly in case Isabelle should hear from upstairs.

'I'm sorry it's not working out,' he said as he stood up to leave, 'and I hope she does find happiness. But she can't cry wolf like this again. Or the police won't be there for her if she does need us.'

6

The search

The missing persons searches went ahead in parallel. Jill concentrated on the possible candidates to be the temenos remains, while Steve kicked off the keyword searches to identify other possible victims with similar characteristics. When Jill came over to compare notes, she found him drowning in a sea of paper.

'Look at this,' he exclaimed, and flourished one sheet from the many on his desk. 'Just last year alone there were over 1000 missing adults reported in Norfolk. Add in Cambridgeshire and Suffolk and you're talking about nearly 3000 missing adults in one year! I'm going to be here all week! A month even!'

'Don't be daft.' Jill sat down at Steve's desktop and pushed the print-offs to one side with one brisk motion of her arm. 'For a start, quite a lot of those people will have turned up since, dead or alive. The first set of data you need is the unresolved cases, those still missing. That'll cut your numbers down to hundreds rather than thousands. Then look at the age profile. You'll find you can exclude the children under twelve, and any adults over thirty-nine. Unfortunately, the majority of missing persons fall into the twelve to seventeen and eighteen to thirty-nine age brackets, but even so, you'll reduce the numbers some more. Then exclude the males, which are usually slightly more than half of the total, and you'll have a much more manageable number you can look into in detail.'

Steve heaved a huge sigh of relief. 'You make it sound so easy, Jill. Thanks.'

'It is, if you just approach it logically,' she replied. 'Anyway, that's what I've just done for the years 2007–2009, and I've narrowed down the possibles to three probables to check with dentists and family members. Of course, our remains might be of someone from out of county, in which case I'll have to widen my search, but for the time being, I think it's worth going with my first three. I'll leave you to get on, then.'

'Yes. Thanks again, Jill.' And Steve turned back to his screen with renewed energy and even a smidgeon of enthusiasm.

Jill took her file and list over to Chris's desk. 'I've three best options,' she announced. 'Am I OK to try the dental route with these?'

'Summarise what we've got,' said Chris, looking up.

'First, a twenty-three-year-old care worker from Poland. Went missing on her way home and was reported as missing by her employers in Norwich when she failed to turn up for her shift the following day and proved uncontactable. No sign of her since. No usage of credit cards or mobile phone since that day. Described as around five foot four tall, dark haired and slim.

'Second, a thirty-year-old community nurse who never

came home from a late evening call out to Cantley. Her car was found in the car park at the sugar beet factory, amongst the staff cars, keys still in the ignition. Again slim, dark haired and mid-height.

'Third, and this one's a bit of a longer shot, a twenty-five-year-old dog walker, by which I mean commercial dog walker. Dogs in her care were found running loose on the dunes near Caister lifeboat station. No sign of the woman. This was treated as suspicious at the time, as her employers and friends were adamant she would never willingly abandon the dogs. She was British in origin, also around five foot four, dark haired.'

'Why is the last one a longer shot?' asked Chris.

'Because of the timing. She didn't go missing until 2009, so she'd have to have been buried on the dig after the trenches had been fully closed up and grown over. But she's still missing and she matches in every other way.'

'Yes, I see your point. And that's all? I thought there'd be more,' commented Chris.

'That's all for the relevant time period and for Norfolk. Other possibilities have either been found since, or don't match the profile so closely, i.e. wrong hair colour, wrong age group. Obviously there're bound to be more if I look outside the county, but I thought it'd be worth checking these for dental records and so on, just in case we get lucky. I can always broaden the search later.'

'Yes. Makes sense and keeps costs down too, thanks, Jill. Go ahead.'

'If it's OK with you, I'll kick off the dental records search, then go and interview whatever friends and family I can find after ten years.'

'OK, yes. Thanks. Let me know straightaway if you turn up anything interesting.'

Chris had no sooner got back to her paperwork when Steve was coughing at her elbow.

'I've got some preliminary findings,' he announced, 'mainly thanks to Jill, I have to admit.'

Chris put her papers down again and looked up. 'What've you found?' she asked.

'First, as of this year, we in Norfolk have 123 long-term missing adults on our books, i.e. missing for more than a year. I can break that down by the year they were first reported missing, but I don't think that matters at this point. Of those, fifty-two are female, and forty-five are adults under thirty-nine. I propose to pull the files on all these and see how many match the characteristics we've been given. And I've shared my approach with Cambridge and Suffolk, and they're happy to do the same. One other thing,' he added. 'I've found a small number of cases of unidentified remains in the three counties. Five in Norfolk, six in Cambridgeshire and twelve in Suffolk. I thought I'd check those out too.'

'Oh boy! That's going to cost us! But I suppose we've no alternative. Thanks, Steve. Good work. You'd better go ahead,' said Chris, already turning back to her desk.

Once Ned obliged with the data on teeth, a mass of emails to Norfolk dental practices was despatched from Jill's desktop and she started the search for family and contacts of the three missing women. Krystina Kaminska, born in Oświęcim, Poland, in 1985, worked as a carer in a home in Norwich, not far from the community hospital in Bowthorpe. Jill picked up the phone and asked to speak to the care home manager, without much hope that, ten years later, it would be the same person. Greatly to her surprise, it was.

'I wonder if I could come and see you about Krystina,' she said. 'Just to be clear, I have no definitive news, but I am following up some details in connection with another investigation.'

'If you must,' said the voice, sounding brisk and slightly hurried, 'although I don't see there's much I can add to the statement I made ten years ago. I'll see you in half an hour, then,' and rang off, also briskly.

Pulling into the small car park at the front of the converted big house, Jill noted that the place looked well-tended. The windows were clean, the shrubbery pruned and weeded, and paintwork in good condition. In the hallway she noted that carpets were clean, albeit a little shabby, as she was met both by a wall of heat and a member of staff neatly dressed in lavender scrubs and a white apron. Mrs Smith rose to greet her as Jill was shown into the small office at the back of the hall.

'I'm sorry to bother you,' said Jill, 'and I do appreciate that a long time has passed since you reported Ms Kaminska missing in 2008. As I said on the phone, I don't have any definitive news for you, but I'm sorry to say we have recently found some remains that could possibly be those of Ms Kaminska, hence the case being reopened. As I understand it, you reported Krystina Kaminska missing at around 0830 on Wednesday 22 October 2008. What led up to you making that call?'

Mrs Smith brushed neatly bobbed grey hair back from her brow. 'I'll have to take your word for the precise date without going back to my old diaries, but that sounds about right. As to why I rang, I remember I'd been ringing Krystina's mobile ever since she failed to turn up on schedule at 6.30. After an hour or so of no answers, I rang the emergency number we had for her in our records. At least I rang the England-based one. It was the mobile number for a friend who shared a flat with her. They did answer, and said they hadn't seen her since the day before. There was a pause while they checked her room, then they came back and said that as far as they could see she hadn't come home the night before. Her handbag and coat were missing, and so were the scrubs she'd been wearing at work that day. That's when I started to get worried. She'd pulled a double shift the day before and I knew she'd have been tired. And she certainly wasn't dressed for going out. I rang off, then rang the Norfolk and Norwich and the local community hospital in Bowthorpe. Neither had any knowledge of her. That's when I rang yourselves.'

'Where did she live?'

'That's surely in your records,' replied Mrs Smith with more weariness than acid. 'She lived in a house near Bowthorpe that was divided into a couple of flats and some bedsits. She shared a flat with this other girl, another Pole. It was, is, only a few miles from here. After a few months of commuting using buses, she saved up and bought a bike so she could travel back and forth more swiftly.'

'Is the flatmate still around d'you know?'

'I don't know, but I doubt it. I'd think she'd have gone home by now, or moved on.'

'Did anyone find the bike?'

'D'you know, I don't know. I never thought to ask.'

Jill made a note. There was nothing about a bike in the records she had from that time either. 'D'you know if she set off on it the previous evening?'

'I assume so. She normally did and the bike wasn't here, so how else would she have gone home?'

Back at her desk, Jill started on more digging, but without much hope of success. The elapsed time since the events she was investigating made all her normal routes of exploration useless. No video footage from ten years ago. No opportunity to look for the missing bike. No one to interview about events on the route between the care home and Krystina's flat. No ANPR data from so long ago. She sighed heavily, frustrated at every turn. She was just about to set off to talk to the family of the missing dog walker, when she had one last bright idea.

Back to the paperwork, a dig in the report filed by DCI Geldard and DS Mathews, and 'Eureka,' she exclaimed, as she galloped from the room clutching paper to her chest.

Chris was on the phone when Jill burst through the door, but curtailed the conversation when she saw the excitement on her face.

'You've found something?'

'I think so. I'm still waiting on the dental reports,' she added with the remnants of caution, 'but it's looking more likely that the temenos remains belonged to the Polish care worker. It seems she had a bike for commuting to and from the care home, and the bike was never found. Yet,' and she waved the paperwork again, 'one of the archaeologists at the Roman site complained in passing about finding what he thought was evidence of fly-tipping at the site. Amongst the items they found, when they reopened work there, was a bike in a ditch, all covered in brambles and undergrowth generally.'

'Come on,' said Chris, rising from her desk. 'You'd better report this to the boss. He's about to start interviewing archaeologists and their volunteers. He'll need to know about this.'

'I thought Jim was dealing,' said Jill, surprised.

'He was, but the chief super has diverted him to some emergency or other, so Greg said he'd deal himself.'

Told about the bike, Greg was less than impressed. 'I think you're jumping to conclusions,' he remarked; then, noting Jill's crestfallen expression, he said, 'That's not to say you weren't right to follow up on the bike, but why would anyone cycling from that care home to their home in the same suburb of Norwich pass Caistor St Edmund? It's way out of their way, and from what you've told me, we have no reason to think she was going anywhere other than home. I'll ask about it,' he added, feeling obscurely guilty at having to pour cold water, 'but it's not very likely anyone will remember much about an abandoned bike ten years later. Unless it was a penny-farthing! Jill, well done so far, but keep looking at your other candidates. Chris, ready?'

He headed for his car and the meeting with the archaeologists, still mentally shaking his head. Chris followed in silence, checking her phone. The excavating team had agreed to set aside space in their temporary HQ for the police to talk to all those from ten years ago currently working on site – a massive total of three, as Greg noted glumly, plus however many others they could round up. However, as his car bumped over the field entrance towards the little circle of tents and gazebos, he was cheered to see a respectable crowd of around a dozen hanging about, drinking coffee out of flasks and exchanging gossip. A figure he recognised peeled off from the crowd and came towards Greg as he climbed out of his car.

'We've been pretty successful,' Jason remarked as he approached. 'It seems most of our volunteers are quite excited at the prospect of being interviewed for a police investigation. Apparently, it's a pleasant change in a day otherwise spent brushing dirt off tiles and bricks or, in some cases, stacking shelves in a supermarket. We've lined up those working on the current dig first, so they can get back to work. The other eight, you're free to see in any order that suits you.'

'Let's have your three first, then,' said Greg, 'and then ladies first, followed by the last three men.'

'Is that a nod to traditional manners, or the fact that most killers are male?' asked Jason with inconvenient perception, then waved an acknowledgement that no reply was expected and left them to it. Chris thoughtfully watched him go.

'Was he here ten years ago?' she asked Greg.

'Not on the list,' he replied, settling at the table provided for their convenience. 'Come on, let's get started. I'm not expecting a lot from this to be truthful, but it needs to be done right.'

The second of the volunteers who had been present ten years ago and was also working the current dig was forthcoming about the bike. 'I'm sure it wasn't there when we cleared up the site in 2008,' he said. 'We'd had a good relationship with the landowner that we didn't want to damage, so we were meticulous about cleaning up after ourselves and restoring the dug areas to usable grazing.

We wouldn't have left anything lying in a ditch, so that bike we found last week must have arrived sometime during the last ten years. And judging from how it was overgrown and the general state of it, not very recently either.'

'We're looking into whether it was contemporaneous with the body,' replied Greg, 'but it's a pretty long shot. And as an even longer shot, I don't suppose you remember anyone cycling round the site ten years ago.' At the rueful grin and shake of the head from the volunteer he went on, 'So, setting that on one side, what can you tell me about movements round the dig in 2008? This time around, access seems to be quite carefully controlled, but was that true ten years ago?'

'As far as I remember, yes,' said the volunteer. Chris checked her notes for his name. Miles Sandiford. Now working as a taxi driver, but pursuing his archaeological interests for as many hours a week as he could spare.

'Even ten years ago, access on to this part of the field,' he waved his hand at the nearest landscape of paddock disturbed by spoil heaps and neatly taped out shapes, 'this was limited to team members and anyone trying to wander onto site was challenged.'

'Why was that?'

'Souvenir hunters and metal detectors,' replied Miles succinctly. 'They're the bane of our lives.'

Ten more interviewees later, and very little additional information had been gleaned. Greg accepted a mug of coffee gratefully as he stood at the entrance to their temporary tent, stretching the kinks out of a spine bent by too long sitting in a camp chair at a rickety table. Chris joined him, mug also in hand, and turned slowly to take in the full 360-degree view. The foreground was all paddock and people earnestly dusting soil off various artefacts with what looked like plasterer's trowels or pastry brushes. To the north a low hill with trees on top blocked the view towards Norwich, while to the west the top of a church tower showed over some venerable yews. Jason, coming up behind them and observing which way they were looking, remarked, 'Interesting, isn't it, that this temenos has served religious communities through many centuries, from the temple precincts here to the church yonder.'

'No doubt even that's seen some changes,' replied Chris. 'Presumably it was Catholic once, before it was Church of England?'

'Like most C of E churches,' agreed Jason. 'They were all Catholic until Henry VIII fell out with the pope over his divorce and broke with the Church of Rome. So, any church that pre-dates the Reformation in the early 16th century was certainly Catholic in origin. This one belonged originally to the abbey at Bury St Edmunds, then fell victim to another of old Henry's money raising ventures: the dissolution of the monasteries. If you're interested in a poke around the church, you'll find its fabric incorporates quite a few Roman bricks, pillaged from this site and the bigger one of Venta Icenorum just to the north of here.'

'Another time maybe,' replied Greg with a look at his watch. As he turned to pick up his papers from the table behind him, the peace was disturbed by the sound of a large lorry grinding up the road and turning in to the farmyard opposite.

'That's something we haven't asked about,' he remarked. 'As landowners, how much access do the farmers have to this site? And how much did they have ten years ago?'

'Well obviously, between digs, the land is entirely under their control, provided they don't do any unauthorised digging or deep ploughing. They graze their sheep and horses on here, when we're not around. When a dig is in progress, they tend to stay away unless invited for a look round or to see anything particularly exciting, but when we've gone home for the evening, well obviously there's nothing to stop them having a wander round.'

Chris was still watching the lorry manoeuvring in front of the grain store in the farmyard. 'I assume visits by grain lorries are fairly frequent,' she said, 'given the size of that store.'

'Is that what they are?' replied Jason, uninterested. 'Yes, we see quite a few of those. And other delivery vehicles too.'

'It might be worth having a chat with the farmer,' Chris said to Greg, 'just to establish what the traffic was like ten years ago. It'd be easy to transport a body in a vehicle that size.' As they watched, a forklift with a bucket on the front began the task of transferring wheat from the store to the back of the lorry.

'Let's pop over now,' she suggested. 'We've time for a quick chat.'

Entr'acte 2

The first ghost

My first malevolent ghost was in Cambridge. I spotted her drifting round by one of the colleges. Other people didn't seem to see her. At least, they never seemed to look at her. But she came up to me. She scared me, with her jet-black hair, red mouth and sharp teeth. She kept showing me her teeth. I thought at first she was smiling, but no one smiles that much. And the teeth at the sides were longer than the ones at the front. I walked away from her, down a side street, but she followed. Still smiling, still making no sense. She seemed to want something, but I couldn't understand her. I kept trying to walk away, but she kept following. Then she grabbed me by the shoulder and pulled me round. The road was quiet and there was no one around to rescue me. That was my first mistake. I tried to shake her off again, but she wouldn't let go. And she kept smiling. Smiling. And I kept looking at those teeth, and the red mouth, until the voice in my head was screaming at me. 'Get away. Get away or she's going to bite. You're going to die here in this quiet street.'

She leaned in for the bite and I grabbed her neck to keep her away. Then I squeezed and squeezed, until she went limp and the dead weight dropped at my feet. There was still no help around, so I just walked away, shaking with fright. That was my second mistake.

I went home and sat down in my bedsit with a can of lager. Then I realised I was still at risk and I got up and locked the door and windows.

'Next time,' my voice said, 'next time make sure you're safe. A stake through the heart. Or silver. That should do it.'

7

Sweet smell of success

Left behind at HQ while Greg and Chris set off for Caistor St Edmund, Jill sighed, brushed her hair out of her eyes, and turned again to her emails. Still nothing from the dentists and nothing new from Ned. She decided she had time to follow up one of her other leads before knocking off for the day. It was a toss-up between the Cantley community nurse and the Caister dog walker. Cantley won, largely on the basis it was on her way home. She picked up her coat, bag and notes, and set off for the sugar factory.

Turning off the A47 she noted the roads to Cantley were much better than in adjacent villages, both broader and smoother. Presumably to facilitate lorry movement. She could smell the factory long before she arrived there; a sickly sweet, but not wholly unpleasant, aroma blew in the wind that was kicking up the surface of the River Yare as it ran past the processing plant. Lorry-loads of the large, lumpy roots were arriving.

Slowing and obeying the signage, she left the lorries to turn off at the beet intake and followed the road a little further round to a visitors' entrance. Pulling up at the main security office, she parked in the small lay-by and took herself in for a chat with a burly security guard behind the desk.

'Hi,' she said, holding out her ID. 'Detective Constable Jill Hayes. I think I'm expected.'

The security guard nodded. 'Yes, that's fine,' he said. 'Please sign in and read the food safety rules on the pad to your left while I issue you with a pass. Have you been here before?'

'No, never,' she replied.

'OK.' He reached behind him for a big aerial photo of the site. 'You need to follow this road down to the river,' he said, pointing first over his shoulder and then at the map. 'Reverse park in the visitors' car park here,' he indicated where he meant, 'then go into the blue reception building here. You'll be met.'

'Thank you,' said Jill. She took the proffered pass and went back to her car. She drove in slowly as the security gate rose, and she looked round her with interest. There was a lorry park on her right with, behind it, what seemed to be a small car park. She drove further along as instructed and the river opened out before her, with visitors' parking signposted on the river bank.

Stretching the kinks out of a spine that had spent too long sitting at a desk, Jill walked a few yards over the tarmac to get a better view of the site. Back the way she'd come, a bulk transporter seemed to be waiting to unload something, while a sugar tanker was headed in the opposite direction. As she watched, it pulled onto a weighbridge, paused and then drove off to the main exit near the lorry park. Turning the other way, she had a view up and down the River Yare. To her right she saw what seemed to be public moorings, empty of pleasure boats at this time of the year, and the outline of a river bank pub. She was startled by what seemed to be a public footpath running along the river bank, divided from the industrial site by sturdy metal rails certainly, but readily accessible in either direction.

The gentleman waiting for her in reception turned out to be one of the human resources team.

'Good afternoon,' said a long, lanky middle-aged man dressed warmly in a British Sugar uniform and hi-vis jacket, a bright yellow hard hat in his hand. 'I'm Joseph Wright, head of HR. We thought I might be most relevant, as I have ready access to the necessary database and I'm also the chap who inducts a lot of the new staff, so I'm used to explaining how this place works. How can I help?'

Jill got her notes out.

'I'm making some enquiries about a cold case,' she explained. 'Around ten years ago, I can give you the precise date, a thirty-year-old community nurse never went home after a late evening call out to your factory here. Her family and her colleagues separately reported her missing the following morning. The community nurse team records showed that the last call in her diary was to a minor injury complicated by some symptoms that might have been a heart attack. It seems someone visiting the factory had a fall in the car park. Your workplace first aid team attended and rang for assistance and the task of first response was handed off to the community nurse team to assess and decide if an ambulance was required. The nurse in question, a Julie Bolton, was detailed to attend, and subsequently made a brief report to the treatment database and requested ambulance support. The ambulance records show the casualty was taken to the James Paget Hospital in Gorleston and the nurse was still on site when the ambulance left. Her colleagues hazarded the theory that she might have stayed on site in order to write up her notes, as this is a location with a rather better mobile-phone signal than many places in Norfolk. After that, nothing. When it was reported to us, preliminary enquiries found that her car was still in the car park here, left amongst the other cars, keys still in the ignition. I'd like to know what you have in your records about this event, and I'd like a look around the car park areas please?'

'I looked out our accident reports for the month in question,' replied Joseph. 'I thought that'd be the best place to start.' He pointed Jill to the open file on the small meeting table, motioned her to sit down and planted a stringy finger on an entry halfway down the right-hand page. 'The health and safety officer on duty that day made the entry. A press visitor to the factory tripped in the car park at the end of his visit. The specific trip hazard seemed to be a piece of a broken pallet from a pile in the corner. The first-aider on duty attended, and recommended a trip to A&E as he thought a stitch might be necessary to a wound on the visitor's forearm. When contact was made with the ambulance service they said they were trialling a keep-people-out-of-hospital service for suitable casualties and offered a visit from a community nurse. The casualty, one Tom Dreyfus, accepted with alacrity. At least,' Joseph looked down at Jill with laughter on his face, 'that's how I interpret the comment recorded in here. He clearly didn't fancy a long wait in A&E. The accident report goes on to say that while waiting for the arrival of the nurse, the casualty complained of chest pains, and so one of the first actions of the nurse was to request an ambulance after all. The nurse is recorded as having arrived on site at 1917 and the ambulance at 1940, but neither were asked to sign in as you did today and neither were issued with a pass. It seems security took the decision to wave through the two emergency vehicles, i.e. the nurse's car and the ambulance. They noted the time the ambulance left, but there is no record of the nurse's car leaving, and because she hadn't signed in, no one went to check.'

'And so her car, at least, never left,' agreed Jill. 'Wasn't it a bit odd that no one noticed a strange car parked overnight? I assume she was in the car park near the entrance? The one I've just come past?'

'That's right,' replied Joseph. 'And no, it's not at all surprising no one noticed it. That car park is always full of strange vehicles. Hire cars, pool cars; you name it, they're parked there. One more wouldn't have been noticeable.'

'So, when was the car noticed?'

'Not until your folk started to make enquiries, I'm embarrassed to say. It was just a standard saloon car, no logo or anything to make it stand out.'

'Are the first-aider and the gatekeeper still employed here?'

'The gatekeeper is, but he's not on duty today. The first-aider is still employed by British Sugar but at the Bury St Edmunds factory, not here. I can let you have details of both, if you like.'

'Yes, thank you. Now, can I have a look around the car park and the outside of the factory please?'

'Yes, of course. You can have a full tour if you like.'

'Not today, thanks.' Jill looked up from her bag, where she

was shoving her notes. 'I'm a bit pressed for time today, and since it seems Sister Bolton never entered the factory, my focus needs to be on the areas she did visit.'

'I'll still need to kit you out with hi-vis clothing though, unless you've brought your own PPE?'

'No, I haven't. The loan of some would be very helpful, thank you.'

'We do our best not to lose people, or have them run over,' said Joseph with a grin, handing over a hard hat like his, a hi-vis jacket, gloves and protective glasses. 'Have these as well, just in case you change your mind about going in the factory.'

As they walked down the river bank to the entrance, Jill looked around with interest. 'I saw the beet deliveries went in a different way,' she said. 'Why would a lorry come down to this side of the site?'

'Well, some delivery lorries come in this way,' replied Joseph, 'whether they be delivering limestone, anthracite or other materials. But the lorries that've dropped off sugar beet would only come out this way if they were picking up something else for their return journey, like wet beet pellets for animal feed.'

'Do they park up in that lorry park?'

'Not always, and not routinely. But if they've run out of hours on their tacho, they might park up for a break. They're not allowed to stay overnight though.'

'Would you know which companies' lorries had been on site on the day in question?'

'Absolutely. And the names of the drivers. The only question would be whether we've still got the records from that long ago. I've got someone checking now.'

*

Towards the end of the tour, Jill walked over towards the river bank. She was surprised to see how little margin there was between the footpath and the surly water flowing beside. In places there seemed to be little more than an inch or two, and she took an involuntary step back.

'Yes, it's high,' remarked Joseph, noting her reaction. 'In fact we got a flood warning from the Environment Agency only this morning. It looks like they may be right.'

'Does a flood threaten the factory?' asked Jill.

'It can do. We've had the river up to the reception area where you met me. If that happens, we drop barriers between the buildings to stop the water going any further. After that we can carry on processing as long as we have beet supplies on the big storage pads at the back. Our main problem would be interruptions to deliveries and collections if the high water persisted for a long time. Once we start the campaign in October, we don't normally stop for anything until it's complete in February. Interrupting processing would cause us a serious problem.'

'What about the footpath, mooring and pub along there? What's to stop members of the public coming on to the site?'

'Very little, if they were determined. Apart from our security team challenging them, obviously. But there's no barrier as such, other than the one which stops lorries going onto the footpath and the signs on gates.'

Jill made a note. 'Thank you, you've been very helpful. I'll be in touch if I need anything else. The main thing is that list of everyone who was on site that afternoon and evening, including any lorry drivers who made drops during those hours.'

'Surely, if we've still got it,' said Joseph. 'I'll let you know ASAP.'

'Thanks then. And good luck with any flooding.'

'Thanks. If I can just have my PPE back?'

Jill grinned and handed it all over. 'Thanks again,' she said.

Back in her car and heading for the exit barrier, Jill looked at her dashboard clock, made a quick calculation and decided to head for her home in Moulton. En route her phone bleeped a few times to indicate incoming text messages but, ever a stickler for the no-phone-while-driving rule, she drove on. It was only after arriving, changing her shoes, pouring a glass of lager and sinking into an armchair to think about supper, that she remembered the missed messages. One was from Steve, still in the office ploughing through missing persons data. The other was from the emergency coordination team. She read Steve's first.

'Progress! We have a match on one of those missing persons you consulted dentists about. The Polish girl, Krystina, is the temenos remains. I've put the details in an email. Good call, Jill.'

So excited she almost dropped her phone, she nearly forgot to read the second. It was an instruction to report to the ops room immediately, to help coordinate flooding assistance. She took the time to ring her DCI first, but he wasn't answering, probably, she reflected, because he had been called out too. Sighing, she put down her half-drunk lager, then she snatched a can of coke and a sausage roll from the fridge, and headed back out to her car.

Entr'acte 3

Next time, I was prepared. I'd been sorting through my stuff just before moving to the new place that went with my new job, and I came across a small box I'd hung on to when my mother died. It was the box of silver thruppenny bits that she used to put in her Christmas puddings. At least, that's what she claimed she did, but if you watched her carefully you could see her slip one into each bowl as she served the pudding out, so everyone she wanted to get a coin, did get one. They always went to family members, because that way she could collect them up after the meal and use them again the following year. Or at least, that was the theory. Clearly some hadn't been given back because there was only one left. I looked at the little box and realised I'd need to get some more. Meanwhile, I put the sole survivor in an old purse and hid it in my cab. That way, it would always be near at hand.

*

When I saw the next ghost, she was at the side of the road like the first. Not far away either. Perhaps there was a nest of them nearby. She came with me quite happily it seemed and got into my cab. Then I drove her to the quiet place I knew, and took her by the throat. She didn't make much of a fight. I think she was quite glad to be released, really. So I laid her out gently and made sure she'd stay safe with the piece of silver in her mouth.

8

Nails and gales

Sarah parked her car in the first spot available, a few doors along from 'Nails Galore'. The shadows of the preceding business were visible in the faded letters beneath the bright green sign. '*Chips with Everything*' read the original, and Sarah wondered whether that meant greasy spoon or mobile-phone shop. She looked at her notes and at the name of the proprietor interviewed by the Gangmaster and Labour Abuse Agency. 'Madame Trieste,' she read.

Pushing the door open, she entered the shades-of-green reception.

'Can I help?' asked the middle-aged lady behind the desk, but her welcoming smile froze when Sarah showed her police ID. 'Madame Trieste?' asked Sarah.

'Not you lot again,' said the woman in green overalls with the long, dyed-blonde hair, darkening along the centre parting.

Sarah sat herself down in the nearest chair.

'Just a few questions,' she said. 'It won't take long.'

'Have you a warrant?' The woman was brusque and failed to look at Sarah, occupying herself with sorting the desk drawer in front of her. 'I'm busy. Too busy.'

Sarah made a point of looking round the empty salon, at the shelves laden with tired bottles of hand cream and body lotion, and at the even more weary adverts on the walls for massages and facials.

'There's no one here,' she pointed out.

'Don't mean I'm not busy.'

'OK, I'll have a manicure while I'm here and ask my questions at the same time.'

'£25 for gel manicure,' said the woman.

'OK,' said Sarah.

She watched in silence while her cuticles were tidied and the nails buffed and shaped. She chose a dark red colour and said, 'I just want to ask you about your visit to Dragan Bakalov.'

'Why?' asked the woman.

'Because no one else has visited him in the months he's been in prison, and we wondered why you.'

'Nothing wrong with visiting a prisoner,' said the woman. 'I follow all the rules. I have all the permissions.'

'But why you? How do you know Bakalov?'

There was a sullen silence while the woman painted the clear undercoat onto the first four fingernails and indicated Sarah should put her hand under the UV light.

'Because he is Romanian. Like me.'

'Romania is a big country,' remarked Sarah, while the

next four fingernails were painted. 'How precisely do you know Bakalov?'

'I don't know him,' said the woman reluctantly, her head down. 'But I was asked to visit him. To pass on a message.'

'What message?'

'Just to tell him he's not forgotten.'

'And who's not forgotten him?'

The woman was silent.

'Who asked you to pass on the message?'

'I can say no more,' said the woman. 'I'll finish your nails, then you go. It'll still be £25.'

And the rest of the manicure was conducted in silence.

Reporting back to Greg later, Sarah said, 'I think she was frightened. I don't think we'll get any more out of her that way. Probably not at all without a warrant, and I don't think we have enough on her.'

'Was there anyone else there?' he asked.

'Not that I saw, but I could hear noises, like there were at least two other people on the premises. In a back room perhaps.'

'OK, thanks, Sarah. I think we need to see if we can turn up any more from the money movements. If we can find a link between Nails Galore and anyone else in the sorry set-up, we can try again; meanwhile…' He shrugged.

Sarah paused on her way out of the office and looked back at Greg's head bowed over his laptop. 'I don't think we'll get anything more out of her,' she repeated, 'not without some real leverage. I got the impression she was pretty determined as well as scared.'

*

That night the easterly strengthened still further. Across Norfolk and Suffolk some older trees gave up the unequal struggle and by late evening the highways patrols were being inundated with calls about blocked roads, while several parts of East Anglia suffered blackouts and the electricity companies struggled to get customers back online. The offshore wind farms were stood down, the vanes left to stand still in a wind that, if allowed to turn them, would have stripped bearings and burned out generators. Just after midnight, Greg and all other personnel not currently on shift or on sick leave got emergency call-outs. The last few days of easterlies hadn't just brought a wind chill that had the whole region shivering. It had backed sea water into the east coast estuaries and this was now being followed by an exceptionally high tide. The Thames Barrier had been raised and the Environment Agency had issued multiple red alerts to areas within river basins, flood plains, and indeed anywhere within a few miles of the east coast. Greg was reminded of his often-expressed view that Norfolk just had too much water. It seemed it was about to get a lot more.

Equipped with the best of his wet-weather gear and a freshly charged mobile phone, Greg headed for Great Yarmouth as ordered. Getting through the screaming gale-force winds was bad enough, as his windscreen wipers struggled with rain and spray. Crossing the Bure by Acle Bridge he couldn't help but notice how high the water was, and wondered how bad things were in the town for him to have been instructed to take the country route rather than the Acle Straight.

'Presumably,' he thought aloud, 'because that road is on the marshes.'

*

Arriving in town and making his way to the first main bridge over the Bure, he found silent streets and few people other than emergency services. He looked over at the river.

The water surged and retreated in the circle of light from the lamppost. Then surged again, almost to the top of the river wall. A thin trickle broke from the treacle-black surface and eased its way down the inside of the sea defences. There was another surge and more trickles, like thin fingers reaching for the onlookers. The light flickered, recovered, then flickered again and went out. The river bank was plunged into darkness just as the fingers became arms, extending across the pavement, stretching out to the grass lawn beyond and grasping the boots of the emergency workers standing by.

'Back to the main road,' commanded the figure wearing a tabard that read 'Incident Commander' Greg watched the mixed bunch of Environment Agency staff, police and a couple of soldiers turn and splash towards the vehicles parked on the rise towards the bridge, then followed, addressing his radio as he went.

'Nothing more to do here for the moment,' he reported. 'The evacuation of the area at risk seems to have gone smoothly. I'm getting the team clear and following the evacuation effort to higher ground. We need to kick off Plan Recover for the morning. For the time being, we just need to make sure folk are evacuated and stay that way. The Environment Agency team tell me pumps are on standby and they can't do any more just now to stop the water overtopping the river wall. Provided the wall holds, the quantity of water coming over is likely to remain low. If the wall goes, then all bets are off. And we don't want anyone trapped down by the river if that happens.'

'OK, Greg. The exercise in Yarmouth has gone well, considering. Handover to uniform and get yourself to Hemsby. That's the next big risk area and it seems there're a lot of people not cooperating. Can you get along and give them a kick in the pants?'

'Will do. Out.'

Greg splashed through the shallow water over to his car parked by the magistrate's court, which he noted was well protected by sand bags at the doors. Back in familiar, and drier, surroundings he radioed Jim Henning, whom he knew had oversight of the evacuation efforts further along the threatened coast. His route out of Great Yarmouth took him parallel with the river. As far as he could see, all houses were dark, but emergency helicopters were still using the airfield near the dog track.

'Jim,' he said, 'I'm through in Yarmouth for the moment and heading for Hemsby. Where're you?'

'Scratby cliffs. So far, the new sea defences are holding. There's a bit of slippage from the rain, but the sea isn't the issue here. Hemsby, however, that's another matter. I'm told part of the cliff's gone already and that means a couple more bungalows are teetering on the edge. The gardens have washed away and also part of the road.'

'Have they been evacuated?' asked Greg.

'One has. The other's a holiday home and was empty anyway. We're trying to clear the row behind and the ones further along the coast road too, but some of the owners are being stubborn.'

'I'll be there ASAP.'

*

Climbing out of his car again was a very different experience at Hemsby than it had been in Great Yarmouth. In Yarmouth, partly protected from the wind by the surrounding buildings, the overwhelming impression had been of the menacing waters surging and retreating in the river. Here, in the full teeth of the easterly powering in from the Urals with seemingly nothing in between, Greg found it hard to stand straight and even breathe. A rain-lashed figure in streaming oilskins proved to be Jim. Half crouching in the lee of the car they communicated in bellows, augmented by waving arms.

Greg was given to understand that part of the cliff face was close to collapse – yet some home owners were still reluctant to evacuate.

'Show me,' he yelled into the wind, his words snatched away even as they left his mouth. Jim got the meaning, if not the sounds, and nodded inside his hood.

'This way,' he waved, and the two of them staggered down a rutted lane towards the cliff edge.

As they came within sight of the sea, Greg gasped. He was used to seeing it in a range of modes, from summer's glassy calm to winter's rolling breakers. This was something else. From the base of the cliff to the horizon was a seething mass of breakers taller than a man, rolling in to besiege the cliff with the force of an entire army of trebuchets. The whole surface was lined and splashed with white foam, catching the glow from the floodlights of the emergency services. Under the scream of the wind he could hear the crash of the waves hitting and overtopping the sea defences, and feel the secondary crash as they hit the cliff beneath his feet. He took a step back involuntarily, and as he did so, with a rumble audible even over the wind, a section of land that had previously been someone's garden tipped, split, and rolled to the waiting sea below. The bungalow hung on a moment or two longer, then lost its fight with gravity, sagged, and slithered over the edge in a long, slow glissade.

The two men turned and stumbled over the rough ground to the adjacent property, set a little further back from the cliff edge. As they approached, they saw that uniformed officers and a couple of men in Environment Agency tabards appeared to have won the argument with the residents. Watching, they saw an elderly couple ushered to the dubious safety of the cars on the road behind. One of the constables broke away and came up to Jim.

'That last cliff fall did the trick,' he said, 'and probably only just in time. That, and finding out what the real problem was.'

'Which was?' asked Greg.

'Their hens in the back garden. Once we promised they could take them, we started to make progress. One of the Agency lads boxed them up and put them in their car. God knows what the volunteers at the Parish Hall will do with them, but at least this lot are safe now. Christ!' he added as a rumble signalled another slice of cliff descending to the hungry sea. 'Really was just in time, wasn't it?'

The first glimmers of yellow light on the horizon showed the extent of the damage. The shattered remnants of two bungalows were balanced precariously halfway down the muddy cliff. Broken timbers and individual bricks, mortar still attached, were all that remained of a third. Scattered along the beach from Hemsby, southward as far as the eye could see, was the sad detritus of homes and lives: fridges and freezers, tables and chairs, sinks, toilets and miscellaneous household wares.

*

Jim and Greg, tired at the end of a long and sleepless night, approached the cliff edge with caution. Ahead of them, taking risks that neither felt comfortable with, was one of the Environment Agency staff. He was peering over the edge and even as they watched, one foot slipped in a manner that brought their hearts into their mouths.

'Get back,' shouted Greg, 'nothing's worth the risk,' but the man ignored him and leaned out again, this time holding his phone out at arm's length to take a photograph. He came back then, and made his way over to Greg and Jim as fast as he could over the uneven ground.

'There's something down there,' he said, gasping. 'I thought so earlier, but now it's lighter, I'm sure. Look.' He proffered his phone. 'I hoped I was just seeing things. But I'm not, am I? It's an arm.'

Entr'acte 4

It was years before I saw another ghost. My new job just didn't seem to bring me into contact with ghosts. Perhaps because I was working nights? I don't know. Anyway, it was only when I changed jobs again that I met the next ghost. I'd just made a journey to a new place. I was doing the boss a favour because my holiday started the next day. It was lucky I made the trip, because I was just about to go home when she appeared. I'd seen someone in a uniform floating around the car park but I took no notice until she came up to me. She had some tale about her car being broken, and wanted to know if I could take a look at it. No way was I going over to that dark corner on my own. Not with her flashing her white teeth at me through her red mouth and laughing in my face. She followed me round the corner still talking about why she was there, as if I was interested, then I turned to her and went up close, my heart beating like a hammer in my ears. I went to take hold of her but this one reacted differently. She started back and opened her mouth to shout. I pushed her away and she banged her head on the side. That seemed like a good idea, so I did it again harder. There was blood on my hands. I didn't like that. I wiped them on her top, put a cloth round her head, pushed her in and drove away. The chap on the gate waved as I went past.

The yard was empty as usual when I got back, so I put her in my car under a blanket and went straight off on my hols. That night, I laid her in the garden with a coin. Another one safely protected.

I'd long since run out of my mother's silver thruppennies. I'd been looking for similar coins at antique fairs and on eBay, but then I had a stroke of luck. The Mint released a whole batch of historic coins, all in one go. That seemed like a good omen to me. I got twenty from a shop in Peterborough.

9

After the flood

After twenty hours on duty and five hours sleep, Jill was still wired when she turned in for work the following morning. She found the room buzzing and Greg, surrounded by a small crowd, over by the whiteboard. To her disappointment, as she got closer she saw that the identification she'd been hoping to announce was already logged on the board. Seeing her approach, Chris spoke briefly to Greg, who turned with a smile.

'Jill, congratulations, that was pretty impressive. That gives us a real step forward with the temenos remains. Well done all round.'

Jill started to feel better and took a seat at the front of the gathering crowd.

'Right, folks, let's review where we're at. Thanks to Jill we have an ID for the temenos remains, and we can now follow up in further detail with friends and family. First of all, we need to tell close relations. Chris, can I leave that in your hands?' As Chris nodded, Greg went on, 'OK. Now to our new body.' Jill looked up quickly, this being news to her. She wasn't alone in that, as she noted.

'Ned is currently over at Hemsby,' went on Greg, 'but, Jim, you bring us up to date with what we know so far.'

Jim stepped forward and pointed at a photo newly added to the board.

'This body was exposed when the cliff fell in last night's storm,' he said. 'All we could see at the start was an arm and shoulder blade, as you can see from the photograph. This body is also mostly skeletonised and also has no clothes nor, so far as we can ascertain, any ID. It's hard to know how she lay in the ground at present, as the ground itself has moved. Ned is seeing what he can find out as we speak. Once the body is recovered from the cliff it will obviously go to the pathologist. At present we don't even know what sex the victim was, although on the basis of the arm, Ned was prepared to say he thought it might well turn out to be a woman. What we did find was this.' He stuck a second photo on the board.

'Which is?' asked Greg, peering at the smudgy picture.

'A coin. Probably a silver coin. Found a few feet down the hill from the body.'

'Any idea what?'

'Not yet. Ned was using a metal detector on the site just before he went ahead with recovering the body, and this showed up. He's reluctant to rub all the dirt off it just yet, until he's checked for other evidence. But he says it's the right size for a silver thruppence.'

*

It was early evening before Greg made his weary way home to his cottage. It was only on the approach road from Acle that he suddenly realised the flood warnings for the Bure might have had a very personal impact. Barriers were in place across some side roads with 'road closed' signs reinforcing the message. His lane was open, but detritus across the trackway showed where the retreating water had left its mark. Piles of twigs, leaves and plastic rubbish lurked wherever the water flow had been impeded, while uneven lines of smaller flotsam and jetsam wavered across his path. Worried now about what he might find when he got home, and the safety of his cat, a random memory reminded him that what he was looking at was probably flotsam since it had entered the water by accident, while jetsam was debris deliberately thrown into the water. He realised he was distracting himself with irrelevancies and concentrated on driving safely over the unusually bumpy surface.

It was with enormous relief that he saw the headlights light up his cottage, still standing, and with even more that he noted the high-water mark, a foot or two short of his walls. The water had certainly come close, and no doubt there would be some damage to garden shed and garage, but his home and his cat were safe. In through the front door, an indignant cat twining round his ankles, Greg headed for the cat food, bread and cheese, and bed. In that order. Noting he had to see Margaret first thing in the morning, he texted a hearts emoji to Chris and turned out the light.

A good night's sleep did a lot to repair the damage of the previous day. Around the county everyone, public and police alike, woke up to clearing skies, dropping winds and falling tides. Local BBC TV reported damage along the coast and inland along the courses of the Yare and the Waveney. The discovery of a body drew a passing mention and a brief shot of the fallen cliff at Hemsby, now festooned with crime scene tape as well as household remains. They did not venture on any speculation as to the origin of the body. If anything, the impression left was that the body might have been historic, and the final comment that police were investigating was noncommittal. Greg was out of the house by 0645 and a call on his hands-free from Chris confirmed that she too was already on her way to HQ. They bumped into each other in the car park, and walked in together. Greg noticed the preceding day had not dented her colour values, today represented by black trousers, fuchsia jumper and bright yellow waterproof jacket.

'I like the hi-vis approach,' he said. 'Very practical.'

Chris thumped him in the arm surreptitiously. 'Where away today, boss?'

'Depends to some extent on what Margaret has to say. I'm seeing her at eight. Then I hope we'll all be able to return to normal duties. We've got enough to do as it is without any more co-option on to flood management.' He pushed the door open for Chris then following her through asked, 'Did you speak to Krystina Kaminska's family?'

'Yes. All done. I spoke through an interpreter, and said we'd be in touch if we had any further questions, or any news. Obviously their second question was when could they have the remains for burial. I explained the issues and said we'd let them know.'

'And the first question?'

'Who did it?'

*

Back in the ops room, Greg stood in front of the whiteboard, the three strands of investigation laid out before him with photos, descriptions and lots of question marks.

'Not made much progress yet, have we?' he said aloud. 'First, the temenos remains, now identified, but no answer yet as to what happened. And now the Hemsby body about which…' He turned and asked of the room generally, 'Anything from Ned yet?'

'Said he'd be in around eight,' replied Steve, not looking up from his computer screen. 'He's back on site in Hemsby with Jim.'

'Bother, I'll be in with Margaret by eight. Tell him I want to see him immediately she's finished with me, will you?'

Greg had just surmounted what felt like an Everest of paperwork in a great hurry and was heading out the door, when Ned rushed in. 'Glad I caught you,' he started as Greg interrupted, 'Sorry, Ned. I'm already running it a bit tight to see Margaret. I'll catch up with you immediately I come out.'

'No, sorry, Greg, you do need to hear this. I'll be quick. We've disinterred the body. It's a slim woman with dark hair. It looks very like she had her hands crossed on her chest when buried originally. The landslip shifted the body and turned it over, exposing just one arm. And the coin found a little way down the cliff face was a silver thruppence. I can't yet say for certain, but it may have been placed in her mouth and fell out when the body moved.'

'So, a good chance she's another in the temenos remains sequence. OK. Thanks for the heads-up, Ned. As I said, I'll catch up with you properly—'

'Sorry,' said Ned, interrupting in his turn, 'but there's something else you need to know before you speak to Margaret. An EDP reporter was hanging about when the girl cleaning up the coin came to tell me what she'd found. And as luck would have it, it's the same one who reported on the temenos remains. She's put two and two together and gone off spouting the words "serial killer".'

To say Margaret wasn't pleased was putting it mildly. In fact, incandescent was probably understating the ambient temperature by several thousand degrees.

'Which bit of "no leaks about serial killers" wasn't clear?' she demanded. 'What was the reporter doing so close to the investigation anyway?'

'It seems she'd been following up on the cliff damage at Hemsby and turned up to ask whether anything was now known about the body found there. It was just bad luck the new girl entrusted with the coin started shouting the odds before she realised who was in the vicinity.'

'So we need a press conference now, whether we like it or not. And you'd better have some news to share that can at least be presented as positive, DCI Geldard. Best case, we're going to look incompetent. Worst case, mass panic!'

Entr'acte 5

My two weeks' holiday went by in a flash, then I saw another ghost almost immediately. There by the side of a busy road with a bike. Seemed she'd got a flat tyre. But that was just a ploy. It was lucky I caught on to her fast, because at first she seemed quite genuine. It was only when she stood up and smiled that I saw the black hair, the red lips and the danger. She died quickly, and for sure I knew how to make certain she stayed dead. I remembered I'd seen a good place for a burial only that morning. It was on holy ground and now I had plenty of silver too, so this one should be doubly safe. I took her with me. And the bike.

10

Conferences

Bowing to pressure, they convened the press conference for 1600, which suited TV and radio, but not the print media so much.

'Tough,' said Margaret heartlessly, the activities of the reporter with acute hearing still rankling with her.

The room was close to full, attendees including all the local press as well as freelancers hoping to sell the story to the nationals. At the back were the BBC East cameras and their reporter was in the front row along with the radio representatives. Greg followed Margaret to the low dais. His heart would have sunk if it hadn't already been resident in his boots. This was his idea of hell. He hoped fervently that he wouldn't have to view the footage after. Seeing himself on screen was the only thing worse than seeing himself in the mirror. They took their seats behind the long table and a silence fell. The cameraman bent to his apparatus, and Margaret cleared her throat.

Margaret introduced herself then said, with only the faintest tone of irony, 'Thank you for attending at short notice. I am going to outline the basic facts as we understand them, and then hand over to DCI Geldard, Senior Investigating Officer for this case, to bring you up to date. We'll be happy to answer questions at the end, subject, obviously, to the needs of the investigation.

'OK. The facts are these. On Monday 15 October, a body was found in a trench on the archaeological site near Caistor St Edmund. Norwich Archaeology did the right thing and called us out promptly. We attended with full forensic back-up and the body was removed for pathological examination. It was immediately apparent that although the remains were no more than a skeleton, they were modern not ancient, and that they had been placed in the dig within the last ten years.'

'Is it true that you found a coin in its mouth?' shouted Ms Jennings from the front row, freelancer and sometime reporter for the EDP. Margaret ignored the interruption.

'The remains have since been identified as those of a care worker named Krystina Kaminska, who was reported missing in November 2008. The family have been informed.'

Ms Jennings tried again. 'But did the remains include a coin?'

'I said we'd come to questions at the end,' said Margaret. 'And may I remind everyone that we are talking here of people, with grieving family and friends. Krystina Kaminska was a young woman, with a career, interests and a future. Let's remember that.

'If I may continue, Krystina's body was found buried with a relatively modern silver coin. A check on the police database for any similar cases turned up two, one in Cambridgeshire in 2002 and one in Suffolk in 2008.'

Heads turned to each other and there was a susurration from the assembled company, which Margaret ignored.

'Neither of those bodies have so far been identified.' She went on. 'The investigation of the case at Caistor St Edmund was underway with the cooperation of Cambridgeshire and Suffolk police, when the recent east coast flood emergency intervened. Notwithstanding the diversion of police resources onto emergency duties, the investigation continued and succeeded in identifying the Caistor St Edmund body as I have already described.'

Greg stirred a little in his seat, feeling that the interruptions seemed to have thrown Margaret slightly off course, but more than happy to keep quiet for the moment.

'That was how things stood, when the sea brought down a section of cliff at Hemsby, exposing part of a body in the process. I'll now hand over to DCI Geldard for the latest in this investigation.'

Greg looked up, hoping he didn't look as startled as he felt. He'd expected Margaret to do more of the talking. He stood up, feeling more comfortable on his feet than seated, and picked up the verbal baton.

'So, we have three bodies that we know were buried with some similar characteristics, in the years 2001, 2008 and 2009 in Cambridgeshire, Norfolk and Suffolk respectively. A fourth body was found yesterday in Hemsby that may also share some of those characteristics, but at present it's too soon to be sure. We're pursuing several lines of enquiry aimed at identifying the remaining bodies and ascertaining what, if any, were the links between them. I cannot say more than that at present without compromising the investigation.' Several arms shot to their maximum height and a number of voices shouted questions that essentially amounted to the same thing. 'Were these deaths the result of a serial killer, and if so, are women at risk today?'

Greg glanced at Margaret to see if she wanted to respond, but it seemed the ball still lay in his court. He took a deep breath.

'The similarities in the burials may indicate a link, and we are investigating with that possibility in mind. That said, it's too soon to answer your question definitively. As to the risk today, while noting that we have no evidence of any connected deaths more recent than 2009, I would always advise women, and indeed men, to take sensible precautions when they are out and about, especially at night. Don't walk alone if you can avoid it. Don't accept lifts from strangers or use unlicensed taxicabs. And make sure someone knows where you are going and what time you intend to return.'

A confusing hubbub of squawking voices arose around him, but Margaret intervened firmly. 'We have no more to say for now. As and when we find more evidence and/or identify further victims we will release updates. Thank you for now.'

In the corridor outside she glared at Greg. 'I suppose it could have been worse,' she said, 'but not much. Couldn't you have been more reassuring?'

'Not in conscience, no,' he replied. 'I stuck with the facts.'

'Humph.' She grunted. 'Well stick with this investigation too. I don't want to find you straying after wild Lithuanian geese.'

*

It was with huge relief that Greg retreated from his discomfort zone to the ops room and the familiar faces of his team. Except one wasn't familiar. In the middle of the room, lounging carelessly across a table strewn with the results of Steve's searches, was a burly man he didn't know. He straightened up slowly as Greg came through the door and introduced himself.

'DC Jeff Fellows, newly arrived from the Met. The big boss told me to report to you. Said something about an extra pair of hands.' He grinned and held out a pair of what were indubitably a large pair of hands.

Greg regarded him with some caution, then told himself not to give way to prejudice. 'Welcome,' he said. 'Always glad of extra resource. Take a seat for the moment, then we can have a chat before I allot you to a team.' Jeff opened his mouth to respond, but Greg had already turned to the whiteboard. 'Right, folks,' he said. 'We've got a big task on our hands, and I think it's a case of back to basics.. For each of these cases we need to consider means, motive and opportunity, then see where the links lie. Data management is going to be key,' he added, turning to Sarah. 'We're going to generate a lot of little bits of information that will mean nothing on their own. It's the checking and cross-checking that's going to deliver us this chap. And if there's one thing we can take away from the story of the Yorkshire Ripper, it's the importance of not missing a link. Let's not find ourselves in that sort of mess here in Norfolk.

'OK. We have two sets of remains in this sequence that have not so far been identified: the fairly complete body found in Cambridgeshire in 2002, and the similar remains found in Oulton Broad in 2008. The first task with these two is the identification. With the assistance of our colleagues in Cambridge and Suffolk, let's take a good hard look at what was tried before, and what we can try now. Why weren't they ID'd at the time? Why did no one report them missing? Why did no one come forward to identify them? What did these two cases have in common, apart from the manner of their burial?

'Yes, Jill?'

'Did Suffolk and Cambs try DNA matching?' asked Jill. 'I couldn't see anything in the files that suggested they did. If not, why not? And if there are relevant samples still available, could we try it now?'

'With no ID, what do we match them against?' scoffed the new boy.

'Records,' said Jill. 'The DNA database gets bigger every year. We might have an exact match; we might find a familial match. Surely it's worth a try?'

'Yes it is,' pronounced Greg with some emphasis. He hadn't liked the way Fellows had intervened. It savoured too much of a put-down. 'Good suggestion, Jill. Can you see to it please? And, everyone, be sure to report everything to Sarah, no matter how minor an issue may seem.

'On to Krystina Kaminska. This is a priority for now. The identification of these remains gives us a lot of leads. Back to where I started. Means, motive and opportunity. We've no evidence that Krystina ever reached home that day in 2008. Who had the opportunity to pick her up on her way home? Who had the means to transport her to the dig site, and the means to bury her in the place she was found? Who had the opportunity to know that the site was there, and that the digs were recently closed up? What motive might link this killing to those in Oulton Broad and Cambridgeshire?

'Jill's going to explore the DNA route.' Greg looked round for another safe pair of hands, and to his relief, landed on a familiar face and pony tail. 'Jenny, can you work with her on that? Obviously you need to start by exploring what materials may be available from Cambridge and Suffolk and see what other details we might uncover about those two cases. Tread tactfully, can you? They might be a bit sensitive.

'Jim, you and Steve keep your focus on Hemsby. You know what to do. Collect Bill on your way and start the door to door. As and when pathology or Ned feed you more data, you pick it up. Chris, you and I will go back to Caistor St Edmund and ask some questions at the farm up the road.'

'And me?' asked Jeff.

'I was coming to you. Come and have a chat first, then I'll decide where you can add most value.'

Back in his office, Greg regarded the man draped in the chair opposite and again tried to silence his prejudices about the Met, derived from his early years as a wet-behind-the-ears constable in central London.

'So, you've just transferred here from the Met,' he began. 'Welcome. We're going to need all the help we can get on these cases.'

'But they're cold cases, aren't they?' asked Jeff.

'In one sense yes,' agreed Greg. 'I prefer to think of them as unsolved. Cold case, to many, seems to imply unimportant. Whereas, these are unsolved murders of young women. And as every one of these bodies has been found by accident, we can have no confidence that the killer isn't still active. I hope you can commit to this investigation as it deserves, otherwise you'll be no use to me.'

Jeff blinked, a little taken aback. 'Well of course,' he started, but Greg interrupted.

'While I'm on the subject, I'd better make something else clear too. I run my investigations with a team, and every team member is valued. Every honest suggestion is given respect, and I don't stand for any sort of macho nonsense such as you may have seen in some parts of the Met. I'm not suggesting that would be your style,' he added hurriedly, 'just that it definitely is not mine and is not acceptable here. It's best we start with that clear, I think.'

Chris noted, with interest, that Jeff had turned a dull red above his collar.

'As you say,' he managed.

'Good. In that case, grab your car keys and you can come with Chris and me to start the interviews at the farm near the archaeological dig. See you in the car park in five.'

After Jeff left the room, Greg regarded Chris in silence for a moment. 'You think I came down a bit hard?' he asked.

'Just a bit,' she replied. 'Was it necessary?'

'I think so, yes. Especially if he's taken in some of the nonsense I saw at the Met.'

'Was it really that bad?'

'It was that bad,' he affirmed. 'You'd have been livid at some of the things police officers said about women. If challenged they'd defend it as just banter, or jokes. And that was when they felt kind. If you criticised a joke as sick, say one about violence to women, at best you'd be mocked for having no sense of humour. At worst you'd be ostracised and ultimately forced out.' He shuffled papers together and dropped them into his out tray with a sigh.

'Was that what happened to you?' asked Chris.

'Not quite. I was lucky that a promotion and a transfer got me out of harm's way in the nick of time. I've felt guilty about not challenging the attitude more explicitly ever since, and I'm not having our working environment contaminated here. So I will come down hard if I have to, and, Chris, make sure everyone knows they can come to me if they need.'

'Got it. Thanks, boss.'

Out in the car park Greg turned to Jeff. 'Chris can give you the postcode,' he said. 'We'll all go in separate cars so we can split our resources when necessary. You'll find that locations are quite scattered geographically in Norfolk. We'll rendezvous at the farmyard. I'll have a chat with the farmer and his family. You and Chris can start with the farmworkers. We've been told the farm manager lives on site, and so do a couple of students. Apart from them, we might find a grain store manager at work and possibly an engineer in the farm workshop. Anyway, let's see where we get to, and review what we've found at around 8pm. Depending on who's been available, we'll decide then if we need to go back tomorrow.'

'And what is it you want to know?'

'Who was on site regularly around the end of the dig about ten years ago. In other words, who had opportunity. Then we can consider means and motive.'

Entr'acte 6

Back on my usual run, I pulled up for a break just outside the port and there was another. She came smarming round where I'd stopped and caught me having a pee by the side of the road. That really frightened me. My fly was undone and she was holding her hand out to take me. She was laughing too. I couldn't think what to do, except to pretend I liked her. I sort of laughed as well and said, 'Come with me, then.'

She seemed quite eager until I got close, then her smile faded and she started to back away. I hit her quite hard. I didn't like that. I didn't like how it made me feel. Both upset and excited. I shoved her into my cab and pushed her face down into the cushion. She didn't struggle for long. I didn't know what to do next. There were people around and one man shouted to me, 'After you, mate!'

I just shouted something back and got in after her. I was driving off, with no clear plan, when I remembered the roadworks I'd come past earlier in the day. When I got there the roads were quiet. So I just dropped her in, with the silver, pushed some earth on top and drove off in a hurry.

11

DNA

The sky was bluer and the sea calmer, but there was still a wicked wind whipping over the clifftop at Hemsby. Jim and Steve found themselves shouting as they trampled over the remains of damaged gardens towards the edge of the disturbingly mobile cliff. To add to his troubles, Steve was struggling with a badly folded Ordnance Survey map that the westerly was doing its utmost to rip out of his hands. He tried to flatten it enough to make the chart of the immediate vicinity visible, but to no avail. In the end, irritated by a crackling noise worthy of a windjammer in a force 9, he resolved his problem by screwing the whole thing up and jamming it into his coat pocket.

'What the hell,' he said. 'We can see where the garden went and where it came from. According to the records, up until three years ago this bungalow was owned by a local cab driver. He was lucky to sell to someone who didn't need a mortgage, and retired to a chalet further inland at Burgh Castle. I've said we'll call round later.' He stopped as Jim, his phone pressed to his ear and head bent in an effort to reduce the wind noise, waved an arm for silence.

'OK,' he said. 'Thanks. Email me the details of next of kin, will you, and we'll call round after we've seen our cab driver.' He put the phone away and said to Steve, 'Back to the car. We've got an ID for the remains.'

Back in the sudden and relative quiet of the car's shelter, both men pulled on their seat belts as Jim said, 'It's the community nurse from Cantley, or rather, I should say she's the community nurse from Cantley. So Jill's scored two out of three so far.'

'It's pretty good going,' agreed Steve. 'She'll be cock-a-hoop. And deserves to be. Where are we off now?'

'Next of kin, only they're not very next. More like distant. Second cousin once removed or something like that.'

'I've always wondered how you remove a cousin,' said Steve.

'No idea,' replied Jim. 'In this case it seems our nearest relation is a cousin of the victim's mother, living in Great Yarmouth. That's where we're going next. We can call at Burgh Castle on our way back.'

The neat semi with disciplined geometric garden was closer to Gorleston than Great Yarmouth, and very close to the river. Although the Yare was out of sight, seagulls wheeled overhead and Jim could smell the salt spray on the wind. They each pulled their coats and ties straight, then Jim knocked on the front door. There was a pause while a safety chain jangled and then a thin elderly lady peered out through the gap that was all the chain permitted.

‘Can I help you?’ she enquired.

‘Are you Mrs Angela Freeman?’ asked Jim, introducing himself as he held out his warrant card.

‘Yes, that’s right,’ she replied. ‘Is it about that complaint I made about the flasher on the bus?’

‘No, I’m afraid not,’ replied Jim. ‘Can we come in?’ He nodded at Steve to hold his warrant card up to the gap too. There was a pause then the chain was removed and a neatly dressed lady in her seventies appeared in the doorway.

‘Sorry about that, but you can’t be too careful, I find. What was it you wanted if it isn’t about the flasher?’

Jim and Steve had made it as far as the hall, but she showed no sign of moving any further in.

‘I’m afraid it’s bad news about your cousin Julie Bolton,’ said Jim. ‘Might we perhaps come in and sit down?’

‘Oh, yes of course,’ she said, flustered. ‘This way. Sorry. I’m forgetting my manners.’ And she led the way into a cretonne-covered sitting room. A pair of tabbies looked up and the smaller one hissed at the new arrivals. Mrs Freeman sat down with a bit of a bump.

‘If it’s bad news, I assume you haven’t found her alive,’ she guessed.

‘I’m afraid not. I’m very sorry to say, Mrs Freeman, that some remains found on the clifftop in Hemsby have been identified as those of Julie Bolton.’

There was a long pause. Long enough that Jim wondered if Mrs Freeman had taken in what he’d said. He opened his mouth to speak again, but she forestalled him.

‘That seems very odd,’ she said. ‘I thought the last sighting of her had been at the Cantley sugar factory. Had she gone on to another appointment after all and then had an accident on those cliffs? But no, her car was still at Cantley, wasn't it? I'm sorry.' She looked up. 'I'm confused. What d'you think happened?'

Jim hesitated, then said, 'I'm very sorry, Mrs Freeman, but the way she was found suggests she was killed.'

'Murdered?' The question came very faintly and Jim looked at Steve.

'Perhaps Constable Hall could make you a cup of tea,' he suggested. 'I think this has come as something of a shock.' Mrs Freeman sank back into her chubby armchair and her hands were shaking ever so slightly.

'Yes, I'm sorry, news like that is always going to be a shock, isn't it? I'd better come and show you where everything is.' She started to get up but Steve forestalled her.

'I'm a really good forager,' he said. 'Just leave it to me.' And he took himself off in the direction of what he assumed was the kitchen. He was correct and while he filled the electric kettle at the sink overlooking the garden, he noted it was as tidy as the living room. As he hunted for tea bags and opened the fridge door for milk, he also noticed that part of the reason for the general air of neatness was that there was very little food in store. Only a few basic tins in the cupboards and little more than milk, a few eggs and a covered bowl in the fridge. Judging from the pile of cat food, the cats ate rather better than Mrs Freeman.

He carried a tray of three mugs of tea into the living room, and after a few sips the colour came back into their hostess's face.

'I'm sorry,' she said. 'Now, how can I help?'

'To start with, how well did you know your cousin Julie Bolton?' asked Jim.

'Strictly speaking she wasn't my cousin; her mother was. Obviously I knew Julie, but not very well. We'd probably meet only six or eight times a year. Mainly at family get-togethers. She was a nurse, as I'm sure you know, so she often worked odd hours.'

'What sort of person was she?' asked Jim. 'You know, quiet and retiring, or a party girl?'

'Well, neither really, as far as I know,' she replied. 'She wasn't shy. Quite self-confident. Perhaps that came from her job. But she wasn't loud or particularly outgoing. Reserved, I think I'd say. But very caring. She'd always ask how you were and it wasn't just a politeness. She genuinely cared. I think she was probably a very good nurse.'

'The records we have from the time she disappeared say she was single.'

'That's right, at least as far as I know.'

'Was she the sort of girl who'd get in a car with a strange man, do you think?' asked Jim.

'Absolutely not,' replied Mrs Freeman. 'Unless, of course, it was with a patient. If someone asked for her help, then yes, I think she'd do whatever was necessary. You think someone drove her from Cantley to Hemsby?' She paused and then added, 'Sorry, I'm being silly, aren't I? Obviously someone drove her over that distance. Either her, or her body.'

Back in their car, Steve said, 'I'm not very happy about leaving the lady on her own.'

'She was emphatic she didn't want us to ring a friend or neighbour,' replied Jim.

'Yes, but I think that was pride. You didn't see her kitchen.

I doubt she's feeding herself properly. I can't help wondering if we should tip the wink to social services?'

'She won't thank you for that,' said Jim. 'That would really hurt her pride.'

'Yes, but pride is all she has. I just think we should keep an eye on her.'

'You can't do the social's job for them,' said Jim, his mind on the road. 'We get enough of that dumped on us. I'm more intrigued by a possible link.'

'What link?'

'Well, think about it. What do our two identified victims have in common, apart from long black hair and a slim build? What might make them part of a group?'

Steve looked blank and Jim said impatiently, 'They were both from caring professions. Perhaps there's something in that. Right, let's get on to Burgh Castle and interview that cab driver.'

'Retired cab driver,' reminded Steve.

It didn't take them long to reach the Burgh Castle Park. Following directions, they pulled up by a neat log cabin with parking space, garden and decking. Their interviewee was clearly looking out for them as the front door opened before they raised a hand to knock.

'Mr Howe?' asked Jim.

'Thass right,' said the man. 'Come in, come in. Coffee? Tea?'

His accent was a strange mix of Norfolk original and a version clearly designed for off-comed-uns. 'Perhaps,' as Jim surmised later, 'left over from his old profession as taxi driver.'

'Whass you want t' know?' he went on. 'Is't about me old place at Hemsby? I saw bits on t' news.'

'That's right,' said Jim. 'No tea, thanks, we've just had one. When was it you left there?' he asked, taking a seat on the plush-covered sofa in the sitting room. He looked along to the kitchen area and noted that everything was clean and tidy, no sign of washing-up left lying around, clean tea cloth hanging over the rails along the front of the cooker.

'Three year this summer,' said Mr Howe. 'An' lucky I was to sell when I did. I thort I'd be theer till she fell into sea, but this chap from London wanted it for him and missus to retire to, so theer I wuz. Sorted. I got the solicitor to get a shift on and we were done in less than a month.'

'I take it the purchaser didn't need a mortgage, then,' remarked Steve. 'I imagine that'd have been a problem if a surveyor had taken a look at the cliff.'

'Thass right,' said Mr Howe. 'Like I said, I thort I'd be there till they carried me out or the sea got me, but this chap was all for a place with a view an' dint seem to care about the warnings from his solicitor. Mindjoo,' he said reflectively, ''e wunt the brightest match in the packet, I reckon. Like they say, if hiss hud wuz a gun it wunt blow 'is 'at orff.'

Jim hid a smile at the old saying, and recalled the distraught retired university lecturer he'd spoken to at the ruins of the chalet in Hemsby.

'He's saying no one warned him of the dangers from the sea,' he said.

'Well thass a load of ole squit,' retorted the ex-taxi driver from his reclining chair in the corner. 'Everyone queued up to warn him, from postman to baker. 'Is trouble is, he's all brains and no sense. An' 'is wife were no better, and bad tempered with it. Never a word out of 'er that wunt a complaint. If she breathed on yer chips yer wunt need no vinegar, I tell yer.'

'And how long did you live there?' asked Jim.

'Just over ten year altogether,' he replied.

'Which means, you were there over the period when the victim was buried in your garden.'

There was a silence and Mr Howe looked down at his own knees. 'So it seems,' he said at last. 'But I can't explain it. All I know is, I dint put her there. I know nuthin' about it.'

'Were you ever away from the property for an extended period?' asked Jim.

'No. At least only a fortnight each May for our 'oliday. And days 'ere and there to visit relatives.'

'And would you have noticed fresh digging in your garden on your return?'

'I'd have thought so,' he replied. 'It wunt that big a garden. We had a lawn, some flower beds an' a bit of veg garden, and that was it. I s'pose if there was digging in the veg patch I mightn't have noticed, but I'm surprised I didn't, if you see what I mean.'

Back in the car, the two men looked at each other.

'I liked him and I wanted to believe him. But everything he said made it less likely that the body got there without his knowledge.'

'Would any villain be that naive?' asked Steve. 'Or is it a double bluff, and that's what we're meant to think?'

As Jim put the car in gear and looked round the estate of chalets and log cabins, the phone rang. 'Yes,' said Steve, and then, 'OK. I'll pass that on.'

He looked at Jim. 'They've turned up an old colleague of the dead nurse,' he said. 'She's based at the community hospital in Bowthorpe, and they want to know, can we call in before the end of the afternoon?'

'Tell them we're on our way,' said Jim, and he turned south for the Acle Straight and the road to Norwich.

Entr'acte 7

I was scared when the ghost from the port came back into the light. That wasn't supposed to happen. Down in the dark, with the silver in place, they should stay put. But it was only a few weeks later and she was back in the sunlight. Back in my world. I had a panic attack and had to go home. The boss was trying to be understanding, but he wasn't pleased when he had to put someone else on my run. At home I hid in my room, ate biscuits, and wondered how to stay safe. Perhaps the problem was how I'd done it. It hadn't been the usual quiet process with a quiescent victim. She'd struggled. I'd had to hit her. And there in my room, with the biscuits, I knew with a hot, red guilt, that I'd enjoyed it. I'd enjoyed holding her down. Feeling the power run through me. Feeling the dominance. Feeling good.

And I'd dumped her in those roadworks. With a coin, yes, but not with much care. Now she was back and I was at risk. It was because I'd enjoyed it too much. I needed to stop for a bit. If I could. I needed to get away.

12

Farm visit

Pulling up in the drive to the farmhouse, Greg looked around him with interest. This was not a farmyard such as he was familiar with. No old bales or broken pallets here. No rusting machinery stood in corners. No accumulations of plastic bale wrap adorned the well-kept fences. The drive to the farmhouse was bordered with a double avenue of almond trees. He reflected that in the spring the blossom must be quite something. A separate drive ran to the farmyard. This was wide and heavily concreted, to take the weight of the large articulated lorries making regular deliveries and collections at the enormous grain stores arranged in three long rows. Even as he watched, a smart lorry in blue livery pulled up the incline from the turning with a growl of engine, and came to a halt with a hiss of air brakes on the weighbridge in the yard. The driver got out and went to the office alongside, while a huge automated spike moved over the lorry and appeared to take samples from its load. The driver returned to his cab, a strip of paper in his hand, and drove off towards the furthest store just as Chris's car pulled up behind it, followed by a car he assumed to belong to the newcomer, Jeff Fellows. He watched as the two mismatched figures, one small and slight in gaudy yellow and pink, the other burly in denim and leather jacket, walked into the grain store office. After scooping up his briefcase, he headed for the farmhouse door.

Ensconced in the spacious kitchen, coffee in hand and warmed by the massive blue Aga occupying a substantial portion of one wall, Greg looked across at the farmer and his wife. Neither looked like their images in Happy Families. Instead of a rubicund chap with whiskers and a cap, Greg found himself regarding a businessman in chinos and logoed sweatshirt. His wife, albeit she was offering biscuits, was a long way from the homemaker he might have pictured. The biscuits came from M&S, the cashmere jumper and skirt reminded him of the wife of a senior director at Stalham Poultry, encountered during his first Norfolk case. She joined the two men at the large pine kitchen table and picked up her mug.

'How can we help?' she asked, and shook her head slightly at her husband, who was surreptitiously examining the emails on his phone.

'My interest is in people who may have been on site here, or visitors to the farm in the autumn of 2008, when the earlier dig on the fields over the road was concluded. But it would help if you first described your operations here. It's a very different farm from those I'm used to.'

Henry Tipton put his phone down with a, mostly hidden, sigh.

'We're not just a farm,' he said. 'That's the main difference.

I describe us as an agribusiness. Yes, we still farm in the sense that we manage land and produce crops, but we go beyond that by providing crop storage and distribution services to our customers. At the last count, we provide field services across around 4000 hectares and provide the storage for both our crops and those of other farmers.'

'What crops?' asked Greg.

'Anything you can put through a combine,' replied Henry. 'Therefore, mostly wheat but also barley, oats, oilseed rape and mustard.'

'So, in the autumn of 2008, what family and staff would have been present here?'

'Well, obviously me and Caroline, and at the weekends our two children, Piers and Lily. Then the farm staff, i.e. the farm manager and the two field staff, plus the grain store manager.'

'Is that all?' said Greg, surprised.

'That's right. We use a lot of heavy-duty machinery, but not very many men. And by the autumn, most of the temporary harvest staff would have left.'

'Are the folk who worked here in 2008 still working here?'

'The farm team hasn't changed much. One of the field hands was promoted to grain store manager, and replaced with a new chap from South Africa.'

'What happened to the old grain store manager?'

'Oh, he went home to Poland.'

'That's helpful, thank you. Other members of my team are in the farmyard as we agreed and will be able to interview your staff. What about regular visitors to the farm?'

'You mean apart from family and friends?' asked Caroline.

'I mean everyone who visited during 2008, as far as you

can recall. Obviously we'd like to check any relevant farm records as well.'

'I'll go through my address book,' said Caroline. 'I can pick out the ones that are very unlikely to have visited, and you can have the contact details for the rest.'

'If I might borrow your address book,' said Greg, 'that would be very helpful.' Caroline hesitated, then went reluctantly to a nearby kitchen drawer.

'Here you are,' she said, holding out a small scruffy book with bits of paper interleaved between its pages. 'But I'd like it back as soon as possible.'

'Of course,' said Greg, and he tucked the book away. 'What about visitors to the grain store and farm premises?'

'The most frequent would be the lorry drivers,' replied Henry. 'Most come from one transport firm. One of their team arrived at the same time as you today. We do get some others in from time to time, and sometimes farmers deliver their own crops to the grain-dryer in a trailer behind their tractor, but mostly it's the lorries from Delta Transport.'

'Would you know which drivers were visiting all that time ago?' enquired Greg.

'No way. But I think Delta might. You'd need to ask them. What the grain store records will show is who visited other than Delta. One-off visits from farmers will be listed separately. But the Delta visits, they're just listed as Delta.'

Back in his car, Greg rang Chris. 'Finished yet?' he asked.

'Just winding up. We're getting copies of the grain store deliveries and collections for 2008, then we'll be heading back to base.'

'OK. I'm finished here. See you later.'

Pulling back on to the road through the village, Greg was passed by another Delta Transport lorry turning in to the farmyard. As he watched it lumber round the corner, his phone rang again.

'It's Jill.' She sounded excited. 'I've got a match for the Cambridgeshire 2001 body.'

Jill was lying in wait for him when he got back to the Wymondham ops room.

'Tell me more,' said Greg.

'Like I said, the victim had been arrested and cautioned for soliciting earlier that year. Hence DNA samples had been taken and profiled.'

'So why wasn't a match made sooner?'

'Ask me another! As far as I can see, because no one looked. Of course, back in 2001 the database was in its infancy and some of what we do as routine wasn't really bedded in. But why no one's checked since,' she shrugged. 'Your guess is probably better than mine, boss.'

'Did no one report her missing at the time?'

'Not as far as I can see. But it's possible they did and it wasn't recorded. You know as well as I, boss, that back then a missing prostitute might not have created much of a stir.'

'Name and details,' said Greg.

'Joey Asher. Aged twenty. Dark hair, thin build. Almost certainly a heroin addict.'

'Any family?'

'Just one son, long since fostered and then adopted.'

'Best find him. And talk to his adoptive parents. This's going to be difficult news.' As he walked away, a thought occurred to him and he turned back. 'Any chance you can perform the same miracle for the mystery body found at Oulton Broad?'

'Already looking,' she said.

Back at his desk, a couple of phone calls soon located the head office of Delta Transport.

'Shouldn't be a problem,' said the despatcher when he eventually got through. 'I'll need to check with the boss obviously, but I'm sure he'll want to help. I'll dig out the old records. Anything prior to 2010 has been archived, but the info should still be there. Just to be clear, you want to know which drivers delivered to or collected from St Edmunds Farm, Norfolk, in the autumn of 2008?'

'That's right. Thank you.'

A noise in the corridor and his office door banged open, Chris entering with more than her usual precipitancy. She slammed the door to behind her and came over to the desk, pulling her scarf off. Greg watched her with affection as she flung herself into a chair, very aware that she was more than usually wound up about something.

'That has been the morning from hell,' she pronounced.

'Do I need a flak jacket?' asked Greg. 'Is it something I've done?'

'Not you, no, although if you pair me with that Neanderthal again, I won't be responsible for my actions.'

Greg had little difficulty recognising the description. 'I take it you mean the new addition to our team, Constable Fellows?'

Chris snorted with a sound remarkably reminiscent of an

angry horse. 'Fellows. He's one of the fellows all right, but not in a good way. He's an unreconstructed bloke in the worst possible sense. He thinks farting in public is funny. He man-spreads every time he sits down, to the point I fear for his pelvic floor, and if I hadn't glared at him at the right moment, I think he'd have whistled at a young girl working in the farmyard. Mind you,' she added, 'perhaps I should have let him go for it. Judging by the way she threw bales around and hitched a heavy piece of kit to an enormous tractor, she'd have eaten him for breakfast and spat out the buttons.

None of which would have mattered so much,' she added, 'if he hadn't brought those attitudes into the interviews.'

'In what way?'

'Well, he started by talking over me, but I soon put him straight on that, so he reverted to staring into space every time I asked a question with the sort of blank look that's as close to a sneer as makes no difference worth a damn. When I asked to see his notebook before we came back, I found he'd made no note of the answers to my questions. When I asked why, he said he hadn't felt that the answers had moved us forward, then implied that I was only at the grade I was because I was sleeping with the boss.'

Greg felt himself get hot. 'He said that?'

'Not in so many words, but that's what he meant. He asked what someone had to do to get promoted and then said it was a pity he was the wrong sex.'

'That's not quite the same thing,' said Greg. 'It could have been a generic comment.' Chris snorted again.

'Believe what you like,' she said. 'I know what I think. And I know he's trouble. He's not going to fit in here, Greg. No way.'

Greg took his time to answer, shuffling papers together.

Entr'acte 8

A new job was the answer. A trip north resulted in me being poached by another company and I started work with them within the month. In the meantime, I kept away from ghosts. I heard nothing more about the one in the roadworks, and started to breathe easier. I tried to keep away from places where ghosts collect. And the times when they're dangerous. It didn't stop me wanting to feel the excitement again.

I tried very hard. I tried volunteering for extra shifts, so I was too tired to do anything but go home and go to bed. Sometimes it worked. Sometimes I lay there, tossing and turning. Wanting to feel the heat again. Wanting to feel powerful again, but afraid of the risks. One day I found myself on a run outside my normal ground. I stopped in a lay-by for a break and a campervan pulled up behind. Out of the corner of my eye, I saw someone get out and a dog ran up to the waste bin and started sniffing it. I watched out of my window, and saw the dark hair, the slim build. I couldn't stop myself. In moments I was out and behind her. She turned and I saw that look in her eyes, then she spun round and made to run away. I reached out and the power flowed through me. I could see the blue glow all around, as though my eyes were firing flames, and the heat rose in my chest.

When the glow faded, she was crumpled in my hands and that damn dog was worrying at my trousers. A car went past and I panicked for a moment, then realised they couldn't have seen anything because I was behind the campervan. But the next car might stop, or slow down. The heat disappeared as though it had never been. I was cold right through; the ghost dragging me down into the earth. I stuffed her into the van and the dog jumped in after her. I was fumbling in my pocket for the silver when another car went by and I gave up. I slammed the van door closed and left, as fast as I could.

13

Catching up

Coffee in hand, sandwich squashed unpalatably under his arm, Greg pushed the door open to Jim's cubby hole and wriggled in past heaps of files. In the corner a semi-rotten hockey stick enjoyed the company of an umbrella with bare spokes sticking out from the crumpled black fabric and the elderly bentwood hat stand was supporting a new laptop bag and something that looked remarkably like a GP medicine case circa 1940.

After ostentatiously blowing non-existent dust off a chair, Greg sat down and unwrapped his lunch.

'I always feel as though I'm going to get food poisoning in here,' he remarked. 'I hope to God none of these relics are evidence.'

'Of course they're not.' Jim looked up from the packet of biscuits he was struggling to open. 'Want one?' He held out an only slightly mangled packet. Greg helped himself to a garibaldi.

'You'll get scurvy living off this stuff,' he said.

'Rubbish. With all this fruit in them, they're one of my five a day. I don't see you turning them down.'

'But I am having a cheese and salad sandwich too. Anyway, I didn't risk life and limb in your cess pit to exchange views on a balanced diet. I wanted to know how you got on with our taxi driver.'

Jim put the packet of biscuits down and took a swig from his can of Diet Coke.

'Not well,' he said. 'I can't rule him out, but I can't rule him in either. My gut says no, he's not involved. But it's hard to see how he could miss a body buried in his garden.'

'What about other evidence? Where was he on the night Julie Bolton went missing?'

'At work he says, and the database at the cab company he was working for at the time, A1 Taxis, supports that. What they don't have, this long after the event, is evidence of what jobs he took that day.'

'What area do they usually cover?'

'All over, that's the problem. Mostly the east coast, so we can't rule out Oulton Broad, but also between Great Yarmouth and Norwich, and airport trips including Stansted as well as Norwich.'

'So he'd be familiar with all the places we've found bodies. Has he been to Cantley?'

'The company has, but when a taxi picks up or drops off at the factory, security only record the company name, not the driver.'

'Did they call at Cantley the day Julie went missing?' asked Greg.

'Still checking. There's one other thing though. He worked

in Cambridge in the early 2000s.'

'Did he though?' Greg finished his sandwich and gulped down some of his coffee. 'Worth a follow-up, then. Chase Cantley about their records.'

'Will do.'

'Right. Next stop Sarah. I need to know how she got on at the nail bar. Oh, Jim.' He poked his head back round the door. 'Ask St Edmunds Farm if they have any particular taxi firm they use for visitors.'

'Will do,' said Jim again. 'But, Greg, that reminds me. We had a chat with Julie Bolton's old colleague at the community hospital.'

'And?'

'She'd had car problems the week she went missing. Something about the engine cutting out and not always starting again. A few days earlier she'd had to use a taxi to get into work. A1 Taxis.'

Sarah had only just got back in the office when Greg came up to her desk.

'Oh hi,' she said. 'I'm not late for something, am I?'

'No, not at all. Only I've had so little time in the office lately, I'm using this afternoon to catch up with everyone. How's your investigation of the Lithuanian link going?'

Sarah finished hanging her coat up and sat down at her desk. 'Slowly is the honest answer,' she said. 'After my chat with Madame Trieste, I went to see Bakalov himself.'

Greg choked on his coffee. 'You did what?'

'I went to see Bakalov. It was the obvious next step. I took Bill with me and did it exactly by the book.' There was just a hint of sarcasm, which, in the circumstances, Greg decided to let go.

'I hope this was before Margaret's embargo on active investigation of the Lithuanian angle,' he said.

'It was, just,' she said. 'I was at the prison while you did the press conference, so I didn't hear about her latest instruction until I got back. Luckily.' She looked up with a grin, which, Greg noted, was the first sign of warming in their relationship since he and Chris had got together.

'OK. What did you find out?' he asked.

'Very little, which was much what I expected. He's as close-mouthed as he ever was on most subjects. He did acknowledge that he'd had a visit from Madame Trieste, and he also admitted he'd met her before being convicted, which was more than she said to me. No other visitors whatsoever, according to the prison records, and he doesn't socialise much with other inmates. He plays a bit of football when possible, and perhaps more surprisingly, he's learning English, or at least improving his English, with the help of a prison visitor and some online courses. Apart from that he mainly seems to glower at everyone from under his eyebrows, like some sort of great ape.'

'Any involvement with drugs or gambling?'

'Not according to the prison staff. And except at the beginning when he was settling in, no violence either.'

'Are they monitoring his internet usage?'

'Yes. I checked that. All the usual restrictions are in place and there's no suggestion he's tried to get around them.' She looked at Greg. 'You're thinking he has some contacts with his old bosses?'

'It would be surprising if he didn't. Not impossible obviously, but surprising. These groups are usually pretty close knit. It's how they maintain the extraordinary loyalty from their teams. Loyalty plays two ways after all. Or not at all.' He paused for thought, playing idly with a couple of paper clips he'd picked up from her desk, unwinding them and then twisting them around each other. 'So the only contacts he's had outside of prison staff have been Madame Trieste and the prison visitor? OK. Two things to check out.'

'I already planned a chat with the visitor,' she agreed.

'Yes. Good. And the other thing. Ask our friends in the funny buggers if they've any concerns about the prison, any whispers of connections with Lithuania and/or organised crime. It's a long shot, I know, but worth the question.'

One last visit to the ops room, and Greg decided to call it a day. Leaning over Chris to look at her computer screen he asked, 'Are you still on for tonight?' in an undertone.

She looked up, hesitated, then said, 'Yes, thanks. But can we make it an early one? I'm whacked.'

'Half six at the Cheapie Greekie?' he asked, using the joke name they'd developed for their favourite bistro.

'Fine. I'll meet you there.' Greg opened his mouth to say something else, thought better of it, and nodded in acquiescence as he left the room. His thoughts on the drive home were not entirely easy. He'd thought she'd come to his place first and they'd go on to the restaurant together. He couldn't fault her dedication to work, but he had a nasty feeling he was walking into something unwelcome.

A mad dash to feed and appease his cat, only partly successful, and he was sitting waiting in the Olive Tree. He'd bagged a table by the window so he could keep a lookout. Chris was uncharacteristically late, by a few minutes, and he watched her walk to the door with a sinking feeling that his premonition was right. Her shoulders were down, her head inclined to the ground and she wasn't looking towards the bistro window. Normally he'd have expected a smile and wave. Today, nothing.

He stood automatically as she came to the table. At last a faint smile, then she sat down and he poured her a glass of sparkling water as the waiter left the menus in front of them.

'I wasn't sure what you'd want to drink,' he said, to fill the silence.

'This is fine,' she said, indicating the water. 'Perhaps a glass of red with the food, but that's all. I'll just have lasagne and salad,' she added, pushing the menu to one side, 'with a side order of difficult conversation.'

'Oh dear.' Greg didn't know what else to say, but after a moment's thought decided to go with straight talking. 'I can see I've upset you,' he said. 'Tell me what I've done and I'll try to put it right.' As he got no immediate response he added, 'The one thing we promised each other was that if we hit difficulties we'd keep talking. It seems like we need to do some talking now.'

Chris sighed and took another sip of the water, before pushing her glass away. She nodded to the waiter as he brought them bread, oils and olives, and she picked up a piece of focaccia. She started to speak, stopped again, then looked up and said, 'OK, the problem is I feel like I'm being a whining cow, but the truth is I'm not at all happy with how things are going.'

Greg took a deep breath and, as she didn't seem inclined to carry on, said, 'Then please tell me what's making you miserable.

Because frankly, to hear you say that terrifies me. Whatever the problem is, let's fix it. What we have is too good to lose.'

She leaned back while the waiter placed the red wine in front of her.

'It shouldn't come as too much of a surprise. I'm not happy about Isabelle reappearing in our lives, particularly as it seems there was no truth in what she said and it was a plain grab for your attention, which you gave her. That's a big part of what's making me unhappy, and I realise that makes it clear I'm jealous.

'But I am. I'm jealous of the hold she has over you and really irritated that you fall for her carryings-on. Then on top of all that, you dump that Neanderthal from the Met on to me because, apparently, I'm immune to his bad behaviour. That was just the last straw today. If our personal relationship is shaky and you're making use of it professionally, where does that leave me?'

Greg opened his mouth to say 'rant over', then fortunately was interrupted by the arrival of lasagne, stifado and salad, and he shut it again on the words unsaid. The pause gave him time to think and he changed his instinctive reaction to an apology.

'I'm sorry,' he said. 'I'm sorry that I underestimated how much difficulty Isabelle was giving you, and I'm sorry I took advantage of your strength of character in deciding what to do with Jeff Fellows. Truth is, you're so strong and resilient I fell into the trap of assuming you could cope with anything, and overlooked how much it costs you. Let's deal with Fellows first. I feared he might behave the way he did, and I didn't want to expose a more vulnerable or more junior woman to him without checking first. Equally, I needed to give him a chance and not act on prejudice.'

'Well, it's good to know you think I'm armour-plated,' grumbled Chris.

'That's not what I meant at all and you know it,' said Greg, relaxing slightly, 'but I did know I could trust you to both stand up to him and to come to me if there was anything I needed to know. Our private relationship had nothing to do with that decision. Fact is, as you also know, you're by far the best sergeant in the place and therefore the obvious choice to deal with a sensitive situation.'

He ate some of his stifado with little appetite, conscious that the bigger issue had still to be addressed.

'Which leaves us with Isabelle,' he said. Chris put down her fork, her lasagne half eaten, in order to concentrate on what he said next.

'Chris, I genuinely don't know what to say to you. I've already told you that Isabelle and I are over. Long over. Even if she did want me back, I could never trust her again, and if I can't trust her I can't love her. That's the God's truth. And that would be true even if I'd never met you.

'But I did meet you and every day I bless the moment I did when, if I recall correctly, you called me a numpty. I wake up every morning with a smile because of you. I look forward every day to the moment when I'll see you. I don't care whether I'm working with you, partying with you, or just sitting quietly on a sofa with you, every moment I'm with you is a joy. So I may be a numpty, but I'm very much afraid, Chris, I'm your numpty and if I have my way it'll stay that way for the rest of my life.'

There was a long pause, while hot lasagne became cold lasagne, before Chris was able to look up.

'I can't match that,' she said with a catch in her voice. 'I'm not so eloquent. But if you can love a jealous cow with no sense of respect for her seniors…' Her voice trailed away. She gulped some wine and said, 'What I'm trying to say, without crying in public, is that I love you too and it's fear of losing you that makes me jealous. But the next time Isabelle rings up in a theatrical panic, I'll try to be the bigger person. However,' she added, 'don't assume the same applies to the Neanderthal. You still owe me for that one.' And a smile gradually spread over her face.

Entr'acte 9

The campervan ghost caused a lot of fuss. Headlines in the papers. Items on the news. It seemed no one had seen anything, and lots of the news reports were asking how could it happen? How could someone be killed in broad daylight without anyone seeing anything? Appeals for witnesses came up with nothing. The police were said to be exploring all the forensic evidence, but that came up with nothing either. The lay-by was in constant use, so there was all sorts of evidence everywhere, but nothing of use. The van had apparently been covered in dog poo when they opened the door, and if they found any trace of me, well, they had nothing to compare it with, did they? I was wondering how to put a bit of space between me and the fuss when my new boss asked if I'd do some longer trips. Overseas. I said I'd give it a go, and set off on my first long haul the next week.

*

I found I liked it. There was nothing to keep me home anyway, and I liked the travelling. I liked staying in anonymous places. And after the first trip, I decided that concentrating my ghost removal overseas would not be too difficult. So that's what I did. One country one week. A different country the next. I went all over Europe. I found that there were ghosts everywhere. And I found that, if I managed to dispose of one a month, I could keep how I felt under control. That was enough to satisfy the cravings for the heat and the blue glow. Well, mostly anyway. Until the job came to an end.

14

Friday morning and Greg thought it timely to do a progress check across the teams.

'Right,' he said. 'Jill, where are we with DNA identification?'

'Nothing new to report, boss,' she said. 'Still trying to find a cross-match for the Oulton Broad remains.'

'And what about your researches at Cantley?'

'One interesting link, I think,' she said. 'A1 Taxis regularly visit there with visitors arriving from Norwich station especially, so Tom Howe, the driver from Hemsby, may well have been there.'

'But no hard evidence he was there that night.'

'No, boss, not yet. But I'm still going through their lists of who visited when. We have a list of bulk deliveries going back years. One more intriguing crossover from that. The lorries you spotted at St Edmunds Farm, they deliver to Cantley as well.'

'Delta Transport?'

'That's right. But I'm still tracking down which drivers when.'

'OK. Interesting. Jim and Chris, any other data from St Edmunds Farm?'

'Nothing of interest from the current team. I've been in touch with the police in Poland to ask a few questions of the grain store manager who went home there in 2016, but I think that's a red herring,' replied Chris.

'But I do think we should have another chat with Tom Howe,' said Jim. 'I'm not satisfied with his explanations about the body in the garden. I just don't see how he could possibly have missed seeing disturbed earth at the very least. And who else could have had the opportunity to bury a body without neighbours noticing? Forensics think it was a couple of feet down, so that's a good bit of digging, even in sandy soil. I keep thinking about the Yorkshire Ripper,' he added, 'and how he was interviewed but missed. I don't want that to be us.'

There was a silence. 'OK,' said Greg. 'Get him in for an interview under caution. This afternoon.'

Running a retired taxi driver to earth proved easier said than done. Mr Howe was supplementing his pension with the odd driving job as a relief driver for a local Yarmouth firm.

'You'd think they'd just radio him and tell him to come in,' said Jim, frustrated.

'Apparently he's taking someone home from the airport and as he hasn't a radio in his car, they rely on mobile phones. That's the problem. Wherever he is, he's out of signal,' replied Steve.

'Or he's ignoring his phone.'

'If he's not in touch soon, put out an APB. Right idiots we'll look if he's made a run for it.'

Phil waved from the corner. 'It's OK,' he said, 'I've got him on the phone now. He wants to know if it's urgent. Says he's got a darts match in Caister this evening.'

'Tell him yes, it's urgent and we need him in here this afternoon. Have you got a location for him now?'

'Says he's in Worstead.'

'Tell him to come straight here, and if you get any resistance, have a word with the North Walsham team.'

Phil turned to his phone and then turned back. 'Wants to know if he's under arrest. And does he need a solicitor?'

'Tell him he's not under arrest, no. We just want him to help with our enquiries. And he is of course entitled to legal advice. He can contact his own solicitor or we can provide one. No, on second thoughts I'll have a word with him.

'Mr Howe, it's DI Henning here. We spoke the other day. We have a few more questions for you and it would be very helpful if you'd come in this afternoon.' Jim listened for a moment and then said, 'That's excellent. Thank you, Mr Howe. We'll expect you and your solicitor at two.'

'On his way,' he pronounced with satisfaction. 'I'll go and tell Greg.'

The afternoon saw a worried-looking Mr Howe come into the station, accompanied by a, if anything, even more worried-looking solicitor in the worst-fitting greenish black suit that Jim had ever had the pleasure to behold. The trousers concertinaed round his skinny ankles, the waistband strained over his ample tummy and the jacket rode up over his shoulders as though he'd forgotten to remove the coat hanger.

'The first thing we need to establish,' he said before he'd scarcely got into the interview room, 'is precisely under what terms Mr Howe is present here. It seems you were quite insistent about him coming in as a matter of urgency.'

'That's right,' said Jim. 'At this stage in our investigation we have a number of questions it would be very helpful if Mr Howe could answer. We'll be conducting the interview under caution,' he added, 'but at this stage Mr Howe is of course free to go at any point.'

While Jim administered the caution, Greg was watching carefully. It was his first meeting with Tom Howe and the question dominating his mind was, 'does this man look like a serial killer?' He could see why Jim was half convinced he was not.

The man in front of him was ruddy with recent exposure to the sun, his bald head beginning to peel. He had pale blue eyes and what remained of his hair was a white ruff round the edge of his head. His shirt and trousers were worn but tidy, and obviously chosen to present a more formal work-day image than the trackie bottoms and T-shirt that Jim had reported him wearing when relaxing at home.

'The first point we'd like to clear up with you, Mr Howe,' started Jim, 'is how you think anyone got access to your garden to bury a body in it.'

'You can stop right there,' interrupted the portly solicitor, Mr Gardner, as he'd introduced himself for the tape. 'You're asking my client to speculate. He can't be expected to know the answer to that.'

'Perhaps I need to rephrase my question,' responded Jim. 'Mr Howe, please describe to me how anyone could access your garden.'

Tom Howe was looking confused. 'Through the gate, of course,' he said, 'or from the conservatory on the front of the house. Failing that, they'd have to climb over the fence.'

'Where was the gate in relation to the house?'

'At the corner. In fact, the hinges were screwed into the wall of the house.'

'And the fence then ran in a straight line?'

'That's right, up to the neighbour's garden.'

'How tall was the fence?'

'Around four feet, I'd say. You've seen it, surely?'

'There's not much of it left now, Mr Howe,' said Jim without emphasis. 'Most of it's on the beach or in the sea. So, to get into the garden a visitor would either have to go through your house, or the gate immediately abutting the house, or climb over the fence?'

'That's right.'

'I think you can see why we find it difficult to imagine someone doing that with a body, without you noticing.'

'Unless I wasn't there,' retorted Mr Howe with some spirit. 'I've already told you I took a holiday for a couple of weeks every year, and visited friends for weekends away in between.'

'Oh yes. And your holiday in 2008 was when?'

'I always go away in May, before the school holidays,' replied Mr Howe, over the raised hand of his solicitor, who could see where this was going.

'And yet, Julie Bolton didn't go missing until October 2008, when presumably you would have been at home.'

'Well, I must have been away on a visit then, like I said.' Mr Howe was beginning to sound stressed.

'But you just said you visited friends at weekends, and Julie Bolton went missing on a Wednesday.'

'She could've been put somewhere else before she was buried,' replied Mr Howe.

'So she could. Let's look at something else, then. How was your garden laid out, Mr Howe?'

'I don't know what you mean.'

'I mean, was it lawns, orchard, flowerbeds or what? What did it look like before it fell off the cliff?'

'Well then, nearest the house was lawn surrounded by rose beds, and the bit furthest away was me vegetable patch.'

'And in October, what would it look like?'

'What d'you mean?' Mr Howe still sounded puzzled.

'I mean, I assume the lawn wasn't needing much mowing by then?'

'Thass right. It wouldn't normally.'

'And what sort of veg did you grow?'

'I 'ad a good little patch,' replied Mr Howe, his accent broadening with the memory. 'I 'ad blackcurrant bushes an' raspberry canes, an' I grew onions, spuds and sprouts. And cabbage, cauliflower; some carrots sometimes.'

'It sounds a very productive patch,' commented Jim. 'Did you work in it often?'

'Most weekends,' said Tom Howe, still oblivious to his solicitor's signals.

'Then you'd notice if someone had been digging in your patch. Especially if they'd disturbed your vegetables in the process.'

There was a silence. Then Tom Howe said miserably, 'I dun't know. I've told you I just dun't know. I'd 've thought I would, but I dint. And I dint put 'er there neether. I can't explain it. But you 'ave t'believe me. I 'ad nothing to do with it. I never hurt no one.'

Out in the corridor Greg looked at Jim. 'It's thin,' he said. 'OK, finding the body in his garden is suspicious, but we don't have anything else yet. Go back in and ask him about Cantley. I'll have another word with Jill.'

Jill confirmed what Greg was coming to expect. Cantley routinely used A1 Taxis, but then, so did a lot of businesses. The factory folk were still trawling through their old records, but hadn't so far come up with anything that tied Mr Howe to the specific day Julie Bolton went missing.

'He does admit visiting Cantley factory in the course of his work,' said Jim. 'But he's claiming he has no clear recollection of which dates so long ago, and says he destroyed his old diaries when he moved to Burgh Castle. Do we let him go?' he asked.

'Is he a flight risk?' asked Greg.

'On the face of it, no. He's a retired taxi driver with no particular links to anywhere else on the globe and nowhere to run to. On the other hand, he's also a retired taxi driver with no family or commitments to keep him here. So…' Jim shrugged.

Greg hesitated, turning a pen over and over on his desk. 'It's a tricky one,' he admitted. 'To be blunt, there's no real evidence tying him to Julie Bolton's death. Only the suspicious circumstance of her body being found in his garden and no realistic explanation of how it could come to be there without him knowing. On the other hand, right pillocks we're going to look if he scarpers while we dither. Jim, ply him with coffee and ask him to stay put for a few more minutes. Say we have a few more questions. Let me know if he walks out. I'm going to have a chat with CPS and Margaret.'

Less than five minutes later he was heading down the corridor to the interview rooms and bumped into Jim, hands full of coffees.

'We're to hold him for a while so we can check out his new home in Burgh Castle as well as finish up the review of the land at Hemsby, what's left of it. We need to do some more digging, metaphorically speaking, into his past life as well. Arrest him on suspicion of the unlawful disposal of a dead body, and we'd better make good use of the time.'

'OK.' Jim hesitated. 'Are you happy with this, Greg?'

'Not entirely, no. But I don't see an easy alternative either. Let's hope we can confirm our suspicions or clear his name. Preferably quickly.'

Entr'acte 10

It was 2018 when everything blew up in my face. I got a message to see the boss in his office and his first words were, 'I need to let you go.'

I was flabbergasted. And panicked. What would I do? With no job I'd have no travel, no home, no way to pursue my… even in my panic I thought, 'My life's work.' That's what I'd been doing. I'd been on a mission and now what? I hadn't taken in his last few words and he obviously realised I wasn't listening because it made him mad.

'That's exactly what I'm talking about,' he snapped. 'You don't listen. You don't pay attention and you make mistakes. Moreover, the other drivers are complaining. You don't turn up when you're expected. You're late. Or off on the wrong route. Now we've trackers on all the vehicles, we can see where you've been, you know. OK you get from A to B, but why you visit C and D in between is a mystery to me, unless you've a lady friend you've not mentioned. Or you're addicted to tarts. That'd be an answer, I suppose, given where you've been going. Anyway, I don't want to know. You're lucky I need to reduce numbers, so I'm going to let you go with a redundancy package. That's a lot better than the boot, believe me. If you go quietly, you'll get a tax-free pay-out and I won't bad mouth you in the industry. Is it a deal?'

What could I say? I didn't like where the conversation had been going. I didn't want anyone comparing my routes to anything else. I went quietly.

It wasn't too hard to find another job after all. In fact, I went back to my old place and picked up where I'd left off, as though I'd never been away. In every way.

15

One step forward

The road to Cambridge was as busy as ever. Sarah reflected that she'd never yet travelled the A11 without a problem. Today it was road closures near Attleborough and she could only be glad that she was going no further than Thetford. Her destination was a Georgian house in Fern Road, home of retired Methodist minister and prison visitor, George Hamilton.

Somewhat to her relief she discovered that the town-centre property had its own parking. She bumped into a gravel-coated courtyard and looked up at the flint and mortar walls towering over her, glistening slightly in the low autumn sun. Space enough to park, she estimated, a good five or six vehicles; but the courtyard provided a grim introduction to the grey-toned house.

As Mr Hamilton welcomed her to his home, shook her hand

and ushered her into what he described as a sitting room, she was mainly preoccupied by hiding her surprise. It wasn't so much the smell, although that was a choice mixture of cats and drains, but the sheer empty barrenness of what must once have been elegant accommodation. The sitting room contained one flat screen TV and two armchairs, one with an occasional table next to it on which reposed what looked like the remains of Mr Hamilton's breakfast. The hall she'd passed through was blessed with the curve of an elegant staircase and two cat litter trays. Both clearly in active use. She sat in the chair Mr Hamilton indicated, with what she hoped was a discreet check for stains, then took out her notebook.

'Thank you for seeing me so promptly, Mr Hamilton,' she said.

'Coffee or tea?' interrupted her host, and she was swift to decline politely, a clear recollection of the district nurse's mantra in her mind: 'Never accept tea unless you've seen the kitchen.' She shuddered slightly at the thought of the probable kitchen and pressed on.

'Could I start by asking for your full name and address please?'

'George Peter Hamilton,' he replied. 'Netherfair House, Fern Road, Thetford.'

'I understand you're retired, Mr Hamilton.'

'Yes, that's right,' he said easily.

'I'm here to ask you about your contacts with Dragan Bakalov,' she said.

He nodded and replied, 'I've been seeing him for some time now. At least six months. I see him on a Wednesday at 1100.' She regarded him thoughtfully.

'Yes, that's what the prison told me,' she said. 'What do you talk about?'

'Oh everything and nothing,' he replied. 'It's mainly practice for him. To improve his English, you know.'

'Do you have any contact with him outside your normal visits?'

'Oh no,' he said. 'That's not allowed, you know.'

'And has he ever asked you to take any messages for him?'

'No never,' he said. 'Not at all. Never.'

'Or to carry anything out for him? A note, a phone or anything else.'

'No never. Nothing. That would be completely against the rules, you know.'

'Yes, I know, Mr Hamilton, but I also know it happens. More often than you'd think.' She regarded him closely again and he looked her straight in the eyes.

'No. Like I said, he's never asked me to take anything for him, or to bring anything in. Never.' She nodded and looked down at his hands fidgeting in his lap. He was rubbing his knuckles and, perhaps realising where she was looking, he stopped suddenly and grasped his hands together.

Sarah glanced round her and embarked on chit-chat about the house, how they'd bought it, their plans for it. Mr Hamilton slowly relaxed and answered more fluently, his hands losing their convulsive grip. After a few minutes she returned to the subject of Bakalov, and wasn't surprised when the tension returned. She regarded him in silence for a while, then, clearly to his surprise, stood up.

'Thank you, Mr Hamilton. I think that will be all for now.'

'I'll show you out,' he said, leaping with surprising agility to his feet.

As they walked through the hall, she admired the staircase and added, 'It must be a lot of work to look after a house like this. Does your wife have some help?'

'My wife,' he said, seeming startled. 'Oh yes, my wife. Well, she's not here at the moment. She's staying with friends in Stoke-on-Trent. For a while.' A big ginger cat oozed past Sarah's ankles as they spoke, and she noted two fluffy white Persians blinking their blue eyes at her from the stairs.

'How would I get hold of her, if I wanted to ask her some questions?' asked Sarah.

'Oh, I, well, I suppose I could give you her mobile number.' He seemed surprised. 'But I'd rather you didn't bother her. She's not been well, you know. And she can't tell you anything about my prison visiting. It's nothing to do with her. No, on reflection, I would really rather you didn't bother my wife. Good day to you.' And he closed the door so swiftly behind Sarah that he caught the corner of her mac in it. She was forced to knock on the door again.

'Mr Hamilton, you've trapped my coat,' she said, feeling rather foolish. She knocked again. 'Mr Hamilton!' The door opened suddenly.

'Sorry,' he said. 'Sorry.' Then it slammed shut again.

Back in her car, Sarah rang Greg.

'I'm pretty certain he's lying to me,' she said. 'He's showing so many of the usual signs it's almost as though he's read the handbook. Fidgeting, too much information, denying things several times over, looking me straight in the eye sometimes and not others. All the giveaways of a poor liar under stress. I'd like to speak to his wife but he won't give me her contact details. I'll see if I can flush any other information out locally and we need to tell the prison to keep a close eye on Mr Hamilton.'

A chat in the local newsagent revealed that Mr Hamilton had cancelled his wife's daily paper a month previously.

'He always has the *Telegraph* and she the *Times*,' said the busy lady behind the counter. 'But it's been just the *Telegraph* for a few weeks now.'

'Did he say why?' asked Sarah.

'Just that she was away visiting family,' she replied, tidying the paper stand as she spoke.

'Some sort of crisis?' asked Sarah. 'It seems to be a long visit.'

'No idea,' she replied, 'but I do know her brother lives in the Midlands because she was sending him a birthday parcel just before she went herself. I remember thinking how wasteful. She could have saved the postage and taken it with her.'

'Do you have the address by any chance?'

'It should be on the system,' she replied. 'But hang on, should I be giving it to you? She's not in any trouble, is she?'

'No, not as far as I know,' replied Sarah, thinking that a few years ago she'd have had her fingers crossed behind her back for luck. 'We just want a word.'

'OK. I'll have a look.' A few moments' tapping on a desktop ensued, and Sarah occupied the time scrolling through her emails.

'Well I never,' she exclaimed, then looking up saw that the newsagent's lady was holding out a piece of paper.

'This is the address the parcel went to,' she said. 'And the name. A Jamie Wentworth.' Sarah took the paper with thanks and rushed back to her car to make a phone call in private.

In the Wymondham offices, Greg was staring at Jill with disappointment writ large on his face.

'Say that again,' he said.

'I said,' repeated Jill, flushed with success, 'that I thought I'd just see if Norfolk attitudes, back ten years, had been similar to Cambridge. So I trawled around the database for missing prostitutes and checked the DNA database for them. There were quite a few missing, so I pulled up the evidence logs, found some materials that had a good chance of retaining DNA, and voila.'

'You found the Oulton Broad victim.'

'That's right. She was a prostitute living near Thetford. Kay Norton. According to the report taken at the time, Kay's main beat was near the American airbase at Lakenheath and she also worked near a garage on the A11, just north of a major roundabout near Thetford. Aged nineteen. Dark hair, white skin, thin. Possibly even emaciated from a drug addiction.'

'Why wasn't a DNA check done at the time?'

'You tell me, boss. But it looks like the same reason as in Cambridge. The disappearance of a prostitute wasn't taken seriously. Checks that might've been done for another missing person weren't done here.'

'I need to take this to Margaret. Thank you, Jill, and well done. Oh, and when Sarah gets back the two of you need to do some record checking. See how many other cases might have been missed.'

Out in the corridor Greg walked into Chris. 'I heard,' she

said briefly and looked at the set expression on Greg's face. 'Not your fault. It didn't happen on your watch.'

'Doesn't make it right,' he replied. 'It really gets to me sometimes – the attitude of some police. It's an embarrassment! Worse! It tarnishes us all.'

'But it's past,' she argued. 'Let's look forward not back. Let's make sure no more are missed and that no one gets written off like that again.' He turned and smiled at her before disappearing up the stairs to the floor above.

'Quite right. As ever. Not on our watch!' echoed down the stairs.

Margaret was pragmatic. 'It happens,' she said shortly. 'Or at least, it used to. You're not framing this right, Greg. This isn't a disaster – it's a step forward. A success. We can report you've identified another of the bodies. Any news on our taxi driver?' she added.

'Not yet no. So far, we've drawn a blank at both properties.'

Entr'acte 11

Being back on my old stamping grounds was unsettling. So much was the same, but so much was different too. The lorries had been upgraded a bit. The cab was more comfortable, but the loads were the same old, same old. Destinations were broadly the same too. I slotted straight back in, no problem.

Actually, that's not quite true. There was a problem. I didn't realise straightaway because, what with the new job, new early hours, new everything, I was tired. I hadn't realised how much impact that would have, but it did. It was weeks before I felt inclined to take any action at all. In fact, it was weeks before I even noticed much outside my cab or took my gaze from my dashboard. When I did, I was so on fire I nearly forgot all my normal precautions. It was a disaster.

I was doing my regular run, up the A11 from Cambridge to

Great Yarmouth harbour. I had a load for export and I'd set off early so I had time in hand. That's when I saw her, by the side of the road near a well-known truck stop. She had all the usual signs, the dark hair and the red lips. I pulled into the lay-by and glanced up and down. There were no other trucks, just one car at the far end, and no one in it as far as I could see. That was my second mistake, but by then I was out of my cab and the heat was rising in me alongside the excitement and the terror. I felt so good. So powerful. I strode towards her as though I was nine feet tall and took her throat in my hands like I was culling a hen. She didn't even get a chance to scream. My head was bursting, my body on fire and I squeezed that small, soft throat just as though she was a baby bird. Then there was a shout that echoed through my head, a tinny shout, shrill and piercing, and another woman powered out of the trees beside the verge and fired a stream of paint from an aerosol directly at my face. I ducked and most of it went on the back of my fleece, some on my hair. Then the screaming was in my face and she threw the empty aerosol at my head. I shook the one in my hands like a dead puppy and more or less hurled her at the second one. Then I fled. Back into my cab and driving off without even checking the road.

Problem was, I was still on fire, my head twice its normal size, my whole body throbbing as I heaved for breath. Just past Norwich I pulled onto another lay-by and tried to calm down. The paint on my fleece had dried. I turned it inside out and put my jacket on over the top. Didn't look too bad. That left my hair. I rooted through my toilet bag and found a pair of nail scissors. Trimmed short, my hair was free of the paint and what was left was on the back of my neck, well hidden by the jacket collar. I rubbed hard but it wouldn't come off. Obviously it would just have to wear off. My hands were still shaking as I looked into the mirror and the heat was still there, tightening a cord inside me from my feet to the top of my head, until I felt everything was being pulled unbearably tight. If I'd been able to deal with the ghost, I'd have been all right. As it was, I felt as though my guts were simultaneously burning and tightening until I could bear it no longer. I slashed with the scissors to cut the cord. The tension went, and as it did the heat started to cool. I looked at the long, shallow slash on my arm, oozing dark blood. I watched a while, then quite slowly and deliberately put another slash alongside the first. More blood oozed. I watched it for a while then pulled my sleeve down. That would do, at least until I could find another ghost.

16

Notwithstanding the weekend, Sarah was in the office bright and early the next day and, judging from the car park, Greg was before her. After checking emails and voice messages, she settled down to some steady phone use in order to find the Rev Hamilton's wife. After repeated no answers she was successful on the ninth attempt at getting a real person instead of a recorded message.

'Hold on a moment,' said the voice. 'Yes, my sister is here. I'll get her for you.'

A pause, and then a cautious voice said, 'Yes, this is Clara Hamilton. Who's that please?'

'DI Sarah Laurence from Norfolk Police,' said Sarah, and before she could say another word she got the panicky response, 'Oh God, don't tell me something's happened to my husband.'

'No, not at all,' responded Sarah. 'I'm just following up a line of enquiry connected to his prison visiting role and had one or two things I wanted to check with you.'

There was another pause and then, 'I knew he'd get into trouble with this,' said the voice. 'And I just knew I should stay home. What's he done now?'

Sarah stopped to think for a moment. This wasn't exactly the reaction she was expecting. But it was close to the one she'd been hoping for.

'Mrs Hamilton,' she said. 'Can I ask, what made you decide to pay a long visit to your brother in Stoke-on-Trent? At this particular moment?'

'Just a family visit,' replied Mrs Hamilton, defences back in place.

'I see. Nothing to do with your assumption that your husband had got into trouble with his prison visiting, then?' A further silence. 'You see, Mrs Hamilton, the story in your neighbourhood is that you left unexpectedly and we have some reason to believe it was in response to a threat from the prisoner your husband has been seeing.' Sarah was making it up as she went along, but with a powerful sensation she could see a route map unrolling in front of her. 'Your reaction confirms it. Your husband has been seeing a lot of a prisoner we know has strong links to organised crime. His associates are not nice people. So, I ask you now, were the threats against you or him? And what has your husband had to do to get them off your backs?'

This time she let the pause drag on, unaware that her fingers were clenched round the phone, hoping Clara Hamilton would not ring off without replying. After what felt like minutes there was the sound of a sigh.

'If you know that much, I may as well tell you the rest,' said Mrs Hamilton, 'and frankly even if it gets him into a spot of bother, it'd be better than worrying about someone knocking him off. The threats were against me. He wouldn't tell me exactly what, just that it would take pressure off him if I paid a visit here for a while and give him time to sort it out. He said with me out of the way he could go to the authorities and call the prisoner's bluff, but from what you say it doesn't sound as though he has. Stupid man. He's way out of his depth, I think.'

'How long have you been in Stoke-on-Trent?' asked Sarah.

'Two weeks, and to be honest, I'm starting to outstay my welcome.' Sarah could hear sounds of expostulations in the background, but Clara Hamilton paid no heed. 'And no wonder. No matter how well you get on with your siblings, no one wants an everlasting house guest. I'll come home tomorrow.'

'I'd like to call round and see you if that's OK,' said Sarah. 'What time would suit?'

'I'll be driving. I should be home around 3pm tomorrow, traffic permitting.'

'Thank you. I'll see you at four.'

About to leave for the day, Sarah had a second thought and popped into Greg's office to bring him up to speed.

'Greg,' she said, barely halfway through the door, then stopped short. Jim was sitting one side of the desk and Greg the other. The space between was occupied by a frozen silence and a crumpled Ordnance Survey map. 'Sorry,' she said, 'didn't mean to interrupt. I just wanted to…' and her voice trailed away. 'I'll drop you an email,' she said and started to back out of the room.

'No. Stay,' said Greg, his voice, as she said later, sounding 'weird'. 'There's something you'd better know. Take a seat.'

She came back in, closing the door behind her and sat

down. The silence continued, then Greg cleared his throat. 'I'm not quite sure how to say this,' he said, 'but we have a problem.'

'Let me,' said Jim. 'It was my fault after all.' Then as Greg made a sound of dissent, Jim went on, 'The plain truth is, we've arrested the wrong man.'

'What? How do you know?' asked Sarah. 'Has he an alibi? Or d'you have another suspect?'

'No, to both, which makes it all worse,' said Jim. 'No. The problem is, the body of the nurse wasn't buried in Tom Howe's garden after all.' Sarah went to say 'what' again, but thought the better of it and waited in silence.

'We assumed, *I* assumed,' said Jim, 'that because the body was buried in the land in front of Tom Howe's old home, it was buried in his garden. It turns out it wasn't. That land belonged to the chalet one plot to the north. Their garden was L-shaped and the land in front of Tom Howe was only his as far as a dividing fence. The next section, between the fence and where the clifftop used to be, belonged to next door. By the time we saw it, of course, all the land between the cliff edge and the chalet that belonged to Tom Howe had dropped down towards the beach.'

'So Julie Bolton could still have been buried in the Howe garden?'

'Possible but very unlikely according to forensics. When the body was spotted, she was halfway down the cliff. There are the remains of the fence between the body and the new cliff edge. All badly damaged, of course, and in pieces, but also very obviously quite new. I've checked with the agents for the chalet to the north and they had a new fence put in only two years ago. Replacing the pre-existing, much older fence. There can be little doubt the interment took place in the other garden. Moreover,' he planted his hand on the map in front of him, 'the Ordnance Survey map confirms it. It shows both gardens and the line of the fence. If I'd looked at it earlier, if it hadn't been blowing a hooley on the day we checked the surroundings, I'd have seen it and at least asked some questions.

'I'm sorry, Greg,' he added. 'I'll go and tell Margaret now.'

'No, you won't. I'll tell her,' said Greg. 'Ultimately it was my responsibility.' At the same moment, Sarah asked, 'But why didn't Tom Howe say something? I'm damn sure I would've if I was being arrested.'

'We've not yet spoken to him about it. That's the next job after Margaret. But I imagine he simply assumed we knew about the garden design and the body was in his section, as we kept telling him. The boundaries are perfectly clear on the map, and if we'd had any doubts about which bit the body had been buried in, we'd surely have been asking some questions. We didn't. We, *I* made an assumption and I didn't check it. My fault, not yours, Greg.'

Greg stood up. 'Still my responsibility,' he said. 'I'll go and see Margaret now.'

'And I'm coming with you,' said Jim.

Sarah stood up as well. 'I'm going to go and do some digging on the ownership of the next-door chalet,' she said. 'I'll see what I can find.' The Bakalov link forgotten in the face of this new challenge; she rushed off.

It was evident Margaret was not pleased. She sat for some moments looking at her desk, twisting a pen in her hands.

'Better get the PR team in,' she said at last. 'The media're going to be all over us. And get legal in as well. We're almost certainly going to face a complaint of wrongful arrest. OK. What can we rescue from this?'

'Nothing for the moment,' said Greg flatly. 'The plain truth is we arrested the wrong man and we don't yet have any other leads. It's back to basics for us.'

Margaret's attention was back on her pen. 'I don't need to tell you there'll probably be an investigation,' she said. 'Nor do I need to tell you, you fucked up. You know that. Go away and put it right. Fast.'

The conversation with Tom Howe and his brief was tricky too. The victim was primarily confused.

'But how could you make a mistake like that?' he kept asking. 'The boundaries are on maps. On my deeds. It's clear enough. Why didn't you check before firing off with your accusations?'

As Greg admitted to Chris later in the day, it was a fair question.

'And unanswerable. What could we say? It was windy and the map kept blowing away? After the cliff fall, everything looked different? We tried to interview the neighbours but they were either at the far end of a transatlantic phone line, or in a state of shock at the loss of their own homes. There was no one we could walk round the site with and ask our questions.'

'All true,' said Chris.

'And all insufficient. Plain truth is, Jim messed up and I did no better. I should've checked.'

That evening Greg sat alone in his cottage, Bobby on his lap.

Chris had watched him head for home with some concern, but he'd turned down the company offered.

'Not this evening, thanks, Chris,' he'd said. 'I won't be good company, and I need some time to think.'

So thinking was what he did.

'We need to go back to the cases we know most about, Bobby,' he said, running his hand over her smooth tortie back, 'and that means the temenos remains and the district nurse, or in other words, Krystina Kaminska and Julie Bolton. What links these two cases? Apart from the obvious, of course, that they were very similar in looks and both buried in identical ways, with arms crossed on their chests and a silver thruppence in their mouths.

'One was taken from the Cantley sugar beet factory and buried in a garden in Hemsby. The other taken it seems, with or without her bike, from streets near the Bowthorpe Community Hospital and buried in archaeological diggings at Caistor St Edmund. So, the other common factor is that both victims were moved some distance either before or after they were killed. That, Bobby,' he went on, 'was the attraction of the cab driver, but that, as we now know, was a big mistake. So, how else could they have been transported, and why to those particular locations?'

He stroked in silence for a while. 'It could be a car or van,' he said, 'especially as we know the Cantley site is effectively open to the general public on the footpath or at the pub. But, and I'm sticking my neck out again here, Bobby, I am very drawn to the lorry idea. According to Jill's report, lorries park at Cantley right alongside the car park Julie Bolton parked in. And lorries hauling the same sorts of agricultural materials also call at the farm across the road from the Caistor St Edmund dig.'

He ruminated in silence for a moment. 'Which brings me to the poor soul buried in the Oulton Broad hole in the road. She was probably picked up from one of her working locations on the A11. Right on a main lorry route to the east coast ports and/or Cantley.

'Tomorrow, Bobby, we take a good hard look at lorry drivers.'

17

'Back to basics we said, and back to basics it is,' muttered Chris, staggering to her desk with another pile of printouts.

'Returned to good old-fashioned paper, have you?' asked Steve, passing by with another enormous mug of coffee. 'Would you like one?' He indicated the coffee. 'It looks like you'll need it.'

'Thanks,' said Chris, stacking paper in different piles. 'Yes, I know you can compare reports on different screens, but if I want to cross-check something, I find paper is best. OK. Let's see what we have here.' And she dived in.

An hour later she emerged, hyper from caffeine and frustrated from lack of progress.

'Jill,' she hollered across the room, 'have you turned up anything new yet?'

'No new links yet,' she replied and was interrupted by Sarah coming into the ops room.

'I've got something on that chalet,' she announced to the room at large. 'It was owned by a chap who divided his time between Canada and England. It seems he let it out as a holiday cottage when he was out of the country and he's given me the letting agent details. I've had a quick word and I've got some info but it's not much more than a list of names at the moment. One of them must be significant if we can only just work out which one. Chris, Jill, can you follow up please?' She swept out again.

'Let's have a butcher's,' replied Chris, taking the sheet of paper from Jill. 'Not much here as Sarah said,' agreed Chris, running her eye down a printout of the letting agent's database. 'Just dates and names, not even addresses. They must have more than this. We'd better get back to them, especially for the dates in the relevant years.' Running her eye down the page, muttering, Chris suddenly froze. Staring so hard at the fuzzy print her eyes started to water, she sat down again. Then she started shuffling paper on her desk so vigorously some went on the floor.

'Poop,' she exclaimed and bent to pick it up. 'It would be the one I wanted, wouldn't it? Yes. Look there. I thought there was a name I recognised. Colin Brown. He's here as a tenant of the chalet in 2008. And again here,' she flourished the sheet she'd picked up from the floor, 'one of the lorry drivers visiting St Edmunds Farm in the same year.'

'It's not that unusual a name,' remarked Jill dubiously. 'There must be lots of Colin Browns.'

'But worth looking into. Jill, you get on to the letting agents as Sarah asked. See if there's an address or occupation for the Colin Brown in their records. Oh, and did you ever get that list from Cantley? You know, of the lorry drivers on their site.'

'Not yet. I know they're doing their best but it was ten years ago and they had a change of IT system in between. Joseph is trying to mine the old system as we speak.'

'Joseph is it?' teased Steve, passing by. 'Didn't realise you were on first-name terms.' Jill made a rude gesture in his direction as Chris said, 'Steve, I think you and I should pay a visit to Delta Transport. Perhaps we'll get a speedier response from them if we turn up on their doorstep. Phone calls and emails don't seem to be getting us very far in either case. Jill, you keep chasing Joseph.'

She headed for the door, scooping up her jacket and tote.

'What about telling Sarah?' asked Jill of her retreating back.

'Sure. I'll ring her when we're on the way.'

Sarah was on her way to Thetford and her meeting with Clara Hamilton when she got the call from Chris. 'OK,' she said, distracted by another incoming call. 'Keep me posted, thanks.' Changing calls she said, 'This is DI Laurence. Who's calling?'

'Madame Trieste,' said the voice. 'I need speak with you. Now.'

'OK,' said Sarah, checking the traffic before pulling on to the A11. 'Go ahead. I'm driving but I'm on hands-free.'

'No. Need speak face to face.'

'I'm sorry,' said Sarah, 'I'm on my way to a meeting. It's been arranged since yesterday. Please go ahead now and I'll pop over when I can.' 'If I need to' was the unspoken addition, which Madame Trieste picked up out of the ether.

'No. Either you come or no talk. You need to hear me. You need this. Come soon or too late.'

'OK.' Sarah sighed. 'I'll make it to you as soon as I can.'

*

The drive to Thetford went well for once and within less than an hour Sarah was pulling up to the big gaunt house on Fern Road. This time there were two cars parked outside: a big old Merc and a little Ford Ka she took to be Mrs Hamilton's runabout. When she knocked on the door there was the distant sound of raised voices and a short delay, before a flushed lady in body warmer and jeans opened the door.

'You must be Detective Inspector Laurence,' she said with precision. 'Please come in. My husband is being difficult but I expect he'll join us in a few minutes. Come through to the kitchen. I've got coffee on.'

The kitchen was still bare, but markedly more welcoming thanks to the smell of coffee rather than cat poo. A French-style coffee pot was simmering on the old Aga, which now gave out a welcome warmth.

'Silly man turned it off when I went north,' said Mrs Hamilton. 'Said he didn't want to waste the oil, but mainly I think he didn't want the pressure to cook proper meals. He's been living off takeaways and baked beans as far as I can tell. No wonder his judgement's off.'

The Rev Hamilton entered at that moment and, glancing at him, Sarah was sure he must have heard his wife's words. He said nothing, however, as he sat himself at the table. Clara Hamilton banged a coffee cup in front of him, and placed another, rather more gently, in front of Sarah.

'I'm so cross I could spit,' she announced. 'Go on, George, tell her what you told me, and hurry up about it. I haven't got all day. I've still got clearing up to do after you let the cats run wild.'

The reverend occupied himself stirring his coffee for

a while, and Sarah decided to help him out.

'I believe that Dragan Bakalov, or at least one of his associates, has threatened you,' she said with as little emphasis as she could manage. 'I'm sure you will have been briefed on his convictions, so you know why he's in the gaol, and that he has links to organised crime. How you could be put in that position is likely to be the subject of a separate investigation. What I want to know for now is what he wanted you to do for him, and what you did.'

'For God's sake,' snapped his wife as the silence looked set to continue. 'Tell her and hurry up about it or I will.' Sarah gave her what she hoped was a silencing look and the Rev George heaved a big sigh.

'First, he wanted me to give a message to another visitor that I met when I left the prison. I felt sorry for Bakalov. Judging from his history, he'd never had much of a chance, and giving a message to the one woman he trusted seemed a small thing. But then he wanted me to bring a mobile phone in with me. I refused but he said that I'd already broken the rules by taking a message, so I was in trouble anyway. I still refused, I'm not a complete idiot.'

'But you didn't report it to the authorities,' snapped his wife.

'No, I didn't. I thought I could persuade him to be more reasonable. Indeed, everything seemed to go back to normal for a few weeks, then he wanted me to ring someone for him. Give them a message and carry one back to him. I refused again, but this time he threatened Clara.'

He stopped and Sarah prompted, 'What was the threat, Mr Hamilton?'

'He said she'd never look the same again if I didn't do what he wanted. He hinted at acid in her face.' This obviously wasn't news to Clara Hamilton, but she paled nonetheless.

'That's why I got her out of the way.' George Hamilton's voice was tired, almost inaudible. 'I thought it would give me time to get things sorted, but he kept up the threats. He said they'd get one of us, one way or another, so I carried the message.'

'What was it? And how did you pass it on?' asked Sarah.

'It was quite short. I was to say that Bakalov had got their instructions and would do as they asked. And there were some numbers I thought might relate to a bank account. To pass them on I just had to ring another number he gave me. He told me to get a phone specially for the purpose, but I didn't bother. I used mine.'

Sarah held her hand out. 'I'll take it, then,' she said. 'When did you make the phone call?'

'Last week. Tuesday.'

'For now, I would recommend you leave here ASAP and stay in a hotel. Once I've spoken to my boss we might be able to sort some protection for you, but in the meantime...'

'I'm not going anywhere,' interrupted Clara Hamilton firmly. 'I'm not leaving the cats.'

Sarah looked at her in silence as Clara sipped her coffee with a determined air. 'We'll be careful, don't worry, and I expect you can have the local police keep an eye on us, but no thug is driving me out of my home.' George Hamilton said nothing, drawing patterns in spilled coffee on the table.

'What about you, Mr Hamilton?' asked Sarah.

'I'll do as my wife wishes,' he replied. 'I've messed her

around enough. If she wants to stay here, I'll stay and do my best to look after her.'

Sarah got up to leave and handed them her card. 'Ring me any time if you have any concerns,' she said. 'I'll have a word with the local team and then let you know what's been arranged. But you would be safer in a big hotel. Are you sure I can't persuade you, even for a few days?' She looked at the two set faces and gave up. 'OK. I'll say goodbye for the moment, then.

'Oh, one last question. Who was the fellow visitor Bakalov asked you to meet?'

'I don't know her name,' said the Rev Hamilton. 'She was about middle-aged, I'd say. Dumpy, blonde hair with a dark streak down the middle.'

'Dyed,' remarked Clara Hamilton. 'Bottle-blonde. That figures.'

'One of the guards at the entrance called her madame,' added George. 'That was all I caught.'

18

Sarah was muttering to herself most of the way back to Norwich. After the reverend's admission, she'd made as swift an exit as she could manage, delayed only by the need to ensure the local police kept as close an eye on the pair as they could. She drove away, fully aware that it wouldn't amount to much more than the occasional drive-by. Her concern for their safety was, however, pushed into the background by her irritation with herself.

'Should have gone straight to Madame Trieste,' she muttered as she queued to join the Thickthorn roundabout. 'Damn. I suppose now she'll clam up again and I'll have missed my chance. Damn damn damn.'

She hammered the steering wheel, oblivious to the slightly alarmed, slightly amused reactions of the passengers in the car next to hers, then surged away once the lights changed and, ignoring the speed limit, made her way as quickly as possible to the nail bar. It was closed.

More hammering, this time on the front door and then the display window alongside. No response. She made her way round the end of the small terrace, past the chip shop on the corner and, clambering over some broken pallets and discarded oil cans, found her way to what she still, harking back to childhood, would call a 'back entry'. Breathing hard she made her way along to where she estimated the back of the salon lay, then pushed her way through a broken gate, trying to avoid the waste food on the ground around her. Something, or someone, seemed to have made a good job of emptying the contents of the waste bins onto the ground around her feet. The air was full of a smell of rotting cabbage, sour oil and old fish skins. It wasn't pleasant.

She made her way through the backyard to the door and hammered again. Paint peeling off the door fell in showers of pigmented dandruff.

'Madame Trieste,' she called, over and over. 'Madame. I came as quickly as I could.'

She was about to give up and was turning away when the door opened. Madame Trieste stood, half concealed by the door, her hair dishevelled and scruffy slippers on her feet. She showed no sign of inviting Sarah in, but Sarah didn't wait to be asked. She pushed past and found herself in a small kitchen. The Formica-topped table was chipped and the electric stove in the corner had seen better days. There was little else on view other than dirty mugs and glasses.

'Don't think I offerin' you tea,' snapped Madam Trieste.

'No, thank you,' replied Sarah, and after sweeping some papers off a kitchen chair, she sat down at the table. She went to lean her elbows on it, then, sensing an ineradicable stickiness, thought the better of it. 'You wanted to see me,' she said.

'An' you didn't come.'

'I'm here now. What was it you wanted from me?'

'I wanted help, like I should from the police.' It was a sneer. 'But police help isn't for the likes of us, is it?'

'Of course it is, if you need us,' replied Sarah. 'But you haven't told me what the problem is. What help do you need?'

'OK. Let's see if you mean what you say.' Madame Trieste sat down on the opposite side of the table. 'I want report a missing person.'

'Who?'

'One my girls. A good girl.'

'Her name?'

'Marilena Dalca.'

'How old is she? And how long has she been missing?'

'Since last night.'

Sarah looked up from her notebook, and paused before saying what she would normally say in such circumstances: '*She may be with friends. It's a bit soon to be worried about an adult. Perhaps she's just…*' She looked at the woman opposite. Never exactly a svelte fashion model, she was looking distressed and disturbed.

She asked a different question. 'Why are you so worried, Madame?'

'Because she's good girl. She's a friend. She work for me a long time. Six years now. She never do anything like this before. And I read about this serial killer. I'm worried for her. But,' she shrugged her shoulders, 'I know you won't care. I know you not interested in working girls. Whores you will say. They get what's coming to them. They desire what they get. I hear it all before.

No one cares about us. But I tell you.' She stood up and leaned over Sarah threateningly. 'Buying a girl for an hour or a night not mean you buy her life. Her soul. These girls deserve better. Deserve respect.' She was spitting her words out. Sarah looked up, calm, unperturbed by the anger on display.

'We care,' she said. 'My boss cares. Tell me a bit more about her. Do you have a photo of her?'

'I have photo,' said Madame Trieste and she left the room. She was gone only moments, and reappeared with a large photo in her hands. The sort you might use for advertising or in a model's portfolio.

Sarah's interest sharpened. The girl in the picture was tall and slim, with long, straight dark hair. In the photo she was leaning forward, wearing only a skimpy black bra and pants, and pouting at the photographer. Her lips were painted bright red.

Chris and Steve had almost reached Cambridge when they got the call from Greg.

'I need you back here,' he said. 'ASAP. Sarah has just phoned in. It's possible we have another case on our hands, and this one is a fresh one.'

'What?' Startled, Chris pulled over into a convenient lay-by, seriously discommoding the lorry behind her that'd been planning to use the same space. He went by with a squeal of air brakes and two fingers held up to his windscreen.

'And to you too,' muttered Chris. 'Greg, what exactly has happened?'

'Missing person from Norwich. Sex worker from the nail bar/massage parlour that Sarah's been visiting. She went missing sometime last night and she's a dead spit for all our victims so far. I'm calling on every favour I have to look for her. So I need all hands on deck.'

Chris glanced at her watch and at the map on the phone screen in front of her. 'Greg, we're less than ten minutes from Delta Transport and I think we have a really good lead. Is it OK if we check this out as fast as we can, then get on the road again?'

'How good's your lead?' he asked.

'Lorry driver at Delta who's called at St Edmunds Farm has the same name as a tenant at ground zero in Hemsby. And the dates match too. At least, the same year.'

'Any connection to Cantley?'

'We don't know yet. That's one of the things we want to check at Delta.'

'It's thin, Chris.'

'Yes, I know. But we've already driven for an hour and a half to get here and we're nearly there. If we're right, it might shorten your manhunt.'

There was a pause, while Chris and Steve sat listening to atmospheric crackles.

'OK. Do it. Then get back here ASAP. I don't need to say, let me know if you find anything, however little.'

'On it. Thanks, boss.' Chris turned to Steve. 'Come on. Let's hope we're right.'

Re-entering the traffic flow with the same despatch that she left it, another lorry driver irritated in her wake, Chris sped through the speed cameras in the run up to Cambridge, then hit the roadworks where a new intersection for the A14 was seriously impeding the flow of traffic.

'Damn damn.' She drummed her fingers on her steering

wheel, unaware that Sarah had earlier been doing exactly the same. 'Do we come off here, Steve?'

'No. Keep on for the moment. There's a turning for Delta Transport just after the crematorium.'

'How appropriate.'

The turning, when they reached it, was clearly signposted and more signs on site directed them to an office beside a weighbridge. Huge grain stores obscured the skyline and alongside was a substantial concrete pad with four Delta Transport lorries parked in a neat row, all displaying the navy and white livery. A fifth lorry was currently being shampooed under a lorry wash. They parked as near to the office as they could get in the limited visitor parking area and, hopping over runnels of sudsy water from the lorry wash, arrived at the open door.

A man was seated at the reception desk, which ran in an L shape from the doorway and in front of the window onto the yard and the weighbridge. Sandy-haired and heavy in build, he was dressed in the same navy and white livery as the lorries, this time rendered in polo shirt, jeans and fleece top with 'Delta' and 'Dave Patterson' embroidered on the shoulder. He looked up as they entered and motioned to two seats beside him, his side of the desk.

'You must be the police,' he greeted them. 'Do you mind if we do this here? I have a couple more lorries due in and I can't leave this place unattended.'

Holding out their warrant cards and introducing themselves, Chris and Steve took the seats indicated. Steve got out his notebook, but before any questions could be asked, Dave handed them a giant wad of printouts.

'Those are the driver records for 2010, all of them,' he said.

'That's what you asked for originally. And these,' he handed over a smaller wad, 'are the driver records for Colin Brown as you asked this morning. You'll find there's a gap. He left us at the end of 2010 and only came back a few months ago. Whoops, I just need to deal with this chap. Give me a minute, would you?'

A huge articulated lorry labelled 'Cambridge Grain' was pulling onto the weighbridge. As Chris watched, the driver removed the cover from part of his load, then came across the yard towards the office, a bundle of papers in his hand. Dave was busy at the terminal by the window and, without moving from his chair, manoeuvred an articulated sampling arm by the weighbridge until it lowered a probe into the load of grain. There was a pause, then a rattle as a small quantity of grain was funnelled from the probe into the office to a unique receptacle, which Dave promptly labelled. The driver was waiting by the desk, looking at the two strangers curiously.

'Got visitors I see, Dave,' he remarked.

'That's right. OK, got your sample and your weight. Tip at Store 2 and I'll weigh you out. There's no one in the queue at the moment.'

'Thanks. Will do.' The driver nodded, took his completed paperwork back and returned to his cab.

'Is that interaction with a driver typical?' asked Chris.

'Well, I suppose so,' said Dave, puzzled.

'What I mean is, do you do everything from here without going over to the lorries?'

'Normally yes. In fact, I'd only go over to the lorries if the probe and sampler weren't working, and that's almost never.'

'So, the driver could have anything or anyone in the back of his cab and you wouldn't know.'

'Yes. I suppose so.'

Chris and Steve looked at each other.

'What can you tell us about Colin Brown?' asked Chris.

'Not very much. At least not much more than you can get from the paperwork I've given you. I only joined DT two years ago, so I never met him until this last year.'

'How did that come about? Did he come here looking for a job?'

'He applied for a vacancy in the normal way. We usually have a vacancy or two for drivers. Experienced HGV drivers aren't easy to come by. Especially not ones that're willing to comply with company rules.'

'Are they so unreasonable?' asked Steve, intrigued.

'No, not at all. But they are strict and we do enforce them.'

'Such as?' asked Chris.

'Well, wearing the uniform, like I am today, keeping lorries clean, making a good impression on customers when you pick up or drop off, no phone use when driving, that sort of thing.'

'Why's any of that a problem? Sounds pretty normal to me,' remarked Steve.

'Well, it would to you, but you'd be surprised how many drivers want to get creative with a uniform or, even more commonly, don't want to be bothered to wash their lorries down. And the boss is really hot on having clean lorries. Anyway, we've usually got a vacancy or two, and when Colin Brown came along claiming to have worked here before, I looked his records up and checked with the boss. That's why I could lay my hands on them quickly. The records that is.'

'Any issues with him?'

'No. No complaints that I could see, and the boss was

happy too. Said he wouldn't be his choice for a night out in Newmarket, but he was an OK driver and punctual as well.'

'Why did he leave in 2010?'

'No idea. You'd have to ask him that.'

'Where'd he go, do you know?'

'We had to do a reference for a firm in Lincolnshire; so as far as I know, that's where he went after us. But that's all I know, I'm afraid.'

'And what d'you think of him? As an employee and as a man?'

'As a driver, he's fine. Keeps his lorry clean, makes his pick-ups and drop-offs. Doesn't seem to go off-piste. As a man, I wouldn't say I knew him very well. The boss throws the occasional party for the team. Usually one at Christmas and another in the summer. He's come to them, but that's the only time I've seen him join in anything like that. When the chaps organise a birthday party or similar, he makes an excuse. And he's not exactly life and soul anyway. You can see what the boss meant.'

'How does he behave?'

'Sits in a corner nursing a pint, generally. If you go and talk to him he's OK, but a bit weird.'

'What d'you mean, a bit weird?' asked Steve.

'Well, his ideas are a bit wacky. He seems to believe any old rubbish you read in the *Mail* or see on the TV. You know, conspiracy theories type stuff. And he believes in ghosts and zombies and that sort of crap. But he's a good driver, and that's all we're concerned with.'

'When's he due back into the yard?' asked Chris as they stood up to leave.

'Not for over a week,' Dave replied. 'He's on holiday now.

Last day he worked was yesterday. Now he's off until next Monday.'

The two police officers looked at each other again, then Steve asked, 'Where's he gone, d'you know?'

'No. Sorry. Could be sitting at home for all I know. You'll find his address in the paperwork I've already given you.'

As Dave politely showed them back to their cars, Chris asked, 'Where do the lorry drivers park their cars? You know, while they're out on the lorries.'

'Mainly behind the grain stores,' he replied. 'One or two might park here if they've got a really early start and they're staying over in the drivers' hostel. But mainly behind the sheds.'

'Can we see?' asked Chris, and she headed over to the nearest grain store without waiting for a reply. A huge lorry inching off the weighbridge, kicking up dust as it went, provoked another thought.

'Which is Colin's lorry? Can we see it?'

'Sorry, it's out today. Not due back until later. He pulled a late shift yesterday, returned about 9ish according to the docket, tipped up at Store 3 then refuelled for the morning and parked his lorry in the line. His car wasn't here this morning, so presumably he left last night and went off on his hols, whatever that means to him. Ray, one of the other drivers, had a problem with his lorry, so he was allocated Colin's instead. He should be on his way back from Yarmouth by now.'

By this time they'd crossed the wide expanse of heavy-duty concrete, dusty with chaff and spilled grain, which small groups of ducks were collecting. A flight of yellowhammers took off as they reached the corner of the buildings and turned to look at the short row of cars waiting in the weak sunshine.

'OK, we've seen enough,' said Chris. 'One final thing. We need Colin Brown's mobile number, and the number plate for his lorry. The one that Ray has taken to Yarmouth.'

'OK.' Dave took his phone out. 'The number's here,' he said, thumbing through his contacts. 'But if you want to know where Ray is now, I can do better than give you the registration number. I can show you on the office GPS.'

The GPS screen showed the big Scania to be joining the A11 at the Thickthorn roundabout.

'OK,' said Chris. 'How can you get in touch with him if he isn't allowed to use his mobile?'

'Radio of course,' said Dave with just a shade of incredulity in his tone, as he indicated the set in the corner of the office.

'Oh yes, of course,' said Chris, mentally kicking herself. 'OK, get him on the radio and warn him we may need to take a look at that lorry.'

Dave hesitated, seemed about to ask something, then sighed heavily and pulled the radio microphone towards him.

'I suppose the boss did say to cooperate,' he muttered. Chris, who'd assumed his next words would be about a warrant, left Steve listening in, uncrossed the fingers held behind her back and went outside, speed-dialling Greg as she crossed the threshold.

'Yes, I am riding a bit of a hunch,' she admitted, once safely out of earshot of Dave and his radio. 'But just listen a second, boss. This lorry driver stayed at ground zero in Hemsby. He visited St Edmunds Farm. He probably visited Cantley sugar beet factory but we're still checking that. He was in Norfolk last night when the latest victim went missing. And get this, he worked here in Cambridgeshire until 2010 then transferred to a new job in Lincolnshire. He only came back this year. Which might go some way to explain the apparent lull in cases between 2010 and now. What's more, his office manager chappie describes him as a bit weird. Apparently believes in zombies etc.'

Greg had made several attempts to get a word in edgewise, but with little success until Chris paused for breath.

'So what's your thinking on the lorry? He isn't even in it at present, from what you said earlier,' he said.

'No, and that's another thing. We need to find him now. I'll have his mobile number shortly and that might help. But going back to the lorry. He came back to the yard here last night. Then went off in his car. If he did take the Romanian girl last night, there should be traces in the lorry cab.'

'Is there anything on the yard CCTV?' asked Greg.

There was a long silence, then, 'Damn damn damn,' said Chris. 'I knew there was something I hadn't asked.'

'If you find anything on the CCTV, let me know and get the lorry diverted to us here, or at least somewhere forensics can take a look at it. But only if you have reason to believe the girl was in the lorry.' Greg was worried his words were falling on deaf ears, but Chris did take them in as she shot off back into the office. Then found Steve was ahead of her.

'Of course we have.' Dave was answering a question. 'The reason you haven't seen it is because it's hidden. When we had a spate of diesel thefts a few years ago we put a lot of extra security in. There's an infra-red beam round the whole lorry area and the grain stores at night. Break that beam by walking through it, and an alarm goes off that you can hear all the way to Madingley. The heavy security gates on all the drives are closed at 10pm and can only be opened by a zapper or a phone call from an authorised mobile number. The cameras we had before got vandalised, so they're all disguised now.' He pointed up at the nearest grain store. 'There's one up there by the grain elevator and another by the grain drier exhaust. And,' he turned on his heel, 'that owl box holds another. There are others.'

'Can you show me what you have from last night?' asked Steve, and on the nod, he sat down at the desk in the corner. Chris went back to her phone.

'Checking the CCTV now,' she said briskly. 'The lorry should be on its way to you. I'll ring back shortly.' And rang off.

Entr'acte 12

I had a few times in the following week when I got stressed. I tried my second solution. It worked, after a fashion. Only problem was making sure no one saw the scars. Luckily the weather was cool, so I could keep my long-sleeved fleece on without too many comments. Even so, I was running out of space. Then I had a brainwave. It was easier, I found, to pull up my shirt and scratch my belly. I was taking a perverse pride in keeping the lines neat, all the same length, and parallel. But it wasn't the same as dealing with a ghost. I started to feel, not just the hunger, but an anger. This wasn't fair, that I should be feeling like this. It was their fault. The anger was growing. The next ghost I saw was going to pay for this.

As it happened, the next ghost I saw was in a lorry park near Thetford. I'd already decided this one wasn't going to get away, when she actually walked right up to my cab. She was the dead spit of the last, so I knew this was my next clean-up job. I didn't take in what she said, but when I opened my cab door, she stepped right in, and smiled at me with those evil red lips. Her teeth shone at me in the light reflecting from the puddles on the tarmac, and the rain was spattering my windscreen. The buzzing in my ears was overwhelming and the heat rose in my body until I thought the top of my head would blow off. I seized her thin throat and, looking anywhere but at those terrifying teeth, I squeezed and shook hard. She tried to say something, but luckily I didn't hear what and she went limp very quickly. I hit her head hard on the door frame, just to make sure she couldn't come at me while I was driving, and pushed her into the back. It wasn't easy. She was heavier than she looked and her arms kept flopping around. One gave me such a fright when it fell into my face I shouted with alarm. Then I pushed hard and at last she fell into the space behind the seats. I was going to get in beside her and finish the job, when a bang on my door almost stopped my heart.

'All right, mate?' said a voice from outside. 'I heard a shout.'

I pulled my sleeping bag over the ghost and climbed back into my driver's seat. I pushed the window down.

'Fine, thanks, mate,' I said. 'Spilled hot coffee on my knee. Gave me quite a shock.'

He waved in response and walked away towards the garage shop. I put the window back up and sat there shaking. That was scary. The fight had taken away some of the urgency. And I was too scared now to get on and sort the ghost out there and then. I looked back at the shape under my sleeping bag. There was no movement but I realised, with a jolt, that a foot was still visible. I glanced round the lorry park, then leaned over and pushed the foot back under cover. Still no movement. I looked at my watch and realised I was now behind schedule. I was going to be late back to base. And I would be even later getting away on my holiday.

I smiled slowly. That was a great idea. I'd take the ghost away with me. That way I could take my time. I might even have a bit of fun first with this one. After all, she was safely dead. I didn't think she'd come back now. It should be safe. And she'd keep for a day or two. I would have her all to myself at the cottage. Then I could bury her with the silver thruppence as normal. I was so distracted, so excited I fumbled the gears as I drove off. I re-joined the main carriage way and headed for Cambridge and Delta Transport HQ.

19

Parallel threads

Greg didn't know whether to clutch his head or his throat. Or someone else's. He put the phone down and strode briskly into the ops room. A trio of call handlers were dealing with calls from the public. The appeal for information relating to a missing young girl seemed to be bearing fruit, judging by how busy they looked. How much of the fruit was rotten they had yet to see. He heard an overly patient response from one of the handlers that suggested a regular nutter on the other end of the line.

'Yes, sir,' he heard her say. 'Thank you for your call. It's very helpful that you keep an eye out on your street and I noted what you said about schoolchildren making a noise on their way home from school.' She looked up at Greg standing behind her and shook her head. 'Nothing so far,' she said, then clicked the symbol on her screen to take another call. 'Norfolk Police,' she said down the headset. 'Thank you for your call.'

*

Sarah was updating her notes with what she'd been told by Madame Trieste. Jenny was talking to another call handler.

'A possible sighting here,' she said to Greg, 'but nothing much. Just someone who saw a girl matching the description at one of the park and rides. And that's all.' Just as he was about to reply, Greg's mobile rang again.

'It's me,' said Chris's voice. 'We've got something on the CCTV. Steve's sorting out a digital copy to be sent to you and I think we might need Jill's friend at the UEA to perform their enhancement magic again. But I think we have enough to move.'

'What exactly do we have?' asked Greg with rather ostentatious patience.

'Sorry. Didn't I say? We have CCTV footage of Colin Brown's lorry entering the yard at 2107. It's weighed in at the weighbridge and he then tips up at the intake for their Store 3. After that we lose him for a few moments then he reappears on the camera that points at the lorry parking area. This one's hidden in an owl box, so its field of view is a bit limited. We can see a person, presumably Brown, getting out of the lorry and walking off screen. A few minutes later a car appears in shot and pulls up in front of the lorry but slightly to the driver's side. The driver gets out, walks round the back of the car and opens the rear passenger door on the other side. Then he opens the driver's door on the lorry. He reaches into the lorry cab, appears to take various small items out and put them in the back of the car. Then he goes back to the lorry cab and gets in. When he emerges he seems to have a long parcel in his arms, which he lowers out of the driver's door. The car hides precisely what happens next but as there's nothing on the ground when he drives away a few moments later, presumably he put it in the car.'

'And your thinking is?'

'It could have been Marilena. As far as you can tell from the murky CCTV picture, it was long enough to have been a body. It also seems to have been heavy but not impossible for one man to lift alone, or more accurately lower out of a lorry cab. It's all consistent with it being a body that Colin Brown transferred from his lorry to his car last evening.'

'OK. I think that's enough for us to check out the lorry. Get it diverted here. Forensics can take a first look.' He looked up. 'Sarah, have we got anything of Marilena's that might yield some DNA?'

She swung round on her stool. 'I got a dirty overall that was hers, and a comb Madame Trieste says several of the girls use, including Marilena. Also, I've got the fingerprint team in there to see what they can find.'

'Better than nothing, I suppose. OK. That's good. Did you hear that?' he said into his phone. 'There's a good chance we can identify any traces we find in the lorry if she was in there and left any DNA behind.

'Other lines of inquiry – can you and Steve go to Brown's home address? I'll get someone from the Cambridge team to meet you there and I'll see about a search warrant. Any news on his mobile?'

'Yes. Got the number.' Chris read it out.

'OK, I'll see if this tells us anything about his current location. Well done, Chris. I won't count our chickens yet, but this is looking promising.'

He turned to Sarah. 'I'm surprised Madame Trieste was OK with having a fingerprint team crawl all over her place.'

'I won't say she was keen,' replied Sarah with a smile. 'But having complained that police never took attacks on sex workers seriously, she could hardly complain when we did. I did say we'd be discreet with any ID that wasn't relevant to the case,' she added.

'Just in case we find the chief constable is a regular?' Greg was grinning as he turned round, then had to wipe the smile off his face in a hurry as he came face to face with Margaret.

'Progress?' she asked, choosing to ignore the comment she'd overheard.

'Possibly,' said Greg cautiously. 'We have a person of interest at least. Just need to find him.'

Back in Cambridgeshire, Chris and Steve pulled up outside a small semi-detached house in the village of Coton at the same time as a marked police car. The two cars parked nose to nose and two uniformed officers got out of one, while Chris and Steve alighted from the other.

'Detective Sergeant Chris Mathews,' said Chris, 'and Detective Constable Steve Hall,' indicating Steve and holding out her warrant card.

'Pleased to meet you,' said the tall, bearded officer facing her. 'Constables Morris and Ford at your service.'

'Not really,' said Chris, suppressing a grin.

'Yes really,' said Constable Morris. 'And believe me, we've heard all the jokes. What's more it gets worse. He,' indicating his colleague, 'is named Brent.' Steve laughed out loud.

'Don't tell me, and you've got a brother named Brad.'

'How did you guess,' asked Constable Brent Ford, deadpan, and for a brief second Steve believed him, then they all laughed as Constable Ford reached into the boot of their car for the ram. 'We've been told the search warrant is through,' he said, hauling the ram out one-handed. 'What's he done?'

'Suspect in a missing girl case, possibly a serial killer,' said Chris, walking up to the door and banging hard on the dolphin knocker. It was a cheap reproduction of a more expensive door knocker, the gold-coloured paint peeling even as she knocked. Steve pressed the bell to the right of the door as Constable Morris disappeared round the back.

'Open the door please, Mr Brown,' called Chris. 'It's the police. We need a word.'

A face showed at the sitting room window of the house next door, then disappeared. The door opened and an elderly gentleman came out onto the doorstep.

'He's away,' he called. 'Gone on his holidays.' Steve crossed the bit of front lawn and spoke to him over the low hedge of straggly lavender bushes.

'D'you know where he's gone?' he asked.

'Not exactly. Norfolk, I think. He said something about the Broads when he was chatting last week. We were bringing our bins in at the same time, and he said something about paying a visit to St Benet's Abbey, wherever that is.'

'Thank you,' said Steve. 'D'you know if there's anyone else at home?'

'No. He lives alone,' the man replied. 'What's he done?' he asked, curiosity overcoming politeness.

'We just have a few questions to ask him,' said Steve. 'Thank you for your time. We'll knock on your door if we have anything else we need to ask you.'

The man took the hint and went indoors, but continued watching from his window. As Brent wielded the ram, Steve saw the neighbour pick up a phone.

'Bet he's ringing *Look East*, or the *Cambridge Evening News*,' he said to Chris.

'Let's hope it is the papers, then,' she replied. 'TV cameras we could do without. Come on. We're in.'

Chris went to the car and pulled out two sets of paper coveralls, shoe covers and gloves.

'OK,' she said to Brent. 'We'll go in first and give you a shout if we need help, but at this stage this is a quick recce with minimal interference. When d'you think your forensic team will be here?'

'I'll get on the radio and chase,' he responded. Chris gave him straight look, guessing that helping the out-of-town team hadn't been high priority.

'Tell them we've good reason to believe the person of interest is a serial killer and they'll need to be looking for traces of a missing person. A missing girl, moreover, we've a faint chance of finding still alive if we get a shift on!' She glanced over at the small garden as she spoke. 'They might also want to check the garden for bodies,' she added.

Brent said, 'Understood. I'll pass the message on. Then I assume you'd like me to stay on the front door and Phil to keep an eye on the back?'

'Yes. Thanks. And if anyone has any queries refer them to DCI Greg Geldard in Norwich.

'OK,' she said, this time to Steve. 'Gloves on and watch where you step. Keep an eye out for surprises too, but our main task at this moment is to make sure Marilena Dalca isn't here, and see if there's anything to tell us where Colin Brown's gone.'

The house was quiet. There was little traffic passing on the road and the double glazing excluded the cawing from the nearby rookery that had been deafening them while they were outside. A quick check of all the rooms in the small house was sufficient to establish there were no live people present and no dead ones either. At least, not in the house and not in one piece. They turned their attention cautiously to paperwork and quickly found there was next to nothing qualifying for that definition in the house apart from a few printed books about the occult and some old newspapers several days out of date. It was Steve who hit gold, going through the drawers of an old bureau in the kitchen diner.

'Look what I've found, Chris,' he said, and held out an elderly iPad mini in a battered case.

'Well done,' said Chris. 'We need to get that back to the experts to see what they can find on it.' She was distracted by a knock on the window.

'Crime scene are here,' said Phil Morris through the window.

'Excellent,' she replied. 'Come on, Steve, let's give them space to work.'

20

Parallel threads 2

Bill couldn't help but be impressed by the size and polish of the huge navy blue and white lorry that pulled into the Wymondham offices' car park. The ease with which the driver manoeuvred it into a space convenient for the forensic team was also impressive. A small thin man, looking more like a jockey than a lorry driver, swung himself down out of the cab and looked around rather bemused. Bill went over quickly.

'You must be Ray,' he said.

'That's right. Ray Bennet. Am I in trouble?' he asked.

'Not you, no,' replied Bill. 'Unless you've been up to something you want to tell me about? No, I just want to ask you some questions about the lorry, how it looked when you picked it up, that sort of thing.'

'Is it Colin Brown then?' asked Ray. 'That wouldn't surprise me.'

'Why do you say that?' asked Bill.

'He's an odd one,' said Ray. 'Bit weird. Believes in ghosts and vampires, that sort of thing. But I don't know of any problems with him,' he added hurriedly, 'just the weirdness, and there's no law against that, is there?'

'Luckily for some of us, no,' said Bill, watching as the paper-suited forensic team began their work. 'But come on in, I'll find you some fairly disgusting coffee and the boss has a few questions for you.'

He took the driver into the offices through a back door and on to an interview room. The coffee and Greg arrived more or less simultaneously.

'Thanks for diverting here,' began Greg. 'It really is very helpful of you.'

'Not my decision,' replied Ray cheerfully. 'I go where I'm sent. It's the boss you'd need to thank.'

'And we will. But first, can you talk me through what happened when Colin Brown handed the lorry over to you this morning.'

'Oh, he didn't hand it over in person,' replied Ray. 'That's not how it works. I reported to the weighbridge office this morning. The despatcher said my truck was still with the mechanics and handed me the keys to Colin's. I went round to the yard, checked the cab and found he'd cleared most of his stuff out the night before, and put my stuff in.'

'Such as?' asked Greg.

'Well, my lunch and supper for starters. My duvet and pillow, and change of clothes etc. Then I loaded, weighed out, and set off for Yarmouth harbour.'

'Duvet and pillow?' asked Greg.

'Yes. Some drivers are happy with a sleeping bag. Colin is

for one, but not me. I like my comforts.'

'Was there anything unusual about the lorry when you picked it up?'

'No. Colin hadn't done his usual good job of washing down the outside – not on his last trip, by the look of it. Probably because he thought it'd be sitting around until he got back. But the boss is fussy about clean lorries, so I had to take it through the lorry wash before I loaded. Sorry, forgot to mention that just now.'

Bill and Greg exchanged glances. 'Damn,' thought Greg, 'there goes forensic evidence. If there was any in the first place.'

'So, to be clear, the lorry exterior was washed by you on pickup, and there was nothing in the cab of Colin's. Any bedding etc in there now is yours?'

'Yes. Well, except for the mattress obviously, and the old cushion Colin uses for his back. That's still in there. His sleeping bag and so on, he must've taken them with him.'

'Can you excuse us for a moment, Mr Bennet?' said Greg and he motioned to Bill to follow him.

'Whip down to the car park, Bill, and ask them to take a particularly close look at the mattress and cushion. It doesn't sound like the other bedding had anything to do with our man, although there's always the chance of some transfer, I suppose.'

'OK, boss,' said Bill, then added, 'I was going to ask him,' nodding at the interview room, 'about the vampire business.'

'What vampire business?' asked Greg.

'He says that one of the ways Colin Brown was an odd bod was that he believed in vampires. It reminded me of how the victims have been buried. You know, with silver thruppenny bits in their mouths. Perhaps it's not the coins that are significant, like you said about paying the boatman across the river. Maybe it's the silver that's significant. Doesn't silver kill vampires?'

'Bill, that's brilliant. Well done. I'll certainly ask about that. In the meantime, hurry up to the lorry and have a word with Ned's team.'

Half an hour later, and Greg was on the phone to Chris again.

'Still at the house?' he asked.

'Just about to leave,' she replied. 'I've given the Cambridge lot a receipt for the iPad mini and I'm bringing it back with us for the IT specialists to have a look at. The forensic team here have been very thorough, but there's nothing obvious to suggest that a drugged, comatose or dead Marilena was ever in the house. Apart from the iPad, it's been a bit of a dead loss. But Cambridge are bringing in a cadaver dog and ground-penetrating radar tomorrow to search the garden. You never know.'

'Have you found anything like a sleeping bag?'

'No. Nothing like that. Normal bedding on the one bed that's in the house. But no camping-style gear. The only other thing I noted was the limited choice of books – mainly about the supernatural, vampires and such.'

'That figures,' said Greg, and he explained Bill's theory. 'Have you found anything that might indicate where he's holidaying?'

'Nothing. The next-door neighbour thinks he mentioned Norfolk, but that's all. No paperwork about a holiday booking. Hopefully that's on the iPad, but it's code-word protected and I daren't meddle. I thought I'd leave that to the experts. One thing did occur to me. He stayed at that bungalow in Hemsby ten years ago, didn't he? Perhaps holiday bungalows are his thing. We might do the rounds of the Norfolk agents and see if any of them have him on their books. In addition to the usual with ANPR data obvs.'

'That occurred to me too,' said Greg. 'I'll get someone to look into it. Meantime, get back here as quick as you can. We need the iPad and I need you and Steve.'

'Up to the last couple of words, that sentence was looking promising,' replied Chris, turning away so that her conversation was private. Greg grinned to himself.

'You know what I mean,' he said. 'Just get back here quickly. And safely,' he added, mindful of to whom he spoke. 'We might even get a little time to ourselves tonight, although I can't promise anything given how things are going.'

'See you soon,' said Chris, looking up as Steve approached across the cracked tarmac of the road.

'Got everything you want?' she asked.

'Got everything there is,' replied Steve. 'Are we off?'

'Yes. Back to Wymondham with the iPad. I'll just check with our two car-dealer colleagues, and then we'll be on our way. They need that iPad ASAP.'

'Who?' asked Steve, confused; then as he caught up, he said, 'Oh, you mean Ford and Morris. Yes. With you.'

Chris spun the car round in the narrow road without delay and headed for the main road to Cambridge and the A14. Almost immediately she found herself at the back of a queue of traffic trailing an elderly Morris Minor doing a steady 28mph in the 40mph speed limit. The four cars between her and the Morris were all pulling out to peer past, then pulling in again as oncoming traffic limited their scope for overtaking.

'What *is* his problem?' muttered Chris, doing the same. As they approached a bend, the Morris slowed down some more. 'Oh God, he's going even slower. Does he think his car will fall over if he goes round a bend at more than twenty-five miles per hour? And what are this lot doing? You'd think they could get past now!'

'Possibly the large truck coming the other way is putting them off,' remarked Steve, taking a firm grip of the dashboard as Chris swung out and back again.

The car immediately behind the Morris found a space to overtake, and the one behind that followed into a diminishingly safe gap.

'There. See that?' exclaimed Chris. 'That mutt in the Morris is going to cause an accident driving like that. I've a good mind to pull him over.' Steve suppressed the comment that came to mind and, looking at his white knuckles, suggested calmly that such a solution might cause yet more delay.

'Think of the paperwork,' he said.

Another car succeeded in passing the old Morris. Chris allowed their car to fall back a little, then gunned the engine and, using the space created to gather acceleration, swung past both cars and made it past the Morris just before she hit the tractor coming the other way. The furious tractor driver gave her the finger as he went past, but Chris was looking at the Morris driver gazing fixedly at the road ahead, fingers clenched on the steering wheel and nose almost touching the windscreen.

'Typical,' muttered Chris, slowing down to the speed limit and then speeding up again as she joined the dual carriageway. Steve heaved a sigh of relief and released his catatonic grip on the dashboard.

'I think the boss would rather we arrived in one piece,' he ventured, 'rather than dead on time.'

In the operations room Greg was catching up with Sarah, back in data manager role.

'So, what've we got now?' he asked.

'In summary, not a lot. Clear lines of enquiry, but not much coming in so far. I've taken a couple of operators off the public phone line to ring around holiday bungalow agents. Nothing so far. I've got one person checking number plate recognition to see if we can spot Brown's car. Again, nothing. Ned's team have taken some samples from that Scania that they say might be promising, but again, we await results.

'Oh, just one thing. Jill's contact at the sugar factory has come good. He's dug out their old records from ten years ago, and he's confirmed not only that Colin Brown was a regular at the factory, usually delivering beet for Delta Transport, but that according to their records he was there on the day that Nurse Bolton disappeared. What they can't say is whether he was there as late as the time of her visit, but he did definitely visit that afternoon.'

'It's mounting up,' said Greg. 'We really need to find him now if there's to be any chance of finding Marilena alive.'

As he spoke, one of the civilian phone operators left her seat and came over almost at a run, leaving her headset on her desk.

'I think you might want to speak to this one,' she said. 'It's someone who says they know where Marilena was working the evening she disappeared. But they're asking to speak to the man in charge.'

Greg looked at her and wasted no time asking for further explanations. He strode over to her workstation and picked up the headset.

'Hello, this is DCI Geldard. What was it you wanted to tell me?'

There was the sound of a smoker's cough, then a husky voice said, 'Are you the boss man? The bloke in charge?'

'That's right,' said Greg. 'What was it you wanted to tell me?' he repeated.

More coughing then, 'I'm told you're different. That you're taking Mari's disappearance serious like.'

'I am taking it seriously,' he said. 'If you know anything that might help, please tell me. The quicker we find her, the better.'

'She was working on the A11, at the truck stop near Thetford. You know she was a working girl, right?'

'I knew she was sometimes a sex worker,' said Greg. 'But I thought she worked in Norwich.'

'So she did. But sometimes she worked the truck stop with a few of us. We have a driver takes us out there and brings us home.'

'A pimp?' asked Greg, then wished he hadn't been so blunt.

More coughing. 'I'm not saying nothin' more. Just so you know. She was at the truck stop that night and she dint come home with the rest of us.'

'Can I have your name and contact number?' asked Greg. 'You're not in any trouble,' he added in a hurry. 'I promise you that. You have my personal guarantee. But I might have some more questions.'

There was a cough-filled hesitation then, 'Krystal, with

a K,' said the voice, 'and this number'll find me.'

'OK, thanks, Krystal,' said Greg. 'Did you see Marilena get into a vehicle that night?'

'No. I saw nothin' after we got out of the car. We went to diffrent parts of the car park. You can't see much what with all them big trucks around.'

'What about the other girls with you? Could I speak to them?'

'No,' said Krystal firmly. 'They saw nothin'. We've talked it over. No one saw nothin'. But Marilena was there and then, when we came to go home, she wasn't.'

'OK, thank you, Krystal.'

The headset was handed back to its owner; Greg turned to Sarah.

'You'll have got the gist of that,' he said. 'Don't pull everyone off the Norwich end, but I think that info's good enough to shift the focus to that truck stop near Thetford. Get someone to check CCTV and number plate recognition for the lorry Colin Brown was driving. See if we can place him at that truck stop. And get someone out there to do some asking around.'

Entr'acte 13

Transferring the ghost to my car was easy. Downhill all the way, you might say. The ghost was safely wrapped in my sleeping bag; there was no risk I'd suddenly come face to face with her and it stopped her arms flopping about as well. I pushed her into the back of my car, pushed my pillow in as well because it had got messy from her face, then stuck my overnight bag in the boot and I was off.

It only took a few minutes at my house to pick up my holiday baggage and put that in the boot as well. The crumpled sleeping bag on the back seat hadn't moved; it seemed that I was safe from her for now. It was quite late when I set off back to Norfolk and my holiday cottage. I was tired from driving, but I calculated it should only take me an hour and a half at most, and if I arrived in the early hours of the morning, that was all to the good. Better there were no witnesses to my arrival. The agent said

I could get the key out of the key safe using the code she emailed to me. In a sudden panic I checked my phone, but yes, I had the email safely to hand.

The cottage was tucked away down a short drive. I was dog tired when I pulled up as close as I could get to the front door. I walked all round it first. There was a view of the beach from the clifftop garden, and tucked in a sheltered spot by the house wall was some decking and a hot tub. I could smell both the sea on the wind, and a chlorine smell from the tub. The rest of the rear wall was taken up by a lean-to conservatory with seats placed to take advantage of the view. There was a six foot fence all round the garden except for the section overlooking the sea. I sighed heavily and would have enjoyed the sea air some more, except that I was so tired. I almost wished I hadn't brought the ghost with me. I was tempted to leave her in the car until morning, but the thought of having to haul that burden out under the nosy eyes of neighbours changed my mind. I unloaded my cases first, and went to find the key safe. It was exactly where the email said it'd be, near the front door, and the code worked. Keys in hand I went back to the car for my cases, picked them both up, one in each hand and froze. I peered into the back of the car. The sleeping bag had moved. No, it hadn't. Or had it? Perhaps it'd moved when I bounced over the drive to my parking spot. Or p'raps it hadn't. I couldn't be sure. I watched for a bit, but couldn't see any other movement.

I took my bags into the house and dropped them in the kitchen. There was a note on the worktop welcoming me to Clifftop Cottage, telling me the rules about using the hot tub and reminding me that I'd find some basic supplies in the fridge.

Sure enough, it was stocked with bread, butter, milk, eggs and some sort of cake. Lemon drizzle, it said on the label. I was too tired to eat then and there, but some egg and toast would be good in the morning. Feeling quite pleased I went back out to the car, and this time there was no doubt the sleeping bag had moved. I could see a hand.

I acted fast. In a second the door was open and I'd pulled the bag out onto the drive. It landed with a thud. I couldn't lift it from there, so I hauled it to the front door and over the step as fast as I could. I wasn't too worried about damaging the contents. After all, they were dead. Or soon would be.

21

Loose threads

It was evening by the time Chris arrived in Wymondham. A pizza delivery Greg had organised for the weary team had just arrived. The still-warm boxes were being spread out along the central conference table along with cartons of coleslaw, salad and piles of cheesy garlic bread. Greg was standing in a corner chatting to Sarah, as Chris was quick to notice. She snagged a can of coke from the desk by the door and went over to join them.

'Seems I arrived just in time,' she remarked, leaving why she was 'just in time' open to interpretation. Sarah smiled behind her can of Coke Zero and said nothing. Greg perched on the edge of the table.

'Is the iPad with IT?' he asked.

'Of course. Have we any news on holiday cottages or anything from Brown's truck?'

'Nothing yet. The team have rung all the major holiday

cottage agents but learnt nothing. Ned's team have some samples from the truck cab, but no results yet, although the DNA typing is being fast tracked. Phil and Jeff Fellows have gone to ask questions at the Thetford truck stop – oh, you don't know about that yet, do you?' Greg filled Chris in on his conversation with Krystal-with-a-K. As he did so, Sarah moved away down the room, stopping at intervals to chat with members of the civilian team.

'You two seem to be getting on very well,' Chris remarked rather sharply.

Greg chose to take the comment at face value. 'Yes, it's good, isn't it? Makes working together much easier.'

'And much more pleasant.' Greg looked at Chris as she took another swig of her coke.

'Are you trying to pick a fight?' he asked in a low voice. She looked up sharply.

'I just said…'

'I know what you just said. And there's no need.' Greg could feel the edges of his temper fraying and took a deep breath. 'Look, Chris, we've both worked more than sixteen hours out of the last twenty-four and nothing's going to change until we've got Colin Brown behind bars or eliminated him from our enquiry. Please don't let's fall out over nothing. I can do this without you, but believe me, I'd really rather not.'

Chris opened her mouth on another tart comment, then thought the better of it and closed it again, words unspoken.

'It was a tiring drive,' she said. 'Sorry if I'm a bit crabby. Time I went home, I think.'

'Time you all went home,' said Margaret's voice over her shoulder. 'You've done good work today but we've another mountain to climb tomorrow. Be off, the lot of you, and I'll see you in the morning. That includes you, Greg,' she said before he could speak. 'Finish your supper, all of you,' she said, raising her voice above the background noise. 'You've done well today and you need a break. Off home now, or I'll know the reason why.'

There were mutterings of 'thank you' and 'good night' as everyone gathered up their car keys and bags, and headed for the door. Sarah was one of the first out, leaving with a couple of the telephone-answering team. Greg and Chris were the last.

'Coming back to mine?' he asked.

'Not tonight, thanks, Greg,' she replied. 'I said, I think I need to go home.'

'Oh.' He looked at her searchingly, his heart sinking a little. 'I thought you meant…' He stopped. 'We're good, aren't we, Chris?'

'We're good,' she affirmed. 'But I *am* very tired. See you tomorrow, Greg.'

Left alone in the suddenly echoing space, Greg aimlessly picked up a couple of empty pizza boxes and dropped them in the bin on his way to the door. He paused by the photo of Marilena Dalca, provided by Madame Trieste.

'Sorry, Marilena,' he said. 'We've done our best. Hang in there and we'll get to you as quick as we can.' He snapped the light off as he left the room and headed for his car.

At the Thetford truck stop on the A11, Phil was growing ever more frustrated by his companion. His conversation on the car journey out had been tediously macho-male. The sort designed to put fellow males on the back foot in order to assert a primacy in pecking order that had little basis in reality. Phil knew with a rock-hard certainty that, if challenged, Fellows would back off so fast he'd probably do a ten-second 0–60mph in reverse gear. Everything would suddenly become 'just a joke, mate'. 'Can't you take a joke?' 'Didn't mean it', or the ultimate cop out – 'you got me wrong, mate'. Phil considered making a challenge at least seven times, but when it came down to it, just couldn't be arsed. He was glad, however, to pull in to the adjacent BP garage and park up.

'OK,' he said, cutting ruthlessly across Fellows' latest tale about how wonderful/hard/quick-witted he was and how he was misunderstood by the ladies/cows/lesbians/man-haters that made up his female colleagues.

'You take the garage. See what they've got on CCTV and what they remember from two nights ago about what they probably think of as the "regular tarts". I'm going to have a chat with some drivers.'

'We not working in a pair?' asked Fellows, taken by surprise.

'No need. Not if you want to be home before midnight. Not worried about a little garage-hand are you?' he asked mockingly, having noticed the substantial stature of the man behind the till.

'No,' said Fellows, plainly on the defensive, and Phil walked away before he could add anything else.

Some minutes later, Fellows barged in on what Phil felt was probably the most promising conversation he'd had all evening. After five blank looks and 'No, sorry, mate. Haven't been here for a week/fortnight/month,' he'd finally found a driver who admitted to being in the truck stop two nights ago and to having spoken to a Delta Transport truck driver.

‘What led up to the conversation?’ Phil had just asked when Fellows strolled over and said, ‘Nothing on CCTV. It’s been wiped.’ Phil turned to look at him, irritated on several counts.

‘Wiped when? That’s convenient, just when we need to look at it. Is that the normal routine?’ he asked. Fellows looked blank.

‘How’d I know? What’s the difference?’

‘You’d know if you’d asked,’ said Phil. ‘Better yet, you’d have stood over him while they showed you what they did have on tape. Wouldn’t surprise me if they wiped it the minute you turned your back.’

‘Now why’d they do that?’ demanded Fellows in an aggressive tone.

‘Because they know there are prostitutes working the site and they don’t want any hassle? Oh never mind!’ Behind him, Phil sensed the driver he’d been talking to getting back into his cab.

‘Look, just go and check again,’ he said and turned back to the driver.

‘Sorry, mate,’ he said. ‘You were saying how the conversation with the Delta Transport man started.’

‘Did I say I spoke to him?’ asked the driver. ‘Not really. Just asked if he was OK, and moved on. That was about it.’

‘Why’d you ask if he was OK?’ asked Phil over the sound of the truck engine starting.

‘I’d heard a bang, and I thought I’d seen one of the prossies nearby. Wondered if he’d got into bother, but he said not.’ He put the truck into gear and it started to move off.

‘Hey, hang on,’ shouted Phil, but the driver just waved.

‘Sorry, I’m behind my schedule,’ he shouted out of the open window, then wound it up.

Phil snarled to himself and photographed the rear registration plate of the lorry as it pulled out of the truck stop. Then turned back to his colleague and the garage-hand.

'The tape from that night is deleted,' said the dark man in green logoed fleece and trousers, with a distinctly self-righteous tone. Phil looked at him hard and he shifted uneasily under his glare.

'When?' asked Phil and then added, 'No, don't tell me. Show me the oldest recording you've got.'

The man fiddled for a moment with the laptop behind the cash desk then pointed to its screen. Phil craned his neck and noted the date and time the earliest recording was made. Approximately fifteen minutes previously.

'Well, thank you very much,' he said sarcastically. 'My boss will probably be in touch about you frustrating a police enquiry.' The garage-hand started to gabble but Phil ignored him and headed back to the car, not much caring whether Fellows caught him up or not. He'd have something to say to Greg about this new colleague, and none of it would be pleasant. The drive north was completed in silence.

Entr'acte 14

Once I'd pulled the curtains to, I put a light on and looked at the crumpled heap in the middle of the wooden floor. It moved slightly. I suppressed a scream. Over by the fireplace, laid with logs, there was a set of black, cast-iron fire irons. I picked up the poker. Iron was poisonous to vampires, wasn't it? Or was that fairies? I couldn't remember. And I don't believe in fairies. This was no fairy anyway. This was a vampire, with teeth, and she was coming back to life. In my panic I wasn't sure which was the head end. I raised the poker and brought it down hard on one end of the sleeping bag. There was a thud and a crunch. Then I did the same at the other end. Then, for good measure, once or twice in the middle. Then I stopped, breathing hard.

When I looked closely at the shape on the floor, I saw a dark stain seeping into the fabric. Then I saw there was more than one stain. I sat down on the end of the sofa in front of the fire and watched silently for a while. I looked at the clock on the wall. It was now 3.35 and it would be light in a few hours. Any idea I could have some fun with this one – well, that'd gone out of the window. The problem now was what did I do with it until I could bury it safely. I couldn't bring myself to go to bed with it lying there in the house. There was no garage to leave it in.

I was too tired to think straight. I had some vague idea vampires couldn't cross water. Or something. I daresn't unwrap the sleeping bag. I hauled it through the house into the conservatory. The hard floors made it easy. Then I dragged it outside. The hot tub had a cover on, to stop birds making a mess in it, I supposed. I unclipped the cover, peeled it back and levered the bundle into the hot tub. Air billowed in the folds for a while, then gradually it sank. I watched for a while but there was no more movement. The dark stains lifted off the fabric, swirled in the water, then disappeared into the filter. I had one final thought, and turned the water heater off. Then I put the cover back and went to bed.

22

Moving forward

Greg sat in his conservatory with the lights off. There was a glimmer of reflected moonlight from the river and Bobby was perched on the window sill, fascinated by the rapid flight of the bats in the gloom. They were clearly visible against the pale sky as they zigged and zagged in the space between the tree tops, and Bobby's head tipped back and forward in perfect orchestration with their movements. Greg knew he should eat and go to bed for a good night's sleep, but his head was full of plans for the investigation and his heart was empty. He missed Chris and wished she was there to discuss the case. He also wished she was filling the cool space next to him on the sofa with her warm presence and making him laugh with a wry comment on the day. He couldn't see what he'd done wrong, or should've done differently.

'And maybe that's the problem,' he thought. 'I can't see how to be different. In these circumstances the job has to come first. Surely she can see that.'

Sighing, he got up, went to the kitchen and opened fridge and cupboard doors. After a busy few days, supplies were depleted. Bobby did her elegant, soundless leap from the floor to the worktop and rubbed her head on his arm.

'You're OK,' he said. 'I've got plenty of cat food. Fancy sharing? No, I thought not. Nor do I, to be honest.'

He emptied a sachet of cat meat into her bowl and got out a can of baked beans and some sliced bread for himself. When he got the butter out it looked distinctly as though the corner had been licked by a razor-sharp tongue, but he decided to pretend he hadn't noticed. He ate his beans on toast nearly as fast as Bobby ate her meat, and both retired to bed.

Contrary to his expectations he slept well; apart from a gaseous interruption, which he put down to the beans, and he commented to Bobby that perhaps it was lucky she was the only one sharing his bed. In consequence of the deep sleep, he woke cheerful and energised. He even whistled as he shaved, and was on the way to the office by 7am.

He was still whistling as he entered the operations room and was unsurprised to find Chris, Jill and Phil all there before him. He smacked his hands together on a cheery good morning and added, 'Right, team, let's get our heads together in half an hour and share what we know. I've got a good feeling about today.'

His attitude was infectious and they were all smiling when they sat down in a circle round the whiteboard.

'OK, I'll have a go at summing up what we know.' He nodded to Ned as he came in and sat down with the rest. 'Everyone chip in when you have something new to add – or indeed if I miss something.

'Marilena Dalca,' he pointed at the photo on the board, 'went missing during last Friday evening. Not, as we originally thought, from Norwich; but from the truck stop on the A11 near Thetford. The last person we know to have seen her alive, so far that is, is Krystal, a fellow sex worker. She saw her walking over to the lorry park at around 1915. Phil, anything from last night?'

Jeff opened his mouth but Phil cut in ahead of him.

'Not much, boss. Nothing on CCTV, the tapes'd been wiped. One lorry driver I spoke to says he spoke to a Delta Transport driver. He heard him shout and asked if everything was OK. The driver said yes, he'd just spilled some hot coffee, so my driver thought no more about it and carried on to his cab. But he had seen a woman near the Delta Transport lorry.'

Chris cut in. 'The only Delta Transport truck in that lorry park was Colin Brown's, so it'd seem that's who the other driver spoke to. Did you get a statement?'

'No.' Phil scowled at Jeff. 'I'll explain later, but I have got the registration number and company name. We can locate the driver no problem.'

'Chris and Steve, you pick up on Colin Brown,' said Greg.

'OK.' Chris started. 'Described by colleagues as a good driver but a bit weird. Believes in ghosts and vampires. Has done drop-offs and/or pick-ups at all our key locations including St Edmunds Farm and the sugar factory at Cantley. Rented the bungalow in Hemsby where the second victim was found.

'Two nights ago, he returned from a trip to Yarmouth via the A11 and the Thetford lorry park. He unloaded at the Delta Transport base outside Cambridge and their CCTV has him transferring something roughly the length of a person from his lorry cab to his car. He then went home and, as far as we can see, left almost immediately for his holiday. Whatever was put in his car at Delta Transport seems to have gone with him but we don't know where. His neighbour thinks Norfolk.'

'And his neighbour is probably right,' chipped in Ned. 'That's one of the things I came to say. IT have found emails on that iPad you brought back: an exchange between a letting agent in Suffolk and Colin Brown about renting a cottage near Bacton. We're following up now to get the precise address, but it's a bit early in the morning for the letting agent, and they're not answering yet.'

'No address on the email?' asked Greg.

'Not on the one we've recovered. If the final one had the address it seems like Brown printed that one off then deleted it.'

'OK.' Greg was about to go on when Steve interrupted.

'One other thing,' he said. 'For the past ten years or so he's been working in Lincolnshire. That might explain the gap in killings here. But shouldn't we also ask whether there've been any similar incidents in Lincolnshire?'

'Quite right,' said Greg and Sarah added, 'I've got calls out both to Lincolnshire police and his old employers.'

'OK,' said Greg again. 'The case against Brown is already looking very strong. Anything else on him specifically? Ned?'

'We found saliva on the mattress in his truck,' he replied. 'From more than one person, as you'd expect in a space that's shared by more than one driver. One trace appears to be a match for DNA from the comb supplied by Madame Trieste. We couldn't pick up anything from Dalca's overalls. Now the problem is, even if it's a match, it could theoretically be from another of Trieste's girls moonlighting as a sex worker, since the comb seems to've been shared between them.'

'No matter. Once we find Brown and hopefully Marilena I'm sure we'll get more DNA. Right, the priority today is find them both ASAP. Chris, you and I will go to the bungalow as soon as we have the address. Sarah, follow up with Lincolnshire please and see what else we can uncover there. Jill, put out an APB for Brown's car. Wherever he moves today, we need to be on to him. Anything from his mobile?'

'No hits yet,' said Steve.

Entr'acte 15

It was past four by the time I got to sleep, but once I did I slept like the dead. When I woke it seemed I hadn't even moved. My neck was a bit stiff and I had pins and needles in the arm I'd been lying on. I was dazed and confused. I vaguely remembered putting the ghost in the hot tub for safety. I remembered there was some food in the fridge, and thought about breakfast. I'd spend the day quietly here, then think about safe disposal of my guest. She'd be OK where she was for a while. The water was full of chlorine after all.

At that point, I realised why I'd woken up. Someone was ringing the doorbell. From the sound, it seemed likely they'd been ringing it for a while. As I looked at my watch to check the time – four o'clock, I noted – the bell stopped ringing and I heard steps crunch on the gravel round the side of the house to the back garden. I shot out of bed so fast I went dizzy, then went to the window. There was a man in the garden in polo shirt and shorts with a canvas bag over his shoulder. His clothes had a logo I couldn't see clearly, and he was heading for the hot tub.

I flung the window open and shouted 'Hey,' then realised I was standing there stark naked and pulled the curtain round me. 'What d'you think you're doing?' I asked.

'Sorry, sir,' said the man below me. I could only see the top of his dark head of hair and his polo-covered shoulders.

'I did ring the doorbell, but I didn't get an answer, so I assumed you were out. I've come to check the chemicals in the hot tub.'

My blood would've run cold if I'd had any. Mainly it seemed to have run down to my feet and disappeared.

'No,' I said in what was almost a squawk. Then, 'No!' I said again. 'Leave it. I got here late and I don't want to be disturbed.'

'It won't take a moment,' said the man. 'And I won't make a noise.'

'No,' I said yet again. Which bit of 'no' didn't he understand? 'Just leave it please.'

'Well, I could come back in an hour,' he offered. 'I have another tub to look at just up the coast.'

'No,' I shouted. 'Just bloody leave it, will you.'

'OK OK. Sorry to bother you,' said the man. 'But you won't be able to use the hot tub until you let me check it, you know. I'll come back tomorrow.' And he went off in what I could plainly see was a huff, even from my distorted viewpoint.

I sat down on the bed for a moment. Then sprang to my feet. I had no time to waste. He was going to come back the next day at the latest, and the ghost needed to be gone by then.

23

Back to the coast

The first breakthrough was a call back from the letting agent.

'Before I release any personal information,' she said cautiously, 'can you confirm your name, rank and number for my records?' The civilian phone operator explained her role and the voice stated firmly, 'Then please put me on to a police officer. I'm not willing to release personal information to anyone other than a police officer.' Putting her headset down on the desk, the girl looked round and the first person to catch her eye was Greg. A bit overawed, she nevertheless waved him over and explained the issue. Greg smiled with relief and picked up the headset.

'DCI Greg Geldard, will I do?' he asked.

The voice now sounded slightly flustered. 'Oh, OK. Yes. Of course. We can't be too careful these days you know, with data,' she explained.

'Yes, I understand,' said Greg. 'Thank you for ringing

back. I believe you've been in contact with a man named Colin Brown about a holiday cottage in Norfolk.'

'Yes. That's right. Is there a problem? Has there been an accident? Do I need to contact the owner?' Once he could get a word in Greg replied, 'No problem that I know of, but we're keen to speak to Mr Brown. Can you give me the address of the cottage please? And confirm when he rented it for?'

'Well, now!' exclaimed the agent. 'He should've been there since Friday and as far as I know he is. There've not been any problems reported to me, so I assume he got the key out of the key safe OK and all that. I can ring him and check if you like, or get our maintenance man round to look things over.'

'No. Absolutely not,' exclaimed Greg. 'You must *not* ring either Mr Brown or send anyone round there. Please give me the address and we'll check it out. I'll let you know if there are any issues for you.'

'Oh. OK. It's Clifftop Cottage, 22 Coast Road, Bacton.'

'Postcode?' Greg jotted it down. 'OK, thank you, Ms…?'

'Ms Jones. Helena Jones.'

'Thank you, Ms Jones. We'll be in touch.'

He handed the headset back to the civilian operator with a word of thanks and set off towards the car park at a run.

'Chris, with me, please. Sarah, can you notify the local team and Ned to meet me there? No one's to make a move without my say so. Put it out on the APB too. May help narrow down the hunt. Got it?'

Both were slightly out of breath when they got in the car. Greg headed for the exit before Chris had fairly got her seat belt on.

'In a hurry, aren't you?'

'I've just got this awful feeling we may be too late for Marilena,' he confessed. 'We're well over the golden twenty-four hours and the chances of finding her alive are diminishing all the time. That's what's putting the pressure on. Here.' He gave Chris a bit of scribble on a torn sheet of paper. 'Put this postcode in the satnav, will you, and let's see how long it's likely to take to get there.'

'If it's Bacton, around an hour,' said Chris, tapping busily. 'Yes, it's saying fifty minutes.'

'As long as that?' Greg was checking oncoming traffic before he joined the A11.

'The North Walsham team will get there a lot quicker,' said Chris.

'OK.' Greg thought quickly. 'It's a balance between urgency and preserving the crime scene,' he said. 'Speak to North Walsham, get someone trustworthy over there ASAP. If Brown's there, get them to detain him and check round for Marilena. Tell them to be careful not to damage evidence as far as possible. In fact, on second thoughts, get them to report to us before they do anything at the property.'

'OK.' Chris did some busy ringing and passed the message on. By the time they got a call back they were on the A149 and heading for Stalham.

'They say there's no one at the property and no sign of his car,' reported Chris.

'Put them on speaker,' responded Greg. 'How far away is Ned?'

'About ten minutes ahead of us, I should think,' said Chris. 'He started from Norwich, remember.'

'Who am I speaking to?' asked Greg of the hands-free.

'PC Rob Bates,' came the reply. 'We met on the terrorism case.'

'Yes, I remember you. Describe the property for me.'

'Typical seaside rental cottage,' said Rob Bates. 'No garage, small garden at the front between the house and the road. Bigger garden behind overlooking the beach. Patio with decking and hot tub. No sign of life at the property and no response to knocking. Wet marks on the decking, which seem to suggest it's been in use this morning. That's about it.'

'The crime scene officer should be with you shortly and we're not far off,' replied Greg.

Chris interrupted, 'Message from the office. We've got the search warrant.'

'OK, Bates. Break the door in. Go through the house quickly and carefully. Just check to see whether Marilena Dalca is there. Check the hot tub too. Use gloves and coveralls and be very careful not to compromise any evidence. Then get out, report back to me, and wait for scenes of crime.'

'OK. Got it.'

There was a pause while Greg navigated Stalham and headed onwards to Bacton. Then the hands-free rang again at the same time as Chris's phone bleeped to signal an incoming message.

'Ned's on the scene,' she said as PC Bates reported, 'No sign of anyone, dead or alive. But there's marks on the floor that could be blood smears and something or someone has definitely been in the hot tub. As well as the damp marks on the decking, now fading with the sun on them, the water's murky. Looks awful.'

'OK. Be with you in five,' replied Greg. 'Give crime scene whatever help they ask for, and thank you.'

Entr'acte 16

Getting her out of the hot tub was the devil. I leaned in and got hold of the sleeping bag. I had to reach in the full length of my arms and the water stank of chlorine. Worse than any swimming pool. Pulling the parcel to the side was easy enough and up to the surface too. But getting it any further was a pain. First time I had to let go and it was back to square one. Then I heard voices from next door. A family and children. The kids were running round their back garden by the sound of it and whining about wanting to get in *their* hot tub. I crouched down behind mine and clenched my fists to stop from swearing. Why weren't the brats in school anyway?

After a moment I heard the parents saying something about the beach and the noises faded into the distance. I noticed the kids were still whining.

I reached into that horrible chlorine water and pulled again. This time I got hold of one end and pulled it over the lip of the tub. It slipped in twice more before I got enough of it over the edge, then I had to reach in again and pull the other end up and over. I got soaked. I thought I might as well get it all as far as the car before I went and changed, so I heaved it across the decking and the lawn over to the side gate. I stopped then and looked round. Everyone seemed to've gone out for the day. There were no cars next to the cottages and bungalows that lined the lane. I left the vampire where she lay, still wrapped in the soaking sleeping bag, and fetched a blanket from the house.

I unfolded it and laid it across the luggage space in the back of my hatchback with one end hanging out across the bumper. Then I looked round again, took a deep breath and unwrapped the parcel. She lay on the gravel behind the car: white as a sheet, her skin crinkled from the water, her hair in long black strands across her staring eyes. I crossed myself. Even now, she looked dangerous. Her mouth was open, her sharp white teeth showing through her bloodless lips. I shuddered and briefly thought of leaving her there. Just driving away and leaving her. But then I'd never be safe from her. I thought of her following me down the road. Or worse, turning up at my home. No, she had to be made safe. Neutralised. And for this most dangerous vampire, I realised, that meant sacred ground. Not just anywhere. I decided to load her into my car, then go looking for somewhere suitable. Then I'd finish the disposal that night, by moonlight.

I took another look round, then lifted her into the car boot. She wasn't at all stiff. I pushed her in, curled her up, and covered her with the rest of the blanket. I threw the soaking sleeping bag over the cliff at the end of the garden and drove off.

24

The hunt is up

By the time Greg pulled up at Clifftop Cottage, Ned and his assistant were already gloved, overalled and on their way inside. Constable Bates was outside managing access and fixing crime scene tape around the property. Greg left Chris having a word, and went to the open door.

'Ned,' he shouted, 'anything for me?'

Ned came to the door and pulled his mask up. 'Blood smears on the floor in several places,' he said. 'Looks as though something was pulled through the house to the patio doors then out to the hot tub. We're sampling the hot-tub water for dissolvable solids – pee and poo to you. With all the chlorine we'll have a struggle sequencing DNA, I'm afraid.'

'No signs of a living Marilena?'

'No, Greg, sorry. All the signs are that she was either dead when she arrived here, or died shortly after. The blood smears are exactly that – smears not spatter. Either the injuries that caused the bleeding were inflicted before she got here, or were muffled by something she was wrapped in.'

'Injuries in the plural?' asked Greg.

'Obviously we won't know for sure until we have a body,' answered Ned. 'But from the position of the smears they look as though they came from more than one source on the body, if body it was, that was towed out to the hot tub.'

A shout came from the front garden that caused them both to turn. Chris was waving at the windows. Ned went over and opened one with his gloved hand. Greg, still un-overalled, stayed where he was by the open front door.

'There's something caught in bushes part way down the cliff. Looks like a sleeping bag. Should I recover it?' Greg opened his mouth but was forestalled by Ned.

'No. One of us will get it,' he said. 'Just in case it's evidence.' He called for his assistant, a young woman Greg hadn't met before, and they went over to the back of the garden and the low fence by the cliff edge. A short conversation, then the woman returned to the forensic service van. She reappeared wearing light trainers and carrying a rope and a large evidence bag. Constable Bates joined them at the cliff edge, and Greg hurried round the cottage to see where the small group was gathered on the cliff edge.

Around six metres down the loose, sandy cliff, a dark blue sleeping bag lay across a gorse bush. The girl – 'Must ask her name,' thought Greg – roped up with a professional air and handed the end of the line to Bates.

'Wrap the end round your waist and pay it out so I have just a bit of slack,' she instructed. 'Be ready to take my weight if necessary. It shouldn't be, unless the cliff gives way.'

She made her way carefully over the cliff edge and down.

It was more of a scramble than a climb but Greg could see why she was cautious. Several times clods and bigger pieces of cliff peeled off under her feet and tumbled down to the beach below. He noticed they were attracting attention from holidaymakers further along the beach. As he watched, several got to their feet and started to move towards them. The girl kept her balance in the moving earth with remarkable ease. He noticed she set off from a point a metre or so to the right of her target, so that the earth she loosened on her way down missed it. Once level she moved across, lifted it cautiously and carefully from the gorse bush and fed it into the large evidence bag tucked into her belt. She paused a moment to check the ground around the bush and above it. Then signalled she was returning.

When she was back at the top of the cliff, Greg was impressed to notice she was scarcely breathing any heavier than before. She handed the evidence bag to Ned.

'I couldn't see anything else in the vicinity of the bag,' she said. 'But it does seem to have faint blood stains in several places. And it's soaking wet.'

'Great,' said Ned. 'Let's see what we can get from this.'

Back at the cottage, Rob Bates returned to door duty while Chris addressed herself to her mobile phone. Energetic conversations ensued, judging by her arm waving and the animation on her face. She looked up as Ned and Greg approached.

'His car's been spotted on ANPR in Stalham and a mast near there's had a ping from his phone too. Seems he's turned it on for the first time for hours.'

'Good. Any idea where he's headed?'

'Well, that's the problem. Just that one ping then the

phone went off again. And the ANPR spot was in the middle of Stalham near the Tesco supermarket. No indication of which way he was headed.'

'Anything on the supermarket CCTV?'

'Just checking that now.'

'OK. I need to speak to Margaret,' said Greg. 'We need an all-hands effort in this area to catch him before he goes further afield. She's going to have to authorise that level of resource. It's beyond my pay grade.'

'Oh, and Sarah wanted a word, something about Madame Trieste. I said it'd have to wait for now.'

'OK.' Greg was distracted by dialling Margaret's number. 'What was that? Sarah and Madame Trieste? Tell her I'll speak to her as soon as we have definitive news about Marilena. It's not looking good, but I don't want to say anything until I know for sure.'

Margaret was cautiously triumphant. 'Said you'd get there in the end, Greg. I take it you *are* confident of your facts on this Colin Brown.'

'Yes, ma'am,' replied Greg. 'As sure as I can be without catching him red-handed. At the very least he's got some tough questions to answer. The main thing is that we secure him now before he disposes of Marilena and/or commits any further offences.'

'I've got some news on that score,' interrupted Margaret. 'Lincolnshire think they have a case that's suspiciously close to our criteria and they've shared what they know with continental colleagues, given the number of trips he made to Belgium and France. So, it may be that if you *can* lay him by the heels, it'll do quite a lot for clear-up rates generally. That being the case, tell me what you need and I'll get it sorted.'

'I need teams on every major road in that corner of the county, from Cromer in the north, to Yarmouth in the south east and Norwich in the west. I want them on the lookout for the car and instructed to stop and search if they spot it. ANPR teams need to back up this effort obviously and ditto those monitoring mobile-phone signals.'

'Not much, then,' said Margaret after a pause. 'OK, I'll do what I can, given the manning constraints I have to work with. Where are you headed now?'

'First off, to Stalham since that's where ANPR and the phone mast had him last. If we hear nothing in the next hour or so, I'll base myself at the station in Yarmouth until we know more.'

Greg looked round as he came off the phone. 'Ned gone?' he asked.

'Yes. Headed back a few minutes ago. He and I did another check round in the vicinity. No signs of any disturbed ground, and we've checked outbuildings too. Nothing. So if he had Marilena here, it looks very like he took her with him. I've set the North Walsham team off on a house to house, but there don't seem to be many people in at present. Off enjoying themselves, no doubt.'

'OK. We're going to Stalham first, then on to Yarmouth station if nothing turns up in the next hour or so.' He brought Chris up to speed as they walked back to his car.

'You think we're close,' said Chris. It was a statement not a question.

'Close,' said Greg. 'I can smell him.'

But night was approaching before anyone made any progress.

Entr'acte 17

My first idea had been to bury her at St Benet's Abbey. I'd thought that after a day or two alone with her, it'd be time to lay her with silver, and a holy place like that would be best. But when I read some more, I discovered it would be really difficult to get to without a boat. And almost impossible to have a hire boat after dark. That left my second choice. The partially ruined church near Billockby. I'd looked it up online and, if St Benet's was out of the question, it was a good alternative.

I was tempted to go there straightaway, to see if it was as good as it looked from the photos, but thought I'd better wait for dark. As I drove down the A149 to Stalham I could see the shattered nave and split tower in my mind's eye. It looked as though some Norse god had riven it from flagstaff to base with a mighty bolt of lightning. It gave me the shivers just to look at it. There had to be some powerful magic still there, to have survived a blow like that. It would be a good, safe place to conceal a ghost.

In the meantime, I needed somewhere to spend the day. Since I was close to Tesco I popped in and bought sandwiches, doughnuts and cans of Pepsi. While I was in the car park, I turned my phone on and checked for emails. The strange thing was there were none. And by that, I mean none at all. All the ones I'd had, work and so on, had disappeared as though wiped off the server. I turned the phone off again and was about to turn it back on to see if that solved the problem. Then I hesitated. If my emails had been deleted accidentally, I could sort it later. If they'd been interfered with, I didn't want my phone on, advertising my whereabouts. Either way, the phone was better turned off.

So, stocked up for the day, I headed for the ruined All Saints Church.

I drove within sight of it on the main road, and even turned up the side road between fields, then thought the better of it. Best I wasn't seen near there in daylight. So I re-joined the main road and drove on through Fleggburgh. I saw a village hall car park that looked promising, but just as I turned in I spotted a sign advertising a craft fair that afternoon, so I turned round and came out again. I didn't want to be round too many people. Further along, the road crossed a Broad and on impulse I turned off into a parking area among trees. I pulled the car into a secluded spot among overhanging branches, then switched the engine off with a sigh of relief. I'd be safe here until dark. I might even put the vampire in the lake. I'd see how I felt when the stars came out.

25

Saturday night 1

It was a frustrating afternoon. Joined in the Yarmouth police station by Jim and Steve, Greg found his only pleasure was greeting old acquaintances from past cases. That aside, and despite frequent recourse to telephones and almost as frequent false alarms from ANPR and mobile-phone data, they achieved, as Chris put it, a big, fat, floppy, zilch.

Feeling sick on the smells of over-boiled coffee, sausage rolls and curry sauce on chips wafting over from the market place, Greg took a short walk down to the river bank. Compared to his last visit a few days ago, the river looked calm and peaceful, almost sparkling in the late autumn sun between its industrial river banks. At this stage of the tide it was making a sedate progress to the sea, undisturbed by reverse tidal flows, winds, or general aquatic misbehaviour in the North Sea. A cruiser, a big one from Brundall with aerials sprouting everywhere and clearly equipped with modern radio and sonar equipment, was making a stately turn into the Yare and the harbour. As he watched its careful progress, memories surfaced of his first visit to Norfolk and the resulting boat chase down the river.

'Thank God I'm on dry land now,' muttered Greg to himself as he made his reluctant way across the road and back up the rise towards the police station. The day hadn't started badly, but progress had stopped dead; stymied by lack of manpower, lack of cameras in rural Norfolk and ditto mobile-phone signal.

Back in the small, and distinctly stuffy, room they'd taken over for the day, he noticed a change in the atmosphere. There was a vigorous argument going on between Chris and Jim, which, while not necessarily constructive, was better than the apathy he'd left behind him when he went out.

'What's going on?' he demanded.

'There's been a 111 call I think is relevant,' said Chris. 'I'd like to check it out, but Jim says to leave it to uniform. Which will probably mean nothing happens until next week!'

'What do we know?' asked Greg.

'The call's from a dog walker in Filby,' replied Jim. 'They say that a car they spotted this morning, parked in the rough ground near Filby Bridge, next to Filby Broad, is still there this evening. They think there's a man in it, and they also think they saw rubbish in the boot of the car, so they think he's fly-tipping. No details on the car except it's silver and small. The lady doesn't know much about cars apparently. No registration number.'

'On the face of it it's worth checking out,' said Greg. 'Why your reluctance, Jim?'

'Because the lady is well known to the locals. She complains about something almost every week: fly-tipping, rubbish thrown from cars, lovers in cars, noise, dogs out of control, once even a report of a big cat. At least we should wait until uniform check the registration.'

'And why don't you want to leave it to uniform, Chris?'

'To me anything that looks promising is a priority. And if it is him, I don't want any clodhopping police presence spooking him before we've got everything in place to make an arrest.' The 'obviously' in the sentence was unspoken but there, nonetheless.

Greg made his mind up swiftly. 'I'm not sure it's worth hanging around here any longer, anyway,' he said. 'We'll check it out on our way back to base.

'Jim and Steve, you go on ahead, go straight past the parking area without stopping, then wait further down the road towards Fleggburgh. Chris, you and I will pull in and check the number plate. If it's the one we want, we'll come out again and wait to the east of Filby Bridge while we plan our next move. If it's an unconnected car, we'll take a quick look and refer it to uniform if we have any concerns. OK. Let's go.'

The sky was glowing slightly in the west by the time they pulled off the road and bounced over ruts and tree roots before stopping near the water. Engine and lights off, they listened for a moment as they looked around them. At first they couldn't see the car, then they heard an engine start up, headlights came on, and a silver vehicle reversed out of a clump of trees further over from the road and turned. For a moment the rear wheels spun on wet ground giving them time to clock the registration number, then the tyres gripped and the car re-joined the main road, heading towards Fleggburgh.

'It's him – at least, it's his car,' said Chris. Greg snatched up the radio.

'All units,' he snapped, 'suspect headed west on the A1064 towards Fleggburgh. Henning, tail at a discreet distance and keep me posted. Despatch, who's nearest me at this moment? I need officers to take control of this area and SOCOs out here ASAP.'

'Unit Kilo2Bravo in Ormesby St Michael. With you in five minutes,' responded despatch.

The five minutes seemed to take five hours and never had a potential crime scene been handed over so quickly. In reality it was less than ten minutes before Greg and Chris were on their way again, but by that time Jim had already signalled that their target had turned off the A1064 towards Clippesby.

'Despatch,' Greg was saying, in the hopes that another car could be despatched to intercept, when Jim was back on the radio.

'He's turned up the track to the old church near Billockby. I've parked across the end of the drive, lights off and keeping a low profile.'

'Well done, Jim,' said Greg. 'Stay there until Chris and I join you.'

Greg turned his headlights off as he took the side turning, then spotted Jim's car as a shadow under the hedge up ahead. He parked as silently as he could behind Jim. Now the two cars blocked both the drive and the side road. Chris took her time unlocking her car door and emerged cautiously, keeping her head down to avoid creating a profile above the hedge that might be visible against the night sky. Greg did the same, remembering to take his car keys with him, and both left their car doors open to avoid the slam of closure. Up ahead, Jim was waiting by his car.

'Steve?' whispered Greg.

'Following the target at a safe distance,' replied Jim. 'As far as I could see, Brown didn't take anything with him.'

'I've got reinforcements on the way,' replied Greg. 'In the meantime, you and Steve keep him in sight from a safe distance. Don't lose him, whatever you do. Chris and I will check out the car. See if there might be a live Marilena inside it.'

Greg saw Jim follow Steve up the gravel drive, then lost sight of him against the dark mass of the ruined church tower. It hung in the sky as though suspended by stars, an impossible crack running down its height from top to bottom. The silhouette was fuzzy with ivy and the shadow it cast absolute, so that from here Greg had no idea of Colin Brown's whereabouts. Trusting to Jim to ensure he didn't go missing, he crept across the gravel to the silver car, trying to limit his footsteps to moss-strewn patches less prone to audible crunching. Chris did the same on the other side of the drive, so both arrived at the car with a pincer movement. They paused in silence for a moment, and Chris shook her head. She could hear nothing either. And it was immediately apparent that the car was empty. Chris edged closer and pressed an ear to the boot. Then stood up and shook her head.

'Can't hear a thing,' she said. She tried again, and shook her head again. 'I think if there was anyone living in there, I'd hear them moving. Or even breathing?'

*

Greg looked sceptical. 'Not sure you'd hear breathing, not through a boot lid and against the night-time noises,' he whispered. He paused as his phone lit up with an incoming text.

'Target is digging,' it said. 'Arrest?'

Greg texted back, 'Yes,' and almost instantly the sounds of night birds, bats and the numerous small rustlings in the hedge alongside the churchyard were overwritten with a warning shout, and then the sharp clicking of a taser being fired.

Running in the direction of the sounds, Greg almost stumbled over Steve on the ground before him. A few feet away, Jim was rolling around with a man of similar size and weight, and notwithstanding the effects of the taser, struggling to subdue him enough to get the cuffs on. Greg jumped in to help, and between them they held him face down on some recently dug soft earth. With a triumphant 'Got him,' Jim clicked the cuffs and, since the struggling showed no signs of abating, sat down firmly in the middle of his captive's back. Greg turned back to check on Chris, now bending over Steve.

'You're going to be OK,' she was saying, and Greg saw with relief that Steve was shaking his head as he pushed himself up from the ground.

'Hit me with his spade,' he said, feeling gingerly along his jaw. 'Luckily the flat of it I think, or he'd have taken my head off. Ow.' He paused in the exploration of his mouth with his tongue, and spat out a piece of tooth. 'Damn, only just got them fixed from the last time.'

Greg picked up the radio from where he'd dropped it.

'Despatch,' he said. 'Suspect apprehended. Just going to check on the car. Need a full team here ASAP. Tell the chief super we'll be bringing him to Wymondham.'

Entr'acte 18

The day passed quickly. I was tired from my long journeys the day before, but I couldn't sleep. The vampire ghost kept pushing into my mind. Even with my eyes closed I could see her smile, her hair, her teeth. They were painted on the inside of my eyelids, and when I opened my eyes I saw her everywhere in the shape of passing clouds and in the branches reaching out across the lake in front of me. When swans passed by moving slowly, apparently propelled by magic across the grey water, I saw her hair in the ripples that spread behind them. Two women passed by with dogs on leads, the dogs tugging towards the swans, then turning and heaving on the leads towards my car, sniffing at the boot and barking with a high-pitched, hysterical note. They could feel the presence, even if their chattering owners with dyed-blonde hair and pouter-pigeon breasts pushing their fleeces out were oblivious.

A couple of hours of this, and I was ready to push her in the lake and flee, but the dog walkers were more or less continuous, as though they were on some sort of bizarre rota. Then I saw a small, silent pleasure boat cross the water in front of me and knew I'd have to go with the secret burial at night. In a secret place and guarded by silver, she'd be safe. And so would I.

I stayed there the whole day. Once a nosy woman peered in at my car. Once another rapped on the window and asked what I was up to. I said, 'Sleeping, until you woke me,' in a grumpy voice, and she went away, muttering.

By the time the blackness crept up on me from the east, the stars showing like holes in a canvas between the darker clouds, I was ready. I turned the car and, with some difficulty, extracted it from the muddy ground and set off for the Shattered Tower.

I found my way there so easily it was as though I was following a predestined path. Perhaps I was. I parked near the more solid-looking end of the church, then hesitated for a while by the back of the car. I needed my spade, but I was frightened of what would happen when I opened the boot. What would I do, if she leapt out at me? I got my penknife out of my pocket and opened it. It was a pathetically small weapon with which to face an angry vampire, but it was all I had. I took a deep breath and, as I did, heard a car nearby. I waited again, but the engine noise stopped and no matter how hard I listened I could hear nothing.

I opened the boot, and stepped back. But nothing moved. The blanket stayed still. No hand emerged to grab, no foot peeped out to leap and run. I picked up my spade with a convulsive grab, and stepped, or almost leapt, back. Still no movement. I slammed the boot lid down and locked the car with a click of the remote. The lights flashed once and then all was still again. I moved round the Shattered Tower and found a smooth spot in a corner. I started to dig.

26

Saturday night 2

Their suspect proved hard to subdue. He wriggled and fought nonstop, seemingly impervious to reason or force. If flesh came within range of his face he bit. Even with his hands pinioned behind his back he kicked and butted, until Greg and Jim between them got him down on the ground again and sat on him out of desperation. Steve tried to help but was told sternly to keep clear, both Greg and Jim worried about concussion or worse, when they saw what he'd been hit with.

'Chris,' gasped Greg, short of breath from the struggle, 'ring for an ambulance as well. This chap's going to need sedating.'

The back-up from Great Yarmouth arrived first, and took over the role of restraint with fresh energy, freeing Greg and Jim to look around them. Chris seized the opportunity to go through the man's pockets and, 'Got them,' she said with triumph, waving the car keys. With Steve and Jim holding powerful police torches pointing at the car, she released all the locks and popped the boot.

There was a silence as they looked at the grey blanket covering something still.

'Damn,' said Greg, as he pulled on plastic gloves. 'Chris, film this if you would.' As she held her smartphone up, he pulled gently at the edge of the blanket, and they all stood in silence as the body of a slim young woman, with damp, dark hair, was revealed, curled in the cramped space. Greg reached out slowly, with no hope at all, and gently touched her neck.

'No pulse. Cold. Been dead for some time, I'd say. Right. We'll wait for the pathologist. Nothing we can do to help her now.'

The first medical team to arrive was the ambulance and paramedics. They assessed Colin Brown swiftly.

'Having a full-blown psychotic episode,' one of them stated tersely. 'He needs to go to hospital. Will probably need to be sectioned.'

'He goes nowhere without police attendance,' said Greg firmly.

'He's sick,' argued one of the paramedics. 'And the force you've used to restrain him hasn't helped. Have some compassion, man.'

'Have some…' Greg was so angry he was lost for words. Taking a firm grip of his temper he breathed hard for a moment then said to Jim, 'Show him.'

Jim stood to one side and shone his torch at the car with the open boot. The paramedic gasped and took a step forward before Greg caught his elbow.

'No,' he said with a finality that struck home. 'She's dead. Long dead. The pathologist is on the way. There's nothing you can do for *her*. But you can sedate her killer. If he goes to hospital, it's with a police escort. And under arrest. Jim, administer the caution and let's get him out of here.'

'Colin Brown,' said Jim, 'I'm arresting you for the murders of Krystina Kaminska, Julie Bolton and Marilena Dalca. You do not have to say anything, but anything you do say will be taken down and may be used in evidence against you.'

Colin Brown tipped his head back and screamed. For a moment even the stars stood still and the bats fluttering round the ivy on the shattered tower seemed to fall out of the sky.

'Get him away,' said Greg. 'Chris, you and Jim go with him. I'll wait here for the pathologist and Ned's team. See you tomorrow.'

Entr'acte 19

I'd already dug a shallow grave when I heard it. The rustle that told me she was coming after me. I saw a shape against the sky. It moved towards me and said something. I heard it. I heard the voice from beyond death. Deep and echoing, it was pulling at me. Dragging me down, down, down into the foundations of the tower and still further down where no light shone, no sun could reach. The spade was in my hands. I swung it at the ghost and knocked it flat. Then I tried to flee but the thing was waiting for me. It had arms, more arms than it should have. It trapped me, threw me down, and no matter how I struggled I couldn't get free. I used everything I had, every ounce of strength. Then I heard the voices again, and I went down into the dark.

27

Sunday morning

Dr Paisley, pathologist, fell runner and mountain climber – in her spare time at least – was hot on the heels of the paramedics. She listened impassively to Greg's account of Colin Brown's meltdown, subsequent sedation and removal by ambulance.

'I wish I'd had an opportunity to observe him,' she remarked, as she struggled into overalls and gloves. 'From what you've said it does sound like a psychotic episode, or else a faked one.'

'Precisely,' grunted Greg. 'Either way, I need him kept secure, hence the escort from my team.'

'Where've they taken him?' asked the doctor.

'They said something about Westgate Hospital.'

'Yes, makes sense,' replied the doctor. 'Fen Ward I'd guess. It's a medium secure unit capable of assessment, and from the sound of it that's what is needed at this point. OK,' she added, pulling up her hood over her hair, 'let me see what we've got here.'

Ned's team had already erected bright flood lights and photographed the car and its dismal contents from every angle. Under their glare, Dr Paisley approached the body in the boot and spent some time viewing it from every possible angle. Then she lifted the blanket away from the girl thus exposed and checked her over carefully, as much as she could without further disturbing her clothing.

'OK, if Ned's ready, lift her out,' she said to the mortuary team.

They lifted the body from the car and laid it on their gurney. There was no stiffness in any part of the body. The pathologist took her temperature and looked carefully at her back and legs, before taking a final close look at her head. She stepped back, sighed heavily and turned to Greg.

'No obvious cause of death at this point, although there are several possibilities. She has a blunt force trauma to her head, and another to her ankles. It looks to me as though one ankle is broken. There may be more broken bones when I take a proper look at her on my slab. She's also been struck in the face but I think that was before the violence that led to her death. As to time of death,' she added, pre-empting the question on Greg's mind. 'All I can say at this point is that it was more than thirty-six hours ago as rigor mortis appears to have been and gone.'

'Where are we now?' Greg looked at his watch. 'Four in the morning. That would put her death at before 4pm Friday. That's a problem. We have a witness who says she saw her, live and well, at the Thetford truck stop on the Friday evening.'

Dr Paisley shrugged. 'At this point, my estimate is only a guess, as you know. That's all I can say. You can see that rigor mortis has fully passed off and that normally takes thirty-six hours from start to finish. I can't tell you any more until I've done the full post-mortem.'

'When will that be?' asked Greg.

'Monday,' said the doctor. 'I'll let you know the time later today. See you.' She waved goodbye. 'OK, you can take her,' she said to the mortuary attendants.

'When can I bring someone over to ID?' asked Greg. 'That's suddenly got very important if she died as early as Friday afternoon. It may be she's not who we think she is.'

'This afternoon should be possible. But you can of course use Ned's photos first. They should be good enough for an informal identification.'

'Of course.' Greg slapped himself on the side of the head. 'I'm not thinking clearly, Doctor. Maybe it's time I got some sleep.'

Standing next to his car, he made a couple of phone calls. Chris first. 'Is he secure?' he asked.

'I think so,' she replied. 'He's in a secure side ward at Westgate Hospital. Both for his safety and everyone else's. In addition, I've got Phil sitting outside the door. No one goes in or out without him keeping a record.'

'OK. Get off home, and get some sleep. We'll interview him tomorrow. Well, later today,' he amended. 'Health service permitting. See you there at midday, hopefully.'

'Problem?' she asked.

'May be an issue about identification.' He brought her up to date on what the doctor had said. 'Best, I think, if Ned gets the photos to Sarah and she tries Madame Trieste for an ID. If the photos aren't sufficient, we may need to get the madame to the morgue for a formal ID prior to the autopsy on Monday. I'm about to speak to Ned now, then head home for some sleep. See you later.'

Ned took the point immediately. 'I'll get the pictures emailed to Sarah ASAP. Will you tell her what you want her to do with them?'

'Yes, I'm messaging her now. She should get it when she wakes, then hopefully by the time *we* wake, we should have some news. Catch up with you later, Ned, thank you.'

Sarah got the message when she woke around 7am.

'Wow, great,' she said aloud at the news that Colin Brown had been apprehended. As she read on, the smile left her face. It seemed that was the beginning and the end of the good news. Their suspect on a secure ward instead of in a cell. That wasn't great. And not finding Marilena alive. Well, that wasn't great either, although it didn't come as a surprise. She'd always thought Greg was being needlessly over-optimistic. She noted the final comment about ID and flicked quickly to Ned's photos. Her immediate conclusion was that she'd need to be careful what she showed Madame Trieste. The woman had seemed fond of Marilena, and some of the photos were pretty brutal. Ned hadn't censored his collection, leaving it to Sarah to pick out what she wanted.

Sarah looked at the time and decided that it was a bit early for a call to the madame. She'd get ready first, then try ringing her. Best part of an hour later, showered, dressed and breakfasted on croissant and coffee, Sarah picked up her phone and rang Nails Galore. The voice that answered was suspicious.

'Yes. What you want?' it asked.

'Madame Trieste,' said Sarah. 'There've been some developments and I need to come and see you. Can I come over now? I could be with you in about half an hour.'

'Why not tell me now?' asked the madame.

'There's something I need to show you,' said Sarah. 'It really would be best if I come over.'

'It's bad news,' said the voice flatly. 'You've found her dead.'

'I don't know,' said Sarah honestly. 'It's possible. We have found another victim, and I have to be straight with you, it may be Marilena. But I need you to look at some photos for me, and tell me what you think.'

'OK,' said Madame Trieste. 'I see you. Bring your photos. But I hope it's not Marilena.'

Sarah spent a few minutes checking through the photos on her iPad and selected half a dozen to print. Four showed Marilena's face from angles that didn't show the trauma to her head, or at least where the damage was obscured with a bit of editing from Sarah. The last two were close-ups of two small tattoos. One on the back of her neck and one on her left wrist. She gathered up the pictures, her iPad and her brown leather shoulder bag before a final glance in the hall mirror and she left the house for Norwich and Nails Galore.

Madame Trieste looked at each of the photos in turn, picking one up and holding it at an angle to the window that maximised clarity. Then putting it down and picking up the next. Sarah reflected that if she ever wanted her to do an ID from a photo line-up, she'd be perfect. When she got to the photos of the tattoos, the hand holding the picture shook, just a little, and

Sarah thought she saw moisture in the corner of the woman's eye. Next moment she put the last photo down and shuffled them together, aligning edges and corners neatly.

'Is Marilena,' she said finally, her tone flat.

'You're sure?' asked Sarah. 'How sure?'

'I'm sure. 100 percent sure,' said Madame Trieste. 'You got the man who did this?' And she planted one short, elegantly manicured finger on the pile of photos.

'We've got a suspect in custody,' said Sarah, 'and he's been arrested for the murder of Marilena and two others.'

'Good,' pronounced Madame Trieste. 'Where he held?'

'Securely, don't worry,' said Sarah.

'OK. When can I see Marilena?'

'I was going to come to that,' replied Sarah. 'It would be very helpful if you could identify her either this afternoon, or later tomorrow.'

'You mean, after post-mortem?' asked Madame astutely. 'I come this afternoon. Where and when?'

'I'll pick you up,' offered Sarah. 'Perhaps two o'clock?'

'Two. Yes,' said Madame. 'You come here at two and I be ready.'

Greg surfaced from his much-disturbed sleep to the sound of yet more incoming messages on his mobile phone. He was vaguely conscious that the five or six hours sleep he'd managed had been interrupted by similar sounds several times.

'I'll feel better after a shower,' he said to himself without much hope, as he caught sight of a gaunt face and huge bags under his eyes. Five hours sleep at the wrong time of day was not a great preparation for a difficult interrogation. But it was what it was. He nearly fell over Bobby as he headed for the bathroom, and then strong black coffee.

Showered, shaved and feeling marginally fresher with the scent of Harrogate coffee wafting to his nostrils, he checked the messages.

'It was Marilena,' he noted. 'So either something's off with the pathology, or it wasn't Marilena at the truck stop. Except it had to be, surely. She'd gone there with people who knew her well. Unless they were lying for some reason.' He gave up the conundrum for the moment while he ate some rather stale toast, then got in his car for the journey to Westgate Hospital.

'Or Madame Trieste is lying,' was his belated thought as he pulled onto the A47, 'for some reason not yet known to me.'

By the time he'd negotiated the security at Westgate Hospital and made it as far as the corridor outside Colin Brown's room, Steve had replaced Phil on duty outside the door.

'I thought you'd be off for a few days,' was Greg's greeting. Steve grinned, by way of showing off his new, startling white, temporary tooth.

'No problem other than this,' he said. 'And this is fixed as far as they can for the moment, so I'm just filling in here until Jeff gets over this afternoon.'

'Anything to report?'

'Nothing, except the big cheese wants to see you.'

'OK. Him or her first?'

'Him,' said Steve. 'Down the corridor and first on the right. He's muttering something about an appropriate adult.'

Greg looked up sharply, then shrugged. 'Predictable,' he replied. I just hope we can get one lined up quickly.'

28

Sunday afternoon

Madame Trieste was silent on the drive to the morgue. Sarah glanced sideways a couple of times, started to speak, then changed her mind and decided to respect her silence. They were greeted quietly and professionally by mortuary staff, and, after a short delay, shown into a waiting room. Sarah glanced round and shivered. The anodyne, minimalist environment would always, she thought, remind her of death. And, as always, she was convinced there was a faint, underlying smell of putrefaction.

The madame seated herself on the taupe sofa, placed her feet neatly side by side on the beige carpet square and regarded them at length, as though checking they were the same size. Her hands were clenched on the handbag in her lap, and she stayed silent. They heard footsteps tapping down the corridor and the door opened to admit a young woman in white scrubs.

'If you'd like to come this way,' she said, and led them

down the hallway to another plain door with no window. She paused outside it and said, 'I should explain that you will only be able to view through a window into the next room. This is because the post-mortem has yet to take place, and we need to ensure that there is no contamination of any evidence. I'm sorry if this is distressing for you, but it is necessary to give us the best chance of catching whoever did this.' She paused for a response but Madame Trieste said nothing. The only sign she'd heard was the tightening of her grip on her handbag.

'I think we can go in,' said Sarah in a low voice, and she preceded Madame Trieste into the viewing room.

Once they were both standing next to a curtained window, the mortuary assistant pulled back the drapes. There was no reaction from Madame other than a slight intake of breath. The face of the girl on the table was clearly visible, although there was a covering round her head.

Madame muttered something, but as far as Sarah could tell it was in Romanian.

'I'm sorry, Madame,' she said gently, 'can you say that again for us?'

Madame took a deep breath and said, 'I think is Marilena, but can I see her arm?'

The assistant picked up an intercom from a bracket on the wall, and spoke into it.

'Can you show us the left arm please?' She turned to Madame. 'Is that right, the left arm?' Madame nodded, and a second assistant, overalled, hooded and masked, standing behind the table on which the body lay, stepped forward and with gloved hands uncovered the left arm and lifted it slightly.

Madame nodded, and turned away from the window.

'Is Marilena. For definite.'

'You're certain? asked Sarah.

'Certain. Is Marilena. When can I see her properly? To say goodbye?'

'I'll have to let you know,' said Sarah. 'In a few days, hopefully. If you're ready to leave, I'll drive you back.' Madame nodded again.

The silence was maintained throughout the drive back to Nails Galore. Only when she got out of the car did Madame break it.

'You been kind,' she said to Sarah. 'I won't forget. I owe you.' And she walked slowly into the salon with an immense, sad dignity.

Over at Westgate Hospital, short of sleep, nutrition and now temper, Greg was feeling that it was time things started to go his way.

'Let me get this straight,' he said to the slight, dapper senior registrar facing him across a cluttered desk. 'My suspect is, in your opinion, probably suffering from previously undiagnosed schizophrenia, which caused him to have a major psychotic episode and/or panic attack last night, when we arrested him. And that our heavy-handed approach to arresting him was the problem.

'You don't think the fact that we caught him in the act of digging a grave for the girl whose murdered body was lying in the boot of his car might, perhaps, have influenced how he was feeling?'

The registrar, 'Dr Fish' according to his 'hello, my name is' badge, as Greg noted, shuffled papers around on his desk and sighed audibly.

'You must appreciate,' he said, 'that my concern is primarily, perhaps solely, for my patient. And I have here a patient who was admitted under heavy sedation, with clear bruising to the upper part of his body and arms, in the throes of, as I've already said, a serious psychotic episode. This manifested itself with both auditory and visual hallucinations and from the report of the paramedics he was also hysterical and not making any sort of sense.'

'And my concern is for his victims and the public. My duty is to ensure justice for the first, and the safety of the second. I do, therefore, need to interview Mr Brown, under caution, as rapidly as possible. I don't yet know, for certain, that he doesn't have another victim, possibly still alive, hidden away somewhere. Interview him I must, with legal advisers and indeed an appropriate adult present, if that's what it takes, but interview him I must.' He paused. 'You are not, in fact, telling me that he's physically or mentally incapable of being questioned?'

Dr Fish fiddled with his papers some more. 'No, I'm not,' he said. 'In fact, given his state a few hours ago, and that his sedation has only recently worn off, he is remarkably lucid. But he does seem to have some entrenched, well, I don't know what to call them. Beliefs? Hallucinations? They seem to be of long standing, and mean he is operating within a frame of reference that is some distance from what you or I would call reality.'

Ignoring for the moment the assumption that he and the doctor shared a common perception of reality, Greg said, 'You mean he's barking mad?' Then regretted his irritable choice of phrase as the doctor visibly bristled.

To his surprise, however, after a moment the doctor responded with, 'Shorn of some of your language that may not be such a bad summation at that. I've only spoken to him a short while, but even within those few minutes he has made it plain that he believes the world to be populated not just by humans, but also by a number of supernatural beings who are antagonistic to the human race.'

'That belief is probably shared by a number of respected figures in various established religions,' remarked Greg, 'who would, I think, be hugely offended at the suggestion such convictions rendered them, to paraphrase you, stark staring bonkers.'

Dr Fish sighed again. 'Can we abandon the pejorative terms?' he asked. 'I've been on duty for as many hours as you, probably, and it's not helping. To put it plainly, your arrestee says he believes in vampires and ghosts and thinks he has a mission to tackle infestations of either. That may explain the activities that attracted your attention. I accept that you need to talk to him. I just need to be sure it's done in the right way, and with the right precautions. Otherwise, you'll be no better off and he'll be a lot worse.'

'Which means?' asked Greg.

'If I understood him correctly, when my staff informed him of his whereabouts and that he was under arrest, he asked for a solicitor. And I would suggest that, given his mental health challenges, he should also be allocated an appropriate adult.'

'OK.' Greg thought for a moment. 'I can go with that, and I'll get it organised. But realistically, I'm unlikely to get it set up today. What I'd like to do is caution him again since it seems, from your account, he's more likely to take it in today than he was last night. I can then establish whether he wants his own solicitor or a duty solicitor. Either way, I still want to interview him under caution today. I have a genuine fear that there may yet be another victim somewhere, and if there's the faintest chance of finding them alive we need to take it. I can proceed without an appropriate adult if I have to, but it would be better if you or one of your staff could undertake the role for today, if that's possible.'

'And if we don't?' asked Doctor Fish.

'Then understand me, I'll proceed without if I have to.'

'OK. Leave it with me. I'll have an answer for you ASAP.'

29

Sunday evening

Greg and Chris, accompanied by Dr Fish and a burly nurse, attended Colin Brown in his private room. Greg noted, as he administered the caution, that Brown was not only calm, but also seemed oblivious to the fact that this was the second time around. His face was expressionless and he made no movement other than to pick at the arm of the chair where he sat, close to the window.

'Did you understand all that?' asked Dr Fish.

'I understood. And I want a solicitor,' was his response.

'Do you have a solicitor of your own?' asked Greg. 'You're allowed to make a phone call if you wish to contact them. I'm sure the hospital would arrange that.' The man in the chair looked uncertain.

'I don't have a regular solicitor,' he said. 'I used one when I bought my house but…' And he hesitated.

'He may not be suitable.' Dr Fish finished the sentence for him.

Greg chipped in with, 'You can still ring him if you wish and ask him to organise legal representation for you. Or we can arrange for one of the duty solicitors to come and see you.'

'Perhaps that would be best,' said the man with some relief.

Dr Fish checked: 'You're sure you want a duty solicitor? Not a family solicitor?'

'Yes, please.'

Less than half an hour later a duty solicitor surprised them all by turning up on the ward.

'That was quick,' remarked Greg, shaking hands.

'Your chief super's had me on standby since this morning,' he replied. 'Roger Makepiece. It seems she anticipated both the need and the urgency. Where's my client?'

'In here.' Greg gestured at the door behind him, now guarded by Phil, back on duty after a break. 'One thing you ought to know. The doc in charge here is recommending an appropriate adult, in light of this chap's mental health issues. Unless the chief super has one of those up her sleeve as well, we'll need to press on today with the assistance of the doc himself, or without any assistance at all, depending on what line his management takes. I can get an appropriate adult sorted tomorrow, but no chance this afternoon.'

'Can't you wait until tomorrow?' asked Makepiece. 'That'd give me time to get to grips with my client and you to line up the necessary.'

'Not a chance,' said Greg. 'It's possible there's another victim out there somewhere, and if so we need to find her ASAP. I'll give you an hour, I hope that should be sufficient for your briefing, then I'm coming in.'

'You realise I'll probably have to advise him to make no comment.'

'You do your job, I'll do mine,' replied Greg.

Waiting impatiently for the hour to pass, Greg checked his phone and found a missed call from Sarah. The message on voicemail was short and to the point.

'Madame Trieste is emphatic the young woman you found in Colin Brown's car is Marilena. She has absolutely no doubts, based on seeing both her face and a key tattoo.' Greg rang back.

'Sorry, only just picked up your message. She's certain?'

'Certain,' affirmed Sarah.

'And she convinced you her identification was genuine?'

'Absolutely. She'd already said so on the basis of the photographs, and seeing the body in person confirmed it. I'd go bail her reaction was genuine too. She was upset.'

'OK. Something's weird with the pathology, then. Perhaps her sojourn in the hot tub accounts for it. Or,' he said, thinking aloud, 'the woman seen near his truck on the Friday was someone else, and he'd picked up Marilena earlier in the day. But why would Krystal have lied? That doesn't make sense. I guess we'll just have to wait until the post-mortem.'

Sitting in the crowded side room with Colin Brown, Roger Makepiece, Chris, Dr Fish and the brawny nurse, Greg reflected that if Brown kicked off there was little he could do to prevent someone getting hurt. The man in the chair by the window would need to move less than a foot in any direction to connect with someone else. He noticed that Chris was keeping a very close eye on Brown and guessed she shared his concerns.

He pressed the button on the portable recorder before him and requested, 'For the benefit of the tape, would everyone please identify themselves.' That formality over, Greg added, 'Colin Brown, I'd just remind you that this is an interview under caution. Do you understand?'

The man by the window nodded, and Greg asked, 'Aloud please, for the tape.'

'Yes, I understand,' said the man in a voice that reflected his East Anglian origins.

'So, Colin,' said Greg, 'you were arrested in the early hours of the morning at the church of All Saints near Billockby. Why were you there?'

Brown looked at his solicitor and replied, 'No comment.'

'Your car, parked beside the church, was found to contain the body of a young woman, since identified as a Romanian national named Marilena Dalca. How did the body come to be there?'

'No comment.'

'Where did you meet Marilena Dalca?'

'No comment.'

'We have a witness statement that Marilena Dalca was taken from the lorry park on the A11 near Thetford last Friday evening. Your lorry was also present at that location that evening. Did you see Marilena Dalca at that location?'

'No comment.'

'Did you take her away in your lorry?'

'No comment.'

Greg looked at Chris. 'OK, let's leave the subject of Marilena Dalca for a moment, as you don't seem inclined to be helpful. Let's return to Saturday night and the events at the church of All Saints. Why were you digging in the churchyard?'

'I was digging…no comment.' Colin Brown corrected himself with a glance at his solicitor.

'Digging what?' asked Greg. This time Colin Brown looked sullen and made no answer. Greg glanced out of the corner of his eye at Chris, and gave her a small nod. As agreed between them, she picked up the questioning.

'Why did you hit my colleague with your spade, Colin?' she asked abruptly.

'Because it was after me,' he burst out. 'It was self-defence.'

'Who did you think he was?' asked Chris. After a silence she said again, 'Who did you think was after you, Colin?'

'The ghost, the vampire. I'd seen her teeth. I knew it'd be coming in the dark. I couldn't see who it was. I didn't mean to hurt anyone else. I just needed to keep it away. I'm sorry,' he added. 'I'm sorry about your friend. I didn't mean to hurt him. I thought it was after me. I thought he was it. I thought it's going to get me this time. It's tried twice and failed. This time it's going to get me. So I had to fight it off. I'm sorry, it was a mistake. But I had no choice.'

Roger Makepiece was doing his best to stem the flow, but his client wasn't paying attention. Dr Fish was wholly focussed on his patient, clearly worried about the increasing animation, and Greg felt that they had only a few minutes before the doc interrupted events.

'Where else did you have to fight it off?' asked Chris quietly.

'At the holiday cottage. It was coming for me. Oh God, it reached out for me. It reached for me. I had to use iron. Nothing else was working. I didn't have the silver to hand, so I used iron. I had no choice. It wouldn't die. It wouldn't stay dead.'

'What did you do, Colin?' asked Chris, ignoring the doctor's signal and quiet comment to Greg, 'I think you should stop now.'

'I didn't know which end was its head. I couldn't tell. I hit what I thought was its head and then I hit the other end. Then it lay still. I put it in the hot tub and went to bed.'

Brown was clearly getting more agitated.

'I didn't plan to do that,' he added. 'I was going to keep it for a bit, but I daresn't. It was too dangerous. It wouldn't stay dead so I could...' He stopped suddenly, the manic energy and animation draining away. 'No comment,' he finished. 'I'm not going to say any more. You said to say no comment, didn't you?' he appealed to the solicitor. 'I'm not going to say any more. I'm not. Whatever you ask me. No comment, no comment, no comment.'

Chris looked at Greg, who was himself looking at the doctor.

'I don't think we'll get any more today,' said Greg. 'Thank you for your help, Doctor.' And picking up the recorder, they withdrew.

Once back in Greg's car, they looked at each other and, simultaneously, both blew out their cheeks in a huge sigh.

'So what've we learned?' asked Greg.

'First, he admitted to striking Marilena,' said Chris.

'Not strictly,' interrupted Greg. 'He's not admitted anything in relation to any named person. He's admitted to striking someone or something he calls a ghost or vampire. He admits to striking them twice at the holiday cottage, then putting them in the hot tub. And he sort of admitted to striking

Steve. And frankly, that's about it. We're going to have to prove that the "vampire",' and he drew quotation marks in the air as he spoke, 'was in fact Marilena. It's all going to come down to the forensic evidence.'

'Again,' agreed Chris glumly.

30

Post-mortem

'Greg,' shouted Chris. 'I can't find that shirt I left here.' Greg stuck his head out of the bathroom and spluttered, through a mouthful of toothpaste, 'In the pile on top of the washing machine. It's clean and dry, but not ironed.'

'Thanks.' Chris galloped downstairs making a noise like a herd of wildebeest, earning a glare from Bobby, who regarded that behaviour as reserved to cats. Holding up the bright yellow shirt, she examined the creases, gave it a shake and decided it would do. The collar and cuffs looked all right. No one was going to see the wrinkled bits under her magenta jumper.

'Aren't you going to iron it?' asked Greg without much hope, watching her do up the buttons.

'What for?' she asked. 'It'll only get creased again. Come on, we need to get a move on if we're going to call at the office before the post-mortem.'

*

Sitting in Margaret's office, waiting for her to complete her call, Greg flicked through his notes and the bullet points he'd put together for his next interview with Colin Brown. Putting the phone down, Margaret pushed her hair out of her eyes and heaved a relieved sigh.

'OK, that's sorted,' she said. 'We've managed to source an appropriate adult, and they're on call from lunchtime today. It's a Mr Alan Nigel Ryan and he's not filled the role before. Completed the training a few months ago after moving on from the Witness Service. Retired tax adviser, it says here.

'Now, the post-mortem, what are the questions you're hoping it will answer?'

'Apart from the obvious – time and cause of death? Not a great deal really, although I've got a lot of questions for forensics,' replied Greg. 'For example, can we place Marilena at that holiday cottage and in the hot tub, and indeed in Brown's lorry cab, and his home in Coton. Can we find any direct links between her and Colin Brown? Once we have cause of death, can we identify a weapon, if any?'

'That's a lot of questions,' remarked Margaret. 'Remind me of the evidence you do have – apart, obviously, from a dead body in his car!'

'We have a witness placing Marilena at the truck stop in Thetford when and where we know, from his company GPS records, he called with his truck on the way back from Yarmouth.' Greg was ticking items off on his fingers.

'CCTV at Delta Transport showing him lifting a wrapped item, long and body-sized, from his truck to his car.

'We have traces of body fluids in his cab and in his car, blood smears on the floor of the holiday cottage and in the sleeping bag found on the cliff behind the cottage.

'The hot tub has mysteriously turbid water in it, which also suggests contamination, and there were wet marks on the decking alongside when North Walsham police first arrived there, suggestive of something being removed from the tub and dragged along to the path round the house. The PC had the good sense to take photographs.

'He's been present at St Edmunds Farm and Cantley sugar factory at the times two other victims went missing and he routinely carried out deliveries on a route that would have taken him by another burial site in Oulton Broad. He lived in Cambridge at a time when the earliest Cambridge deaths occurred, and they stopped, or at least we haven't found any, during the period he was living in Lincolnshire.

'In short, I have no doubt we've got the right man and we may eventually be able to charge him with more deaths.' Greg paused for breath.

'Compelling, I agree,' said Margaret. 'But after the fiasco that was the arrest of the cab driver, I think you'll understand why I wanted to be sure.'

'Of course,' said Greg. 'But equally, I think you'll understand why I'd rather we kept all this quiet until we have the forensic evidence in place. No press this time, please! As we have him in secure accommodation, albeit not yet in our cells, I think the risk of further attacks has been removed.'

'Ah, yes, that brings me to his mental state,' said Margaret. 'Is he going to be fit to plead?'

Greg shrugged. 'Ask me another,' he said. 'I suspect it may depend on his state at the time. If he's like he was yesterday, then in my opinion, yes. If he's in the state he was when we arrested him the night before, then probably not.'

The morgue was cold as always. Dr Paisley, in coveralls and hair netted, nodded a welcome.

'I've carried out the autopsy,' she said, 'and I'm satisfied I have everything I need. As far as I'm concerned, the body can go back into cold storage in case the defence want to take a second look. But I don't think there'll be anything to quibble. There were a couple of things I wanted to show you though.'

She led the way through the double doors and into the tiled room where Marilena lay on the steel table. Greg paused in the corridor before following her in, just long enough to apply a smear of Vicks to his upper lip. He noticed Chris had done the same, and he smiled inwardly as he entered the room. The Y-shaped cut had been crudely stitched as usual, and he was relieved to note that Marilena's scalp had been returned to its normal position.

'First, I need to show you this and this.' She rotated the head slightly to show Greg and Chris two abrasions on Marilena's head: one at the back and one close to her left temple. 'These were inflicted on two separate occasions: the one on the back of the head first, and the one on the side most recently. Both would, in my estimation, have been sufficient to cause unconsciousness. The second, this one here,' and she held her finger close to the wound near the temple, 'is the more serious of the two. If you look closely there is a distinct depression in the skull, and the damage I found beneath would have been sufficient to cause death.'

'You said "would have",' remarked Greg.

'That's right. Very astute of you, DCI Geldard. Neither of these blows caused death, although the second one almost certainly would have, except that before that happened, the victim died of drowning.'

'Drowning!' exclaimed Chris.

'That's right. She experienced two major injuries to the head and further blunt force trauma elsewhere.' Dr Paisley pointed to Marilena's lower body. 'There were probably two blows to the abdomen and a further blow that broke her ankle. In my estimation these injuries occurred at the same time or thereabouts as the second injury to the head. But none of them caused her death. She had chlorinated water in her lungs and without a doubt the ultimate cause of death was drowning.'

There was a silent pause, while Greg did some thinking. Chris looked at him, opened her mouth then changed her mind and remained silent.

'Can I be sure I've understood this fully?' said Greg. 'Marilena first received a blow to the back of the head, which at the least stunned her. Sometime later – how much later by the way?'

'I'd estimate about twenty-four hours,' replied the doctor.

'So, roughly a day later she was struck several times at various places along her body, hard enough to generate a mortal wound to the head and to break her ankle, then, while still alive, she was drowned in chlorinated water.'

'That's right.'

'The first blow happened in the lorry,' said Chris. 'The second lot of injuries a day later were probably in the holiday cottage, where we found a smear of blood on the floor.'

'And she was probably tied up in the sleeping bag at the time,' added Greg. 'That would fit with Brown's assertion he didn't know which end of the body was which when he struck it again. Then, he dumped her, sleeping bag and all, into the hot tub and left her there to drown.'

'Incidentally,' added the doctor, 'the hot tub explains the discrepancy in timings. If she was left in hot or even warm water, rigor mortis would have both come on and cleared faster than if she was left in cool night air.'

'Do we have anything from Ned yet on the blood smears and fluids in the sleeping bag?' asked Greg.

'Not yet,' replied Chris. 'He said it was a challenging task to sequence the DNA from the sleeping bag adequately because of the chlorine in the water that'd soaked it. On the other hand, at least one of the contaminated areas contains skin and possibly brain cells, so we're still hoping. The blood smears in the cottage are easier.'

'Judging from the wet marks that were found on the decking, she was still in the sleeping bag until he got her to the car. He probably decided he didn't want a soaking quilt in his car, and unwrapped the body at that point. Are we sure we've checked the gravel for any evidence near where he must've been parked?' asked Greg.

'I'd be very surprised if Ned missed anything, but I'll check,' said Chris.

'I'll let you have my report ASAP,' said Dr Paisley. 'Thank God you've stopped this man.'

Greg said nothing until he was back in the car with Chris. He started the car, then waited before driving off.

'You realise what this evidence means?' he asked. Chris looked at him in silence, thinking she knew what was coming next.

'Marilena was still alive sometime on Friday evening. If we'd traced him quicker, she might have survived.'

31

Returning from the post-mortem, Greg called a meeting of the whole available team in the operations room. Ned and the dark-haired girl from the Bacton clifftop were both present. Greg did a discreet check with Ned and discovered her name was Alicia. Jill and Steve occupied chairs to one side, Sarah and Chris on the other.

'Phil around?' asked Greg, then corrected himself. 'No, he's still keeping an eye on our vampire killer, isn't he?'

There was a mutter of 'Buffy', from somewhere and Greg glared around. 'I can understand the temptation to supply a nickname,' he said, 'but let's not, hey? Too many women have died at the hands of this man and joking about him is disrespectful to his victims.

'Let's review the evidence, old and new. To avoid going over it all yet again, we're going to focus on the gaps and fill in as many as possible. Then we can see whether we have a case that can go to the CPS and, indeed, how many charges we can include on the sheet.

'First, let's look at Marilena Dalca. We know she was found dead in Colin Brown's car and that she died of drowning after suffering blunt force trauma on at least two separate occasions. We think we know how and when she travelled from the Thetford truck stop via the holiday cottage in Barton to All Saints churchyard, Billockby. What new evidence do we have that supports our theory. Ned?'

Ned stepped up to the whiteboard, a marker in one hand, and started to put red ticks against the list of questions.

'We have Dalca's DNA on the floor of the cottage, in the filter of the hot tub, and inside the sleeping bag recovered from the cliff. We have Brown's fingerprints all over the cottage including on the hot-tub cover. We've also lifted his fingerprints from the handle of the iron poker found at the cottage. In shape and size, it's a good match for the wounds found on Dalca's body, and the pathologist is convinced it was the weapon used to deliver the last three blows. The first head injury was almost certainly caused by her head being banged forcibly on the door frame of Brown's truck, and we have found her blood there too.'

'So, good evidence to back up the charge of murdering Marilena Dalca. How about nurse Julie Bolton?' asked Greg.

Sarah chipped in. 'Well, there, we know he was holidaying in the chalet at Hemsby the week that Nurse Bolton died and was buried in the chalet garden at the top of the cliff. And we know his lorry was parked in the area adjacent to where Julie Bolton's car was found on the night she was called out to the Cantley sugar factory and where she was last seen alive.'

'Anything from you, Ned?' asked Greg, but got a shake of

the head in reply. 'So, it's all circumstantial in relation to Julie Bolton.'

'Same applies to the prost…the girl found in the roadworks at Oulton Broad. There we have nothing except the link of the silver thruppence in her mouth, the similarity in body type and the evidence that Brown was collecting from Lowestoft port on or around the dates in question,' commented Chris.

'How about the body that started this whole investigation? The temenos remains – Krystina Kaminska?

'There we also have a little but not much,' said Chris. 'We've evidence he called at St Edmunds Farm on the date in question. But nothing that directly ties him to her death.'

'Nothing helpful from you, Ned?'

'Nothing, sorry,' said Ned. 'Of course, now I've got his DNA we might find something that links him to one or more of the other girls. I'll keep you posted.'

'OK,' said Greg slowly. 'So, to sum up, we have a reasonable case against him for the murder of Marilena Dalca. We have nothing that would stand up in court regarding any of the other cases. So, either we find something, or we're reliant on a confession.'

'A confession certainly wouldn't hurt,' remarked Sarah.

'Agreed, but I'm nervous about how it would play in front of a jury, given his evident mental health challenges, the fact he's been deemed to need an appropriate adult, etc etc.'

'We have him bang to rights for assaulting a police officer,' said Steve with some feeling.

'Quite right,' said Greg amid laughter, then was interrupted by Jill.

'There's something that's been nagging away at me,'

she said. 'It's the coins. I'm right, aren't I? They were all silver thruppences.'

'Yes, that's right,' said Greg.

'And how many do we know he's deployed?'

'Two here in Norfolk/Suffolk, at least two in Cambridgeshire that we know of, and...'

'Were there any in his car with Marilena?'

'Good question, Jill. Ned?'

'I didn't check,' said Ned, furious with himself. 'Alicia?'

'Just checking the database,' she replied. 'Hang on.' She scrolled down her screen muttering, 'Car jack, remains of sandwiches. Here we have it, contents of pockets: iPhone, keys, loose change, wallet with notes, value £75, and medallion. Medallion.' She looked up. 'I'll bet that's a silver thruppence. I'll check.'

'OK,' said Jill. 'But that wasn't really my point. Although, it'd be interesting to know if Cambridgeshire have found any at his home in Coton. Where I was coming from was, where did he get them? I mean, where did he source a number of silver thruppences? It's not as though you just find them in your change, is it? He probably bought them specially. And they're sold by coin specialists. Perhaps we can find where he got them from.'

'Well done, Jill,' said Greg. 'You've done it again. Alicia, please confirm whether there was a silver thruppence in his wallet. Sarah, can you check with Cambridge police exactly what was found in the Coton house? If they didn't find any, perhaps they could have another look. Chris and Jill, start checking out coin specialists. I'd start in Cambridge then widen your search if need be. Thanks, everyone. Anything you find out, let me know so I can use it in my next interview with Brown.'

32

Interviews

Back in the operations room, Greg called Sarah and Chris over.

'I'd like you two to start the interview,' he said, 'with me watching from the next room. In view of the nature of his crimes and the peculiarity of his beliefs, I think it might rattle him if he's questioned by two women. You're across all the detail, Sarah, and Chris can provide continuity from the earlier discussions. OK, both?'

The two women looked at each other without notable warmth but each said politely, 'Fine by me.'

'OK. Half an hour to prep your lines of questioning and agree tactics. OK?'

'Fine,' said Sarah again and Chris asked, 'Anything more yet from forensics or from the hunt for the thruppences? Last thing I had from Jill, we were getting nowhere with coin merchants, and I don't know what they found at Coton.'

'Nothing,' said Sarah abruptly, 'but they're having another look.'

Greg hid a sigh. It was clear there was still a distinct chill between the two. He just hoped that his cunning plan of forcing them to work together might pay off, without incurring blood on the carpet.

Watching from the one-way window a little later in the afternoon, Greg thought they looked like a couple of iced pints of Guinness, Sarah in her usual white jumper and black skirt combo, Chris, for once, surprisingly monochrome in a white collared jacket over black trousers and shirt. They sat side by side facing Colin Brown across the table, flanked by Alan Ryan on one side and Brown's solicitor, Makepiece, on the other. The preliminaries just completed, Sarah was about to lead off with the first of their prepared questions when there was an interruption. A uniformed constable entered the room and handed Sarah a piece of paper, which she unfolded and showed to Chris. At the same moment Jill came into the viewing room and handed Greg a similar note, gave him a thumbs up and left again. Intrigued, he unfolded the paper on a note in Jill's handwriting.

1. "Coins and Medals" in Peterborough supplied a batch of 20 George V silver thruppences to a Colin Brown in 2010. They have the purchaser records on their database and the address is the one Colin Brown logged with Delta Transport as his home address when he first joined their employment.
2. Cambridge police have found a cache of 7 George V

silver thruppences in a makeshift safe behind Brown's living room fire.

3. The so-called medal found on him this weekend was a silver George V thruppence.
4. And forensics have extracted Brown's DNA from the sleeping bag.

Greg returned her thumbs up and focussed his attention again on the interview proceeding on the other side of the glass.

Sarah had taken up the questioning.

'Sorry about the interruption, Colin,' she said with a wide smile. 'Back to what I was asking you before. I think you were about to explain to me how Marilena Dalca found her way from the truck stop in Thetford to the boot of your car in All Saints churchyard near Billockby.'

'No comment,' said Brown and he looked at the smiling Sarah uneasily.

Chris cleared her throat and he turned his attention to her. She too smiled, slowly and deliberately, as she said, 'That's just not going to wash, Colin. We know too much.'

He stared from one to the other then looked down and away as he said again, 'No comment.'

'Let *me* tell you, then,' went on Sarah. He switched his attention back to her, went to say something, but she overrode him.

'We know Marilena was at the truck stop in Thetford on Friday evening because we have a witness who travelled there with her. We have your truck showing on your company GPS system as being there too. We have Marilena's DNA found on the interior of your truck cab and we have you on CCTV removing something very like a body from your truck at the Delta Transport HQ and putting it in your car. Then we have Marilena's DNA on the floor of your holiday cottage, in the filter of the hot tub there, and on the interior of a sleeping bag found discarded on the cliff. That gives us a pretty clear route from Thetford to All Souls, wouldn't you say?' Sarah paused, looked at Chris, and the latter picked up the story.

'Even more interesting is what the post-mortem told us,' she said. 'The pathologist found a wound on the back of Marilena's head that matches the part of your cab where her DNA was found. Seems you banged her head on the door frame hard enough to stun her but not hard enough to kill. Then you wrapped her in the sleeping bag and drove her to Cambridge. But those weren't all the wounds were they, Colin?'

Makepiece attempted to intervene.

'I believe you're supposed to ask my client questions,' he drawled, 'not tell him fairy stories.'

'This is just context,' said Chris. 'I'm coming to the questions, believe me.

'So, Colin, when you took the sleeping-bag-wrapped body into the holiday cottage, what happened then?' She paused, but he seemed mesmerised. 'I'll tell you, shall I? You picked up the cast-iron poker out of the fireplace and then you struck her on the head, in the belly and on her ankles. Why did you attack her again, Colin? You'd already knocked her out once. Why did you hit her again? Even harder? Three times?'

There was a pause. And Alan said quietly, 'Did you understand the question, Colin?' Brown turned to the appropriate adult as though relieved to turn away from the two women opposite.

‘Yes, I understand the question,’ he said, almost eagerly. ‘But he said I was to say no comment.’ And he pointed at Makepiece.

‘And you have a perfect right to say nothing,’ said Alan. ‘That’s correct, Colin.’ Chris interrupted.

‘But I don’t understand, Colin. I don’t understand why you hit her again, and again and again.’ She tapped her hand sharply on the table top three times, not loudly but clearly. ‘Once, and you cracked her skull. Twice, and you ruptured her spleen. Three times, and you broke her ankle.’

Colin fumbled with the words but managed to say ‘no comment’ again. Chris took no notice.

‘But even then, she wasn’t dead, was she, Colin? She was still alive.’

‘Yes,’ he burst out. ‘It wouldn’t stay dead. It just wouldn’t. It reached out to me.’ He shuddered. ‘I had to hit it with the iron, then I had to put it somewhere safe.’

‘Safe for who?’ asked Chris ungrammatically, and Sarah added, ‘Definitely not safe for her, was it, Colin?’ He switched his gaze to her as she said again, ‘Definitely not safe for her, Colin. She survived you beating her head on the truck cab, she survived you beating her with an iron poker. But she drowned in that hot tub, wrapped in your sleeping bag.’

Alan Ryan looked both sick and fascinated. Makepiece sighed heavily.

‘Do you actually have any further questions,’ he asked, ‘or just more of your fairy tale?’

‘We have more questions, don’t worry,’ said Chris. ‘Colin Brown, did you wrap the woman you picked up at Thetford in your sleeping bag, take her to the Bacton holiday cottage in your car, and after hitting her with the iron poker from the fireplace, put her in the hot tub until morning?'

'No,' said Colin. 'I don't know any Marilena.' Makepiece breathed a sigh of relief that strangled in his throat as Colin Brown went on, 'I did hit the vampire again and put it in the hot tub. What else could I do?'

Chris paused with her mouth open and Sarah took up the slack. In the viewing room Greg could hardly breathe as he watched and listened.

'What did you do with the vampire in the morning?' asked Sarah.

'I put it in the car. It was dead for the moment. Then I took it away to bury safely.'

'What do you mean by safely?' asked Sarah.

'In holy ground, with silver,' he replied.

'Is that where you usually bury vampires?' asked Chris.

'Not always,' he replied. 'Sometimes it's not possible to find somewhere holy. Sometimes it just has to be somewhere safe. And the silver helps.'

'Was that why you buried one in the Roman remains?' asked Sarah.

'God, that's a long time ago,' he said, almost laughing. 'Yes. There was a temple there. I thought that would be better than nothing.'

'And the garden at Hemsby?'

'That wasn't so good,' said Colin, his demeanour flattening, losing the energy and bounce of the last few minutes. 'But I had no choice. I couldn't think of anywhere else, not just on the spur of the moment. But I did use the silver,' he added, as though keen to reassure them he'd done the best job he could, in the circumstances.

‘Ah yes, the silver,’ chipped in Chris. ‘According to Coins and Medals, you bought twenty silver thruppences from them. But we’ve only found seven in your home in Coton. Oh, and one was in your pocket when you were arrested. Where are the other twelve, Colin?’

‘Oh, I’ve used them,’ he replied.

Greg found he was holding the edge of the table so hard his knuckles were white. Both Alan Ryan and Makepiece were rendered silent with shock, but Chris went on, ‘Where did you use them, Colin?’ He started to count on his fingers.

‘Well, there was one in Cambridge, one in the St Edmunds Roman remains, one in the garden at Hemsby, one I had to bury rather hurriedly in a hole in the road in Oulton Broad. How many’s that?’

‘That’s four,’ said Alan rather faintly, surprised into speaking up. Sarah shot him a warning glance, but Colin went on, ‘In that case the others must have been in France and Belgium. Oh, except for the other one in Cambridge. But I was in a bit of a hurry with that one, so the coin was on its chest rather than in its mouth. I think the mouth is better, don’t you?’ he asked chattily.

There was a pause while Sarah and Chris looked at each other, then Sarah asked, ‘Which was the one you buried in the garden in Hemsby, Colin?’

‘Oh God, I forget,’ he replied with an air of ‘don’t ask me ridiculous questions’. ‘They get a bit confused after all this time. But hang on.’ He seemed flattered by their attention and suddenly determined to be helpful. ‘It wasn’t the one from Lowestoft because it went into the hole in Oulton Broad. And it wasn’t the one from Norwich because I took it to the Roman temple and buried it there. The bike was a pain,' he added. 'I had to put it in the ditch and I got scratched on the thorns. So, it must have been the one from the sugar factory. I had to take it back to Cambridge with me then bring it to Norfolk in my car, just like the last one,' he said.

There was a pause, then Sarah said, 'Just to be clear, you're telling us that you killed at least four vampires in Cambridge and Norfolk and buried them in Cambridge, Hemsby, Oulton Broad and the St Edmunds Roman remains with a silver thruppence in their mouths. And that you planned to bury Marilena, I mean the latest vampire, in the churchyard at All Saints, also with a silver thruppence.'

'Yes, that's right.' He looked round at his legal adviser and, taking in his expression, said, 'Sorry, shouldn't I have said that?'

Makepiece opened his mouth to answer, but Chris got there first with, 'And you also said you killed four more on the continent?'

But the moment had passed. 'No comment,' said Colin Brown.

33

A debt paid

Outside the interview room, Sarah turned to Chris and they were celebrating with a high five when Greg emerged from the observation suite.

'Well done, both of you, you played a blinder,' he said. 'By the book and on the tape. That should see us home and dry on those four. I'll have a word with CPS about next steps.'

'And I'll chase up Lincolnshire,' said Chris. 'If we can get the same sort of travel information from the company he worked for there as we have from Delta Transport, we can share intelligence with France and Belgium.'

'Right! How they handle it is up to them, but let's be on the front foot as regards cooperation.'

Sarah's phone was buzzing, and she stepped to one side with an apologetic gesture to answer it.

'Hello,' she said and then, 'Oh hello!' again, as she recognised the caller. Greg heard no more as he and Chris walked towards his office, until Sarah called after him, 'It's Madame Trieste. She wants to know if there's any news.'

'You can tell her that a man has been arrested for Marilena's murder and will be appearing in court shortly,' he replied. Sarah turned back to the phone, spoke for a moment, then called to Greg again.

'She wants to see me. She says she has some information we'll find helpful. OK with you if I go? I kicked myself for days after I missed the last opportunity.'

'Of course, no problem. I was going to suggest I pick up the interviewing after lunch. Chris can be winger, and we'll try to tidy up some loose ends. Let me know if the madame has anything I need to know about.'

'Of course. See you, Chris.'

'See you,' replied Chris, and Greg hid a smile. His cunning ploy seemed to have worked in more ways than one.

Over at Nails Galore it was evidently business as usual. Madame had requested Sarah come in by the backdoor in a manner that tended more to instruction than invitation, presumably to avoid offending her clients with the sight of a police officer, even in plain clothes. Nonetheless, she was ready and waiting in the kitchen at the back, with a pot of coffee bubbling on the battered cooker. A young lady wearing a skimpy and rather grubby negligee with not a lot underneath made a muffled excuse and left the room. Sarah took no notice in a way designed to signal that she had noticed but was choosing not to.

'Coffee?' asked the madame.

'Thank you,' said Sarah, sitting down at the kitchen table and trying not to check the chair before she did so.

'You treated us good,' said Madame Trieste. 'You and that boss of yours, you listened and you acted, as though Marilena was anyone. Not a working girl, I mean,' she elaborated.

Sarah started to speak but was waved to silence. 'I told you I owed you, and I meant it. And I pay my debts,' said Madame Trieste. She pushed a crumpled Post-it note across the table. 'That what you wanted to know,' she added.

'What I wanted to know?' Sarah had asked the question so long ago, she'd forgotten it.

'The man who's interested in that Dragan. The man he works for. The big boss,' she said. 'That's his name and his phone number.' Sarah picked up the bit of paper, and looked at the pencil marks on it. The name had been written by one hand, and the phone number by another, the latter in thick black drawing pencil.

Madame's hand came down on top of Sarah's and the bit of paper.

'Put it away and never say where you got it, or I'm a dead woman,' she said dispassionately. 'You not get this from me. Understand?'

'I understand,' said Sarah. 'And thank you. But I will need to tell DCI Geldard where the intelligence came from.'

'OK. Him. No one else. Not even in police. He,' and she tapped the Post-it, 'he has long arms. He reach everywhere.'

'Not Norfolk Police,' said Sarah with certainty.

'You think?' Madame Trieste laughed. 'If you want me dead you tell. If not, then your boss only. No one else.'

'OK, Madame,' said Sarah. 'I promise.'

'And I believe you. Or I not help you. You keep your word, you've proved that. Now go, before anyone sees you.'

*

Back in her car, Sarah picked up her phone to ring Greg, then changed her mind.

'Ridiculous,' she said to herself, but without much certainty. 'Even so, I'll tell him when I see him.'

The journey from Norwich to Wymondham had never seemed so tedious. Sarah was tapping the steering wheel long before she pulled in to the car park and left her car rather badly positioned between a pool car and the Range Rover belonging to the chief super. Rushing in to Greg's office she'd already started to say, 'You'll never guess what the madame wanted to tell me,' before she noticed the room was empty. 'Damn,' she said, and poking her head round the ops room door, she asked, 'Where's the boss?'

'Interviewing again,' replied Jill, 'in the same…' then realised she was addressing empty air and a swinging door. 'Room,' she finished, then shrugged and turned back to her laptop.

Sarah entered the observation suite quietly, noting that the interview seemed to have already been underway for some time, judging by the collection of empty coffee beakers scattered around. Phil glanced round from the window and smiled a welcome. Alan Ryan, the appropriate adult, was looking tired and more than a little queasy. The solicitor was holding forth, while Greg and Chris wore identical expressions of impatience. She turned the sound on and the loudspeaker woke to life with '…not going to say it again. In view of the state of health of my client, in particular his tendency to self-harming and his unique perspective on reality, I'll demand a fitness to plead hearing.'

'What's this about self-harming?' demanded Greg. 'Is there any suggestion he's done so while in custody?'

'Not yet,' replied Makepiece, 'but it's surely only a matter of time, given staffing shortages and lack of supervision in prisons.'

Chris had seized the moments while he was speaking to push a photo over to Greg.

'From the medical report on his admission,' she said. Glancing down at the photo he'd skipped over earlier, Greg noted that the wounds on Brown's belly were old and healed.

'Then I say again, that in view of the fact he is charged with no less than four murders, to which he has both confessed and to which we can tie him with forensic evidence, bring it on. I'm happy to leave it to a jury to decide the appropriate means of making sure young women with dark hair are kept safe from your client.'

'More forensics?' asked Sarah quietly of Phil, with a lifted eyebrow.

'Just in. Ned's been able to tie him to all four. Once he had his DNA profile he took more samples from materials found with each body.'

'Wow, I didn't realise that would be possible!' exclaimed Sarah, her current preoccupation pushed to the back of her mind.

'Well, as Ned said, they can get DNA from woolly mammoths and that's been in the ground one hell of a lot longer. In fact, he said buried a few feet down is a pretty good way of preserving DNA. Mostly he found it on the silver coins,' he added.

'That's great.' Sarah was a little abstracted. 'But I do need to talk to Greg urgently. D'you know how much longer they're likely to be?'

'Not much longer,' said Phil, stroking his beard in what Sarah recognised with some irritation as a new mannerism. 'There, they're getting up now.'

Sarah joined Chris and Greg in the corridor, and interrupted the general congratulations.

'I need a word, Greg, urgently!' she said.

'OK.'

'Just you,' she said, and even without looking Greg felt the new rapprochement cool between the two women. 'Bother,' he thought but didn't say as he ushered Sarah into his office.

34

New threads

'Let me get this straight,' said Greg. 'Madame Trieste says this is the name and phone number of the Lithuanian head man that's linked with Dragan Bakalov and probably behind a whole heap of crimes in Norfolk. And we're to say nothing about where this intelligence came from because he has contacts in Norfolk Police.'

'That's the long and short of it,' agreed Sarah. 'Madame was clear that I could tell you, and only you about the source of this name. And that she'd be at risk if it went any wider.'

'OK. Treat her as you would any confidential source,' said Greg. 'But be extra careful. If she's right and this is our man,' he tapped the Post-it note on the desk in front of him, 'then revenge for betrayal won't take the shape of a beating. Likely she'll be dead and the body never found.'

'That's what I thought,' said Sarah with relief. 'How d'you want to handle this?'

'Well, for a start, this piece of paper goes in my safe. Have you noted the name and number?'

'First thing I did,' said Sarah, waving her phone.

'Good.' Greg glanced down at the yellow square in his hand and turned away to the small safe in the corner. When he turned back, the paper had gone. 'Ironic this comes up now,' he said. 'Just when we've got our hands full with Mr Brown. However, it is what it is.

'First thing, can you do a discreet search on this name. See if we've got anything on him. Anything at all. Then have a look through other sources and see what you can turn up. If that includes your contacts with the funny buggers…'

Sarah looked up sharply and noted that Greg was wearing a wry smile.

'Might as well call in some favours,' he said. 'Sarah, I'm going to leave this in your hands for the moment. Both because I'm going to be busy with our friend Brown, and because it helps with confidentiality if it stays with you.'

'Fine by me,' said Sarah. 'Thank you for trusting me.'

'Keep me posted, but only me, and only face to face,' replied Greg. 'Let's assume that Norfolk is compromised until we prove otherwise.'

'And Margaret?'

'I said just us, and I meant just us, for the moment,' said Greg.

That evening, Chris collapsed onto the sofa in Greg's conservatory with a sigh of relief and a large glass of Chianti. Awaiting her on the kitchen worktop were Tuscan-style sausage pappardelle, garlic bread and salad – all courtesy of Marks and Spencer's and therefore requiring no preparation whatsoever. She lifted her legs across Greg's lap and wriggled her toes. Raising her glass, she toasted him.

'To a successful prosecution.'

'Hear hear,' said Greg, taking a slurp of his wine and narrowly missing spilling some on her legs.

'That was quaffing, not drinking,' she reproved him. 'As defined by the late great Terry Pratchett.'

'As in?'

'Like drinking only you spill more,' she replied.

'Tonight, I'm all for quaffing,' he said, resting his head back on the sofa. Bobby leapt lightly from the floor and settled down alongside Chris, purring loudly.

'Early start in the morning?' asked Chris.

'Yup. Need to be in the office promptly for a discussion with CPS before the bail hearing.'

'Any worries?'

'No. In view of the offences and likelihood of further crime, I think remand is a no brainer. I was a bit concerned about Makepiece mouthing off about fitness to plead, but CPS think the defence barrister will decide against.'

'Because?'

'Because there's no chance the judge will go for it. There are four tests.' Greg listed them on his fingers. 'Can he:

1. Comprehend information presented to him,
2. Understand the importance of that info,
3. Make sound decisions,
4. Understand the potential impact of his decisions.

'Just because he's self-harmed in the past and has some downright screwy notions about vampires, doesn't mean he fails any of those tests. Anyway, until we're told otherwise, we carry on as normal.'

Silence fell for a moment, disturbed only by the loud purring from Bobby.

'Toss you for who goes and puts supper in the microwave,' said Greg.

'Toss what?' asked Chris.

'Good point. Nothing in my pockets. How about you?'

'Nothing. So if you've got to get up to fetch a coin, you might as well put the stuff in the microwave while you're at it.'

'We could play rock, scissors, paper,' said Greg without much hope, but Chris laughed.

'Come on,' she said, swinging her legs down. 'We'll do it between us.'

In the kitchen, garlic bread in the oven and microwave pinging, Chris set the table and poured more wine.

'What did Sarah want?' she asked. Greg had been waiting for the question.

'Oh, she wanted to pass on some info from a confidential source,' he said.

'What about?' asked Chris.

'I can't say,' said Greg. 'Sorry.'

Chris stopped what she was doing and looked up.

'Can't say?' she asked. 'I thought we could talk about anything.'

'And we can, normally, but this is confidential, like I said. I can't tell you what it's about without giving too much away, so best I say nothing.'

Chris looked down at the table in silence.

'Come on, Chris,' said Greg. 'You know work's different sometimes.'

'Apparently,' she said, and although they ate together, cleared up together and went to bed together, the atmosphere had changed.

In the office bright and early, Greg was ploughing through piles of paper when Sarah came in and closed the door behind her.

'I've got something,' she said. 'I did some digging through our databases and we have an address for that name.'

'Why's he in our records?' asked Greg.

'It seems we pulled him in more than five years ago in connection with a cannabis factory in Great Yarmouth. The suspicion was he was running what today we'd call a county lines operation. We got as far as asking him to attend for interview in Yarmouth, but we couldn't tie him to the property in question. There were too many cut outs. And none of the people we'd arrested were willing to give evidence against him. Anyway, we do have a home address on the record and it should be worth checking out.

'I also did as you suggested, and had a word with Newton, our old friend from the funny buggers.'

'What did you tell them?' asked Greg.

'I was careful. I didn't give them the name. I just gave him the phone number and said we had reason to believe it'd been used in connection with a serious crime and asked if they had it in their sights. And they did.'

'What'd they come back with?'

'A name. The same name we have. And they have more

information, but Newton said he'd need clearance to share more with us.'

'OK.' Greg thought for a moment. 'Get someone to check out that address. See if he's still living there, then we can think again. Don't say any more to the funny buggers. I'd need to talk to Margaret first.'

'And our promise to Madame Trieste?'

'That stands. Her involvement stays between us. Where is the address?' asked Greg.

'It's a house near a village called Great Ormesby. It's in an isolated location according to the map. Near one of the Trinity Broads.'

35

Endgame

Looking round for someone to check out the suspect address, Sarah felt she was scraping the bottom of the barrel. Jill, her first choice, was taking some hard-earned leave. Steve and Phil were out and about. That left her with the egregious Jeff, for some reason always everyone's last choice.

'Jeff, a word,' she said, accepting the inevitable. 'I need you to do a job for me.'

Having despatched him to Ormesby, she watched him swagger out with a sinking feeling that all her warnings about discretion had fallen on deaf ears.

'If ever someone had male-pattern deafness, he's the one,' she thought, and only realised she'd said it aloud when one of the girls clearing up the ops room from the big effort sniggered.

'Don't repeat me, for God's sake,' she said, and the girl put a finger to her lips, with a big smile.

*

If Sarah could have been hovering over Jeff's shoulder, she would have seen all her misgivings played out. His first move was to drive past the house in question twice. First one way, then back again, in a liveried Norfolk Police car. He didn't have the blue lights on, but that was the sum total of his discretion. Then he parked a little way down the road and sat in his car making notes. The house was set back from the road behind a high brick wall, only the upper storeys visible from the road. The wide verge was neatly mowed and a row of flowering cherry trees decorated the approach. Jeff noted the tall solid gate and the camera overlooking the entrance to the drive. He failed to notice the one in the tall tree the other side of the wall that monitored the whole approach. Consulting Google Maps he saw that the house sat in substantial grounds. The wall protected three sides. The fourth was occupied by the lake side. Judging from the aerial view, there was a small boathouse at the water's edge and a big garage near the house.

A noise made him look up. A sit-on lawnmower had emerged from the drive and begun work on the apparently pristine verges. Jeff looked at the driver through his rear-view mirror, hesitated, then made a decision. He got out of the car, pulled his cap on and walked over to the mower.

'Morning,' he said. The man pulled up and regarded him in silence.

'Just doing some routine checks,' said Jeff. 'Is the owner in?'

'No,' said the man.

'Oh,' said Jeff, slightly nonplussed at the brevity of the reply. 'Is he going to be back soon?'

'No,' said the man.

'Oh. OK,' said Jeff, and went back to the car, making his mind up to ask around in the village. By the time he headed back to Wymondham he'd drawn a blank at the village pub, post office, garage and newsagents.

It was scarcely an hour later when Sarah got the heads-up from DI Newton.

'Hi,' he said. 'I think you've been rattling some cages.'

'What?' she said, startled.

'I've got a report from GCHQ. After what you said about that phone number I put a flag on it and they're reporting an unusual level of activity. They haven't translated everything, but it seems our subject's been alerted by an unusual level of police interest locally.' Sarah had a sinking feeling.

'Damn,' she muttered.

'You haven't heard the worst of it,' she was told. 'It seems it's made them do some checking. They're after their leak. Wherever you got your information from, I hope your informant is tucked away somewhere safe. These people don't mess about. If they're not, then I suggest you do something about it. Fast.'

For a moment Sarah paused in the centre of the room, irresolute. Then making her mind up, she returned to her desk and the phone. Her first call was to Greg, but as he was locked away with the CPS team she failed to get through. The next was to the Reverend Hamilton. It was his wife who answered.

'I'm sorry,' she said. 'He's out at the moment, doing a spot of shopping. Can I take a message?' Sarah reflected that, in the circumstances, she'd probably get more sense from Mrs Hamilton than from Mr.

'I'm sorry to tell you that your threat level has just increased significantly. It's important you listen to me and do what I say. When do you expect your husband back?'

'Any minute,' said Mrs Hamilton, sounding confused. 'Are you sure you wouldn't like to wait and speak to him?'

'No time,' said Sarah. 'Please listen and please do what I say. Pack a bag for the two of you sufficient for at least a few nights. As soon as your husband gets home leave the house and go and stay in an hotel somewhere. I'll get back to you as soon as I can with further advice. Hopefully you'll be able to go home within a couple of days.'

'But why?' asked Mrs Hamilton. 'And what about the cats?'

'All I can say is that we've had new intelligence that suggests you're at immediate risk. Can you ask someone to feed the cats for you? If so, don't tell them where you're going. Have you still got my mobile number?'

'Yes. OK. I'll pack straightaway and ask our neighbour to feed the cats. You'll let us know as soon as we can come home?' she appealed.

'Yes. ASAP,' promised Sarah and rang off. She tried Greg one more time, and getting no answer again, after a moment's thought she left a brief message before leaving for Norwich and Nails Galore. By the time Greg picked up the voicemail, it was late afternoon and an impatient Chris was audibly wondering why he was prioritising messages from Sarah. For once, he took no notice and tried Sarah's number several times. Nothing. The only other message he had was from Margaret, demanding an immediate explanation for recent calls to her from the funny buggers.

'Talk about never rains but it pours,' he muttered.

'So, I gather our evening's on hold until you've seen Margaret,' said Chris.

'It's on hold until I find out why Sarah wanted me in such a hurry,' said Greg. 'I need to sort that first. Tell you what, how about we go via Nails Galore and then have dinner in Norwich? I can see Margaret in the morning.'

'If you think that's wise,' said Chris. 'But why Nails Galore?'

'Sarah was following something up for me,' replied Greg.

'The Lithuanians,' said Chris flatly. 'I knew you hadn't given up.' Greg didn't reply. 'Come on,' he said, 'sooner we sort this, sooner we can get off out.'

Chris scrabbled her seat belt into place as Greg swung the car round in the car park.

'What was the CPS verdict on Colin Brown?' she asked.

'What?' asked Greg, distracted. 'Oh yes. They think we've a very good chance of getting him on all four counts of murder, as well as his attack on Steve, so they're confident as they can be he'll be put away. The only question is prison or Broadmoor and frankly, in this case, I doubt it matters which. It'll be for a very long time either way.'

'No court date yet, I imagine?'

'No, but not far ahead as he'll be in custody.'

'Good. That's one problem sorted, then. Just leaves us with our East European friends,' remarked Chris.

Greg glanced across.

'Don't fish, Chris,' he said. 'As soon as I can I'll tell you.'

The grunted response was clearly audible and the rest of the drive into Norwich was silent, and cool. Chris was still keeping a lot of thoughts to herself when they drew up outside the salon. At this time in the evening, parking outside would normally be at a premium, but all the windows were in darkness and the door shuttered. One man, middle-aged and affluent-looking in a smart dark overcoat, was peering in through the unlit windows with one hand over his eyes. He turned away sharply as Greg approached and hurried to a silver Range Rover parked down the street.

'Seems the clientele weren't expecting it to be closed,' remarked Chris over his shoulder. 'Try round the back?'

'I'll try,' said Greg. 'You get back into the car.' Chris shrugged and moved away as Greg walked round to the back of the salon. He wrinkled his nose at the smell coming from the rubbish in the backyard and rattled the backdoor.

'Sarah's car is parked just up the street,' said Chris behind him. 'And she's not in it.'

'I thought you were going to wait in the car,' replied Greg quietly. Chris ignored the comment as not worthy of a response.

'I don't like this,' said Greg.

'Nor me,' replied Chris. 'Doesn't make sense, the salon closed up like this on a working day. And where's Sarah?'

'Call for back-up,' said Greg. 'I'm going in.'

Chris pulled out her radio and made the call as Greg stepped back, then kicked sharply at the backdoor. It shook but held.

'Wait for the team,' urged Chris, but Greg was looking in the garden shed and came up with a rusty spade.

'I'll try this first.' After pushing the blade of the spade between the door jamb and the door, he levered. There was a splintering sound and the door opened with a whine as the wood gave way. Still holding the spade, Greg went in, Chris on his heels with one eye behind her, just in case. He stopped dead, and made a choking sound. Chris stepped to one side to see past his broad shoulders, then turned out of the door to be sick on the doorstep.

The air was full of a metallic smell they'd both come across before. Madame Trieste stared at them from empty eye sockets. She was sitting on the floor, nailed to the kitchen cupboards through her neck and outspread hands. Sarah's car keys were on the kitchen table. Of Sarah, there was no sign.

THE END – FOR NOW

Someone is reported missing every 90 seconds in the UK.
Most, thankfully, are found within days.

There is help out there for the families and friends of those who may be missing. The obvious first port of call is the police. Dial 101, or if there are immediate welfare concerns, 999.

Missing People is a UK charity devoted to helping anyone affected by someone going missing.

Ring 116 000 or contact www.missingpeople.org.uk

Printed in Great Britain
by Amazon

61704634R00180